Shakespeare knew his small towns, apparently

The last time Tara Hillerman saw Timothy Swanson, he'd been an unformed college boy, out to raise hell, and darned attractive then. Now, with a man's build, a man's strength, and a man's awareness, he was far more than just attractive. Compelling was the word.

Gorgeous, maybe?

No. Never. And even if he was, she hoped he never found out she thought so.

Some people were born with it, and some weren't. Dr. Timothy Swanson had it in spades. But then he always had, in her book. Even back when they were kids, best friends palling around together. Before puberty arrived and made them aware of each other as more than just buddies, before it made them uncomfortable unless they were fighting. Long before she'd started noticing his physical attributes. Before he'd started noticing her.

She'd have been better off if he hadn't noticed her in that way at all.

He wouldn't be home long, though. Long enough to celebrate his dad's birthday with him, then Tim would shake that infamous Campbell sawdust off his feet again.

She could survive his father's matchmaking efforts till then.

Books by M.M. Justus

Much Ado in Montana

*Cross-Country: Adventures Alone Across
America and Back*

Unearthly Northwest

Sojourn

Time in Yellowstone

Repeating History
True Gold
"Homesick"
Finding Home

Much Ado in Montana

M.M. Justus

Carbon
River
Press

Much Ado in Montana

Acknowledgements

Thanks to Elizabeth Stowe for beta reading, and to Elizabeth McCoy for editing, both of them perceptively.

MUCH ADO IN
MONTANA

Chapter 1

Timothy Swanson stamped the dirt from his boots and shoved open the swinging doors to the Red Dog Saloon. He was glad he hadn't given into the admittedly juvenile impulse to wear his normal Saturday night duds that evening. He'd have been as out of place here in Italian wool and leather as his Prius was out in the Red Dog's gravel and mud parking lot.

Still, he had to resist the impulse to shoot the cuffs of his flannel shirt, one of several he'd bought specifically for this visit. At least it wasn't plaid. This one was navy blue, shades darker than his jeans. He'd grown up in flannel shirts. Gone to college in them. But as soon as he could ditch them and still fit in, he had. Stupidly enough, they made him feel like a hick. But when in Rome...

No one had noticed him yet. Tim couldn't decide if that pleased him or ticked him off. The big, low-ceilinged, wood-paneled room was packed with people. Everyone looked as if they'd just come off shift at the mill or in the forest, which most of them probably had. Peanut shells littered the scarred plank floor. Country music poured from enormous speakers that looked like they dated from thirty years ago because they did. The place smelled like beer and sweat, and, whether he wanted to or not, Tim felt himself relaxing after the eight-hour drive from Seattle.

Then one head turned, and another, and another, astonishment chased by ear-splitting grins and shouts. Tim braced as he was engulfed by the crowd. As he fielded their boisterous greetings. Got slapped on the back. And was yanked forward as the door swung shut behind him. A mug of, yes, that was Budweiser, was shoved into his hand – Tim hid his grimace as he took his first sip and wondered if the Red Dog had anything else on tap these days.

He was home again. Whether he wanted to be or not. Then he saw *her* face, and froze.

* * *

It took him longer than he liked to break free of his impromptu welcome-home party and make his way to where Tara Hillerman sat, big as life and twice as beautiful, as if she was holding court at one of the battered tables. She leaned forward, an elbow on the red-checked plastic cloth covering the rough planks, and watched him approach.

At least she looked as astonished as he felt. Her gray eyes were wide, and, as he came closer, she almost seemed to shrink away, even though he could have sworn she hadn't moved.

The last time he'd seen Tara had been at the University of Washington five years ago. She'd been snuggled under the arm of a fellow library school student. The guy could have won a "least likely to be taken for a librarian" contest with no problem whatsoever, given his abundance of tattooed muscles and shaved head. The last Tim had heard, not that he'd tried to find out or anything, she'd been planning to follow him, and a job, to Portland.

Tim glanced around. No bald heads stuck up out of the crowd, but then most heads here were covered with cowboy hats or gimme caps. Maybe she was visiting home on her own. But why *this* weekend? Tim almost felt like that line in *Casablanca.* "Of all the gin joints, in all the world," he muttered, "you had to walk into mine."

Tara's expression of consternation didn't last long. By the time he reached her table, her expression had gone from shocked to sly. But she shifted in her seat. Was she uneasy to see him? No, of course not. After all, *he* wasn't nervous about seeing *her* again after five years. Then again, she'd dumped him, not the other way around.

"You came a long way for a party," Tara commented dryly. "I try to draw the line at a three-hour drive unless it lasts overnight."

Tim leaned forward onto the back of a wooden chair on the opposite side of the table and set that god-awful beer down. The chair's occupant, little Becky Thorstein, picked up her glass of soda and toasted him. Tim grinned at her briefly before aiming his gaze back across the pitchers of beer at Tara. "The drive or the party? Or do you make a habit of spending all night on a three-hour drive?"

Tara glowered at him. "I suppose you terrorized the state police and got here in six?"

Tim straightened and folded his arms in front of him. "I'm a law-abiding citizen these days."

"Meaning that you've got enough traffic tickets to make you worry about losing your license."

Her smug expression made him long to wipe it off her face. "Who was it almost took a header into the Ship Canal trying to beat the drawbridge?" He could hear snickering, wanted to laugh himself but it wasn't worth ruining the effect.

"Better than getting caught by the campus police popping wheelies in Husky Stadium."

Her smug expression was back. Of course she'd have a comeback, he thought. Why would he expect things to change in five years? "Which didn't do any damage. That bridge will never be the same."

"Neither will you, Tim," said a new voice. Tim turned to see Jack Rasmussen striding toward him, the saloon doors of the Red Dog swinging behind him. He was brown from a summer in the plains of eastern Montana digging for dinosaur bones, and it looked as if he'd come straight here, not bothering to change clothes and get cleaned up on the way. His jeans and plaid flannel shirt wore dust like a badge. His worn boots crunched on the peanut shells and other debris strewn over the plank floor as he came closer. Voices rose in welcome again, this time sounding more like the people in the bar on that old TV show. Jack was obviously known and loved here. Tim was *not* envious of that fact. Jack went around the table slapping backs, and gradually made his way to Tim.

Jack clapped Tim on the back, too. "I figured you wouldn't be in town till at least next week."

Tim turned gratefully from Tara's frustrated glower to the mile-wide grin on the face of one of his oldest friends. "Plans change. I see you got home from the back of beyond in one piece this time."

"Sure did. Found some interesting stuff, too, but I won't bore you by dragging you out to see it."

Tim chuckled. "Thanks. I appreciate that."

"Is that your itty bitty rice burner out there?" Jack nudged Tim away from the back of Becky's chair, leaned down, and kissed her.

Hello, Tim thought, bemused, watching Becky wrap her arms around Jack, dust and all, and return the kiss with interest. What's going on here?

A few long moments later, Jack pulled up a chair, placing it as close as physically possible to Becky's. He pulled her hand into his lap, where she seemed quite content to let him play with her fingers. He then resumed the conversation as if nothing had happened. "I sure wouldn't want to take a toy like that up the Yaak," he said, referring to the rugged, sparsely populated area north of town.

"Huh?" Tim tore his eyes away from the unexpected display and took a surreptitious glance around the table. No one else seemed surprised. He guessed it was what he got for staying out of touch so long. What were they talking about? Oh, yes. The Prius. "I wouldn't want to take anything with less than two feet clearance up the Yaak, Jack," he replied, as the half dozen people seated around the table groaned at the familiar rhyme. "I drove here from Seattle on one tank of gas."

"I'm sure you did." Tim turned back to Tara as she spoke. His surprise at Jack and Becky had only deepened the smug look on her face. "And you probably even managed to cram a change of clothes in there, too. So, to what do we owe this rare appearance in our fair city?"

Tim cleared his throat, prepared for a small dose of crow. "Ah, I came home for a visit. Dad's going to be seventy-five this month. The least I could do was show up to celebrate it with him."

Tara eyed him. "You can't possibly be here for that party yet. It's still three weeks off. People were taking bets –" She broke off, blushing slightly. Tim wondered that she had the grace to be embarrassed. He suddenly remembered why he hated small towns. Everyone knew everyone else. Butting in on private business was a common pastime. And no one was ashamed to wager on anyone else's behavior.

Well, he had to salvage something. "How much money did you just lose?"

"What do you mean?" Tara tried to look innocent, but Tim wasn't buying it.

He leaned forward on the narrow table across from her and watched with satisfaction when she pulled back in her chair. "How much money did you lose because I showed up?"

"None of your business."

"Must have been a lot." Someone snickered. Tim ignored it, the same way he ignored the heads following the conversation as if it were a ping pong match. Having Tara on the defensive was something he hadn't been able to accomplish frequently. Certainly not often enough to be blasé about it.

"I didn't say that."

"You didn't have to."

"Children, children." Becky glanced up from where she'd been gazing at Jack as if he was a mirage and laughed, but the sound was distinctly uncomfortable. Tim could hear her tone over the female singer belting out how she wished she hadn't shot him, the rattle of glasses, and the half-dozen loudly-conducted conversations in his immediate vicinity. Becky Thorstein had never been very fond of the way Tim fought with her best friend. All the way through their lives, right up till five years ago. "You don't have to kill each other tonight."

Tim smiled down at her and noticed the look of relief in Becky's eyes. And then, inevitably, his gaze wandered back over to Tara, who naturally looked triumphant. "No, I suppose not. But don't ask us to declare a truce, Becky. You might get struck by lightning." As he went to the bar to get himself a real beer, Tim shook his head. The more some things changed, the more they stayed the same.

Tim couldn't see that five years – or her bald, tattooed librarian – had changed Tara one bit. Her gray eyes still shot sparks, and she still had a line of malarkey a mile long.

She'd never been classically beautiful. Her features were too strong for that description. When Tim had been young and stupid, they'd always struck him as being perfect for her quick intelligence, even when she'd used it to aim snarky barbs at him. Her mouth, though, was another story. Her mouth was a work of art, wide and pink and soft, and it brought back unwanted memories that didn't involve snark or barbs. She'd left it unpainted tonight, the way he'd always liked it. He refused to wonder if bald and tattooed liked it that way, too.

The little he could see of her figure hadn't changed, either. He wondered, absently, if she would still fit against him as well as she had five years ago, and brought himself up sharply as he reached the bar.

The chances of him finding out if Tara Hillerman was still as desirable as he remembered in his fantasies were less than none. And if he was to maintain his sanity over the next few weeks while he figured out what had his mother so upset, he'd better remember that.

Too bad, though.

"Any microbrews, Charlie?" he shouted to the bartender over the noise.

"Got some Moose Drool —" The beefy man in the dirty apron turned around and beamed. He stretched out a huge damp paw. "Tim Swanson! Come home to take over your daddy's practice?"

Sighing inwardly, Tim shouted back the answer he knew he'd be repeating till his eyes crossed. Till he managed to escape back to Seattle. "Nope. Just visiting."

Charlie frowned. "Your dad said you were."

And so it begins, Tim thought ruefully, as he tried to explain over the racket to Charlie that, no, he hadn't changed his mind, that, yes, he'd just taken on a perfectly good position at Harborview Hospital in Seattle now that he was done with his residency, and, much as he liked the good people of Campbell, he didn't want to come back to the sticks to live. Or words to that effect.

It was going to be damned hard to keep explaining all this without hurting anyone's feelings.

* * *

Tara surreptitiously watched Tim from her spot at the table as he leaned over the bar, yakking with Charlie. Nice butt, she thought wistfully. But then he'd always had a world-class butt. It matched his world-class temper.

Tim Swanson had come home. It made her wonder if there wasn't a fatted calf roasting over coals in the county somewhere.

He wouldn't stay, though, Tara thought. Not that she wanted him to. The gossip running through town like wildfire recently notwithstanding. Most of it originated in the clinic, anyway, and anyone with any sense at all would know better than to believe Tim's father's wishful dreams.

Tara would bet her life on it. Timothy Swanson was too sophisticated for Campbell, Montana, population two thousand, six hundred, and fifty-three, sixty miles east of Idaho and eighty miles south of Canada. A hundred and twenty miles from the nearest mall and the nearest hospital, and – okay, Tara thought, enough already. It was big enough to have a library, wasn't it? *Her* library.

She'd memorized all the statistics during her high school years, while she waited to make the great escape herself. It was just that, for her, the wide world had become too lonely. Her attempts at adventure had been just that, attempts made because she couldn't simply give in to her own nature without at least trying to be a rabble-rouser just once. A nature that craved home and security more than it did the troublemaking she'd caused during her brief college years in the big city. She'd tried, but without Tim, she'd found that the wide world wasn't what she wanted. She'd rather have the comfort of people who knew her. Family nearby. And friends.

Still, he was awfully good-looking. Five years hadn't darkened that beach-boy blond hair, now clipped short and stylishly. The last time she'd seen him, his hair had been carelessly dragging at his collar because, as she well knew, he couldn't be bothered to get it cut regularly. The closely-trimmed beard, just a bit darker than the hair on his head, was new, too. It looked good. Gave him a layer of class. His baby face was gone forever.

The last time she'd seen him, he'd been an unformed college boy, out to raise hell, and darned attractive then. Now, with a man's build, a man's strength, and a man's awareness, he was far more than just attractive. Compelling was the word.

Gorgeous, maybe?

No. Never. And even if he was, she hoped he never found out she thought so.

No, his hair was no closer to dirty dishwater blond than it had been then. She'd wished that on him, along with warts and klutziness and anything else she could think of when he'd betrayed her. His face was smooth-skinned where his beard didn't cover him *and* he was athletically graceful. So much for wishing curses on him.

Some people were born with it, and some weren't. Dr. Timothy Swanson had it in spades. But then he always had, in her book. Even back when they were kids, best friends palling around together. Before puberty arrived and made them aware of each other as more than just buddies, before it made them uncomfortable unless they were fighting. Long before she'd started noticing his physical attributes. Before he'd started noticing her.

She'd have been better off if he hadn't noticed her in that way at all.

He wouldn't be around long, though. Long enough to celebrate his dad's birthday with him, then Tim would shake that infamous Campbell sawdust off his feet again.

She could survive his father's matchmaking efforts till then.

Because that's what she'd been putting up with lately. Dr. Swanson – the other Dr. Swanson, Tim's father – had visited the library a record number of times during the last month, chatting up the big question, which was, of course, whether or not Tim would show up for the party. Tara had to give the good old doctor credit, though. There were very few people in town whose first impulse wasn't to run for their lives when she and Tim were in the same state, let alone the same room.

Tara sighed. It wasn't that she hated Tim, exactly. She just wanted to skewer him with his own scalpel for what he'd done to her. Then wipe that smirk off his face with a kiss he'd never be able to get over. Nature could then take its course. Maybe with a tornado. It was probably the kindest thing nature could do.

Tara deliberately reached for an empty glass and the pitcher of beer Jack had plunked on the table moments ago, ignoring both her soda and the curious glance Rebecca aimed at her. Carefully she poured the lager, stopping just short of spilling foam all over her fingers.

So what if the last – and first – time she'd had a beer was two sips at a microbrewery in Portland four years ago when Hans insisted she at least give his favorite substance on the planet a try? So what if she'd hated the stuff so badly she thought she'd never want to taste it again? She needed some kind of courage to deal with Tim, even if it was the dutch variety.

Making a face, Tara took a mouthful and gulped it down like medicine. It insulted her tongue and burned all the way to her stomach. And the smell... Taking a deep breath, she swallowed another gulp. Anything had to be better than dealing with Tim. Even getting drunk on beer. Deliberately Tara turned toward Rebecca's friend Cindy, seated next to her, and started a conversation as Tim headed back toward the table. If he found out she'd been watching him, he'd never let her live it down.

Chapter 2

The gathering lasted until the wee hours. Which would have been fine if the party hadn't been on top of the eight-hour drive from Seattle. Tim felt like propping his head on the Prius's steering wheel and going straight to sleep in the middle of the rutted meadow the Red Dog called its parking lot.

At least he hadn't had too much to drink, even if the microbrew Charlie'd served him had been as tasty as anything he'd drunk in Seattle in spite of being called Moose Drool. Tim had rationed himself carefully enough to draw attention from Jack, who'd razzed him about it, but he wasn't about to take a chance with his brand-new car. It was the first car he'd ever bought new, and he loved it, not just because it was good for the environment and economical, the latter a necessity because of his med school loans, but because it was his. Wiping it out somewhere on the fifteen miles of one-lane gravel road into town would break his heart.

Tim was just about to turn the engine on when he heard a tap on his window. He glanced up to see who it was and found himself staring squarely at two silver gray eyes gazing right back at him. He tapped the window opener. "Tara? Cripes, you about gave me a heart attack."

"Hi." She gave him a wavering grin.

"Hi," he replied cautiously, and waited. Nothing more seemed to be forthcoming from her. Tim watched her curiously. She hadn't spoken to him since he'd returned from the bar. As a matter of fact, he'd have sworn she'd deliberately ignored him the entire evening, as busy gabbing with old friends she'd no doubt not seen in – how long since *her* last visit here? He wondered if she came home on a regular basis, then wished he hadn't. He wasn't going to feel guilty about how few and far between his own visits had been. His father had gone through med school and residency, too, once upon a time. He understood. "What's up?"

She gestured vaguely. "I, uh, lost my car keys."

And she was asking *him* for a ride? "Do tell. Don't you have a cell phone? Or did you lose that, too?" He glanced around. The parking lot had emptied remarkably quickly. His car and a little blue jeep that must be Tara's were the only rigs still occupying it, and the Red Dog's windows were dark. How long *had* he been sitting here? Tim pulled his own cell phone out of his pocket and blinked at the too-bright readout. No service out here in the boonies, but at least he could see what time it was. He should have known. He glanced back up at her and sighed. "I suppose you want a lift."

She grinned at him again. This one seemed to have a bit more oomph behind it. He eyed her, sniffed. Was it his imagination or was the smell of beer stronger since he'd rolled down the window? She leaned on the door. He sniffed again. Nope. Not his imagination.

"Do you mind?"

"Of course not." He wouldn't leave her out here on her own. He wouldn't leave his worst enemy out here to fend for himself. Well, obviously, he thought. They were one and the same, weren't they? He'd thought so for the last five years, anyway. Tim tapped the button to unlock the doors on her side and his. He climbed out of the car and walked around to open the passenger door for her. She was still standing by the open door on the driver's side, so he went back and took her by the arm.

"Your seat is over here."

The hazy glow in her eyes blinded him worse than his cell phone's light.

"Oh. Thanks." She allowed him to lead her around the car and help her in.

He rested an arm on top of the open car door. "Just tell me if you're going to be sick so I can stop. Chances are I won't forgive you if you heave in my car."

She gave him a vaguely puzzled look. "Just too much beer. That's all." Her voice was starting to sound slurred.

That she'd had too much beer was becoming more obvious by the moment. It was also so unlike the Tara he'd known, even in their hell-bent college days, that Tim began to wonder if this was a new habit or a special occasion. The stray thought occurred to him that *he* might be the special occasion.

No, that couldn't be right, as he was sure she'd inform him if he ever demonstrated enough stupidity as to mention the possibility to her.

Surely, since she'd been the one to dump him, since she'd had no problem replacing him so quickly his head had spun, and, most importantly, since it had been five years since he'd lost her in the first place, for him to be any kind of a special occasion to Tara Hillerman had to be a dream on his part. Or a nightmare.

When Tim realized that he'd been standing there leaning on the car door long enough for a curious expression to filter through the haze in her eyes, he told her, "It's okay, I'll take you home," and closed the door firmly.

He walked back around to the other side of the car, slid into the driver's seat, and glanced over at his passenger. She was already curled up in the leather seats he'd had put in, her warm brown curls contrasting with the black material.

Tim sighed, started the engine, and gently edged the Prius over the rutted grass out onto the gravel road. This was an interesting development, to say the least.

* * *

Tara didn't have any more to say, and, indeed, looked to be sound asleep by the time the car rumbled over the Flathead River bridge and into town. Tim drove down the late-night-deserted main drag, vaguely noticing some new sidewalks and changed businesses. Under the cosmetic changes he was still in the same Campbell he'd always known and, well, not hated. But definitely not loved, not the way his father loved the place. The silhouette of the Cabinet Mountains rose in front of him, silver snow and black rock against the moonlit night, silent walls of the jail he'd once felt so trapped inside of.

At the first stoplight, one of three in town, Tim leaned over and shook Tara by the arm. "Are you staying with your folks?"

"Mmbghmph." She pulled her arm back and curled up again.

"Tara." The light turned green. Not that it mattered. His car was the only moving rig in sight. Tim pulled over to the side of the empty street, anyway, and took the car out of gear. He reached over to shake her again.

"What?" Her voice sounded petulant and warm and sleepy, a tone he wished he didn't remember in a completely different context. He wondered exactly how much she'd had to drink. And still, exactly why she'd done it tonight.

He nudged her, her shoulder soft beneath the cotton sweater she wore. "I don't know where you're staying. Are you at Becky's?"

Her eyes slowly focused on him. "Why would I be staying at Rebecca's?"

"How should I know?" he replied, frustrated. "Where are you staying while you're here?"

"My place."

That startled him. "I didn't know you had one here."

She stared at him curiously, then rubbed her eyes with a fist. "Of course I do. I live here."

"No, you don't. You live in Portland. With what's his face." What's his face had been the only reason Tim hadn't gone after her once he'd gotten over the shock of her thinking she could just dump him like that. Well, that and his pride. Mostly his pride, he thought ruefully.

Tara stared at him. "Who?"

Tim shook his head in frustration. "The bald guy. The one with all the tattoos. Where is he, by the way?"

"Hans? How should I know? I haven't seen him in years." She blinked at him, then licked her lips.

Tim absorbed the shock. So she'd dumped bald and tattooed, too. Tim could almost rustle up some sympathy for the guy. Almost. He wondered if he and Hans were only the first two in a long line of dumpees. Or if she was in a relationship now. No one had been cozying up to her at the Red Dog. It was none of his business, he decided firmly. He wasn't going there. No matter how tempting that beautiful mouth was. "If that's the case, may I have some directions?"

Three minutes later he pulled up in front of a little white frame house on the edge of town. Two enormous Douglas fir trees swept the ground in front of it, partially blocking the moonlight and the mountains.

Tara appeared to have spent the time doing her best to wake up, and she was out the door before he could make it around the car to open it for her. He trailed her to her front door, anyway. Some habits of good manners simply refused to die.

Her smile was a bit sheepish, but a little less fuzzy. "Thanks for the ride, Tim. I'm glad I didn't make a mess in your car."

Tim chuckled. "I'm glad you didn't, either. I didn't know you'd come back home –"

She interrupted him. "I'm sure I'll see you around while you're here." She fumbled with her key in the lock until Tim took it gently from her. He unlocked the door, noticing that her car keys were still on the ring with her house key. He was glad she'd asked him for the ride, anyway. The last thing he wanted was for her to end up in his father's clinic, or worse, airlifted to the hospital in Kalispell after wrecking her car.

She turned to face him, leaning on the doorframe. "I hope you realize I don't make a habit of this."

"What, accepting rides from ex-boyfriends? That's probably a good idea."

She smiled up at him. Tim sternly ignored it. One, she was drunk and probably had no clue she was aiming that lethal smile at him. Two, when she was sober she probably still hated him. And three – three went completely out the window when Tara tilted her head up, reached a cool hand around behind his neck, pulled him down to her, and kissed him.

Ohmygod. Where the hell had this come from?!? Warm soft lips and warm soft breath and sensations he'd thought relegated to his dreams for the last five years. She tasted like beer and peanuts and deep dark turbulent Tara, and she kissed as if the world had stopped spinning. Maybe that was because it had, Tim thought dazedly. His world certainly felt like it.

No soft breeze in the trees, no gentle light from the porch lamp. More like a tornado with fireworks attached. The cataclysm only got more disastrous when she opened her mouth on him. Her tongue came searching for his, and he gave it up without a whimper.

He'd completely forgotten how wonderful she tasted. And felt. But his body hadn't. Tim felt his arms wind possessively around her of their own accord as she swayed against him. Felt her soft breasts flatten against his chest, felt himself stiffen against her. Half of him waited for her to realize how far things were going and pull away. The other half simply took the good fortune and ran with it.

Just as he was about pick her up, open the door, and carry her inside, even if it would have been the most idiotic thing he'd ever done, the inevitable happened. Tara saved him from his own stupidity by breaking the kiss. She lifted her hand from its warm clasp of his nape and stepped back out of his embrace. Tim braced himself, ready to withstand anything from tears to a slap.

He didn't think he could be shocked any more than he had been in the last five minutes, but then she grinned sloppily at him and glanced down at the keys in his hand.

"What do you know? There's my car keys. Silly me." She turned to open the door. Reached out and hooked the keys from his limp hand with a finger. "'Night."

She vanished into the house, leaving Tim standing dumbfounded on the doorstep.

Chapter 3

Tara woke slowly the next day, the midmorning sun warming the covers on her bed before she opened an eye.

She stretched luxuriously, unusually aware of her body. Such dreams she'd had. Warm dreams, sensual dreams. Familiar dreams, though she hadn't had one like that in years. Her lips, gently devoured. Her skin, caressed and cherished. Her breasts, fondled and kissed. Her –

Tara sat up, swayed from side to side, and crashed back down on her pillow. A cold sweat broke out on her forehead as jackhammers started a drumbeat inside her skull. She clapped her hand to her mouth in the hope that it would keep down the contents of her stomach.

What the – ?

Lie still, she told herself as the sunlight streaming in the window threatened to pierce her retinas. She'd be all right in a minute. She had to be.

Long moments later, she opened her eyes again, shielding them from the light with the hand she'd gingerly removed from her lips. Okay. So far so good. She lifted her head. The room moved a bit, then settled down again.

Slowly Tara sat up, trying to ignore the double-time drumbeat against the inside of her skull, holding her stomach with one hand as she used the other for leverage against the bed. It was a very bad move. She moaned.

Bathroom. She had to get to the bathroom.

Five minutes later it was all over but the banging in her head. Leaning weakly against the bathroom counter, Tara eyed herself balefully in the mirror. The flu was simply not an option right now. Not with school started and the library entering one of the busier times of the year. Not to mention the budget proposal she had to give to the board this week. Never mind that she'd been exposed to it a week earlier when Rebecca had come down with the nasty stuff.

Unless... Tara straightened. It wasn't the flu. She'd had the flu before, and it didn't taste like beer smelled.

No. It wasn't the flu. It was her own stupidity. Tara reached over for her toothbrush and squirted a ribbon of toothpaste onto it, barely managing to get the two connected as memories of the night before began to filter through her cloudy brain.

Tim was back in town. He'd been at the Red Dog the night before, and, in self-defense, rather than deal with him she'd gotten drunk for the first time in her life. Brushing vigorously, trying to remove the sour, dusty taste from her mouth, Tara made a face at herself in the mirror. Not the brightest thing she'd ever done – but then Tim had always inspired her to depths of idiocy she'd never have aspired to reach without him.

But what else had she gotten herself into? Done with the toothbrush, Tara filled a cup at the tap and rinsed as she puzzled through what little she could remember after her second glass of beer.

They'd squabbled, but then they'd always squabbled. He'd looked better than he had any right to. Yes, she definitely remembered that. His offended attempts at ignoring her had set her off, and – oh, geez.

She'd pestered him into a ride home. Something had to have happened to trigger those dreams again.

Tara sank against the counter once more, the cup in her hand sloshing with water, the pounding in her head reverberating once more.

She couldn't remember a thing.

* * *

"Um, Rebecca, did I do anything dumb last night?" It had taken half an hour, three aspirin, and a shower before Tara could work up the guts to call her friend.

"Well, I've never seen you drink beer before." Rebecca's normally bright, cheerful voice had Tara wincing.

"That's because last night was the first time."

"Oh." The syllable was pregnant with meaning.

"I know, I know. Bad timing on my part."

"It was because of Tim, wasn't it? I knew we should have told you, but I was afraid you wouldn't come to the party –"

"You knew he was coming? When?" Her voice had gone up half an octave and a few dozen decibels, but Tara didn't care.

"The prodigal Tim?" Rebecca answered with a question of her own. Tara gave a half-smile at the nickname Jack had bestowed on Tim the night before. Which Tim had protested mightily. She did remember that, with relish. "When he called the school office about a week ago and asked Cindy why he couldn't get hold of Jack to tell him he was coming home for a while."

Cindy the high school office secretary and, Tara thought, friend to both of them. Tara vaguely remembered talking with her last night. "And neither one of you bothered to tell me."

"You didn't ask," Rebecca said innocently.

How was I supposed to know to ask you, Tara thought wryly, but let it slide. "I didn't punch him out? Kick him in the shins?" Kiss him?

Rebecca chuckled. "Verbally, maybe. But not literally. At least not in the Red Dog. By the way, Terry said she saw your rig parked up there when she drove into town this morning. How did you get home?"

"Don't ask."

Something in Tara's tone must have given her away, though, because the next words out of Rebecca's mouth were, "Tim? You rode home with Tim?"

Tara winced again. "I think so. I told you, I had a little too much to drink."

"Speaking of which –"

Tara cut Rebecca off before she could start asking the really hard questions. "I didn't feel safe driving home. Tim offered me a ride. It's no big deal."

"Jack and I would have given you a ride. All you had to do was ask."

The way Jack had hung all over Rebecca last night, the last thing they'd needed was a third wheel on the ride home. They didn't get enough time together as it was. "You guys have been apart for almost two months. He just got back yesterday. You think I was going to butt in on you?"

"But I thought you hated Tim."

Tara fidgeted with the phone cord. "I'd hate crashing my rig because I was too drunk to drive it more."

"Oh." Rebecca was getting a lot of mileage out of that word today. "Well, if you're having a hard time remembering what you did last night, it's probably just as well you didn't attempt the drive."

If only Rebecca knew. Tara sighed. "Okay, well, thanks." She had to get off the phone, now, or Rebecca was going to start badgering her again. "Mom's on her way up the walk, so I'll talk to you later."

"Sure. Tara?" Rebecca's amusement came through quite clearly now.

"What?"

"Take some aspirin and learn to lie better. I can see your mom working in her garden from my window as we speak."

"Right. Bye." She hung up the phone. If Rebecca wasn't such a good friend, she'd be tempted to kick *her* in the shins.

And she still didn't know why she'd dreamed that way about Tim Swanson last night.

She'd gotten drunk for the first time. On purpose. She wasn't proud of herself for it, but when Tim had come back from the bar and parked himself across from her, then begun flirting with every female person at the table but her – he'd even teased Rebecca, and it was obvious to a blind man that Rebecca and Jack were tighter than fur on a rug – she couldn't stand it. Short of getting up and leaving, which would have raised eyebrows and started tongues wagging like mad, the beer had seemed like a logical alternative. At the time.

And then not only had she set tongues wagging and eyebrows raising, but apparently she'd managed to do something to start those dreams up again. Nightmares, more likely.

Maybe it was just the shock of seeing him again, she thought hopefully. Just the vague memory of climbing into that funny little car of his with him, which did not have enough room for two people who didn't like each other. Maybe it was nothing more than that.

Tara reached out for the doorjamb and leaned on it, suddenly weak in the knees. No. It wasn't just all that. She'd kissed him. She could remember it now. He'd stood on her front porch under the soft golden light, looking like temptation personified, and she'd reached up and kissed him.

Tara concentrated, trying to remember through the haze covering her actions of the night before.

The keys, yes. Tapping on his window. Being ushered into his car. A long blank until he'd – like a gentleman, no less – walked her to her door. Then...

Yep. She'd kissed him. Not the other way around. Wasn't that just grand. Tara grimaced. How was she going to spend however long he was going to be here in the same town with him now? Surely he couldn't leave that fancy practice of his in Seattle for more than a few days. But the party wasn't for three weeks. He wasn't going to spend the entire time here, was he?

Tara supposed she could hope he'd continue to be a gentleman and realize that she'd not been herself. Maybe he'd even pretend nothing had happened. But unless Tim had undergone a complete personality change since he'd been gone – and, judging from his actions and words most of the previous evening, it was highly unlikely – the chances of him doing that were less than slim.

He was probably bragging about his conquest this very minute.

If I'd been kissed like that by anyone else, Tara thought miserably, I'd have told Rebecca by now. He certainly hadn't forgotten how to push all her buttons. Kissing Tim had always been a whole-body experience, and last night had been no exception. Tara closed her eyes, remembering, the pleasure coming with the memory almost against her will.

His arm slipping around her waist, holding her firmly to him, his other hand reaching up to her hair, fingers sliding through it as slickly as ice on a pond. Hot ice. Like his mouth, warm and firm and melting her against him.

Tara's fingers lifted to rest against her lips. How had she ever lived five years without that? How was she going to live without it ever again?

Because that was her only option. Tim Swanson may have been the only man with the power to send her to the mountaintops with only one kiss, but in every other way they drove each other crazy. And not in a pleasurable way.

Besides, she couldn't count on him, Tara thought. Remember the blonde?

She'd just have to be the one pretending nothing had happened – and hope like anything that he'd at least have the good grace to play along with her.

Sighing, she headed into the kitchen for something to settle her still-roiling stomach.

Her four Saturday hours at the library started in less than two. She was going to have to get a ride out to the Red Dog to pick up her rig at some point, but fortunately one of the joys of living in a small town was that almost anything was within walking distance of anywhere else. Given that she really didn't want to compound things yet by asking Rebecca to help her fetch her car, that was a very good thing.

*   *   *

Tim rolled over, glanced at the clock on his bedside table, rubbed his eyes, and stared at it again. It couldn't possibly be that late, but apparently it was. He was surprised his father hadn't come up and banged on the door with a chorus of, "lazy bones, sleepin' in the sun, how're you ever gonna get your day's work done?" the way he had when Tim was a boy. Although Tim had to admit, the light coming through the blinds was hardly bright sunshine.

He scrubbed his face with his hands again as he sat up and remembered why he really didn't like coming back to visit with his parents. It hadn't been so bad when he'd been a college student, coming home for Christmas and for a few weeks between summer school and the beginning of the fall semester, but even then he'd felt like he was being squeezed back into a space he didn't fit into anymore.

His room looked like a damned shrine. To what, or who, he didn't want to consider. He wondered if his mother would ever take it over as a sewing room the way she'd threatened to do when he left for college.

Maybe it wasn't big enough to bother with. He'd swear the room wasn't much bigger than the bedroom closet in his apartment in Seattle, and that was saying something. A twin bed, which he'd outgrown while he was still in high school, a desk, and a nightstand barely left room enough to turn around in. The space had been carved out of the attic dormer of the tiny bungalow, and the ceiling slanted down to unusable space on either side, with built-in cupboards that he'd used in lieu of the chest of drawers that wouldn't have fit.

It did have a nice window at the end of the dormer, looking out into an enormous maple tree, its leaves in the midst of turning school bus yellow. It had once been a very useful tree. If he took the screen out of the window and climbed out onto the downstairs roof, he could reach branches sturdy enough to support his weight, allowing him to climb down and go out without his parents' knowledge. At least they used to, until he hit his growth spurt in high school.

Tim smiled ruefully. He remembered how disappointed he'd been when he'd discovered — the hard way — that those branches wouldn't hold his weight anymore. He almost wished they would now.

He'd hardly stopped to drop off his suitcase and say hello to his folks last night before he'd headed out to the Red Dog. Oh, he'd have stayed home this first night, but his dad had insisted he go on, and his mother hadn't said stay. She'd just looked at him in that way she had, her mouth smiling but her eyes —

He did not want to face those eyes this morning. Or the rest of her.

But he couldn't stay up here forever. Sighing, Tim got up and began to get dressed.

* * *

His mother was alone in the kitchen when he went downstairs, putzing around, wiping already-clean counters. Tim hoped she hadn't been waiting for him, but he knew she had.

"Where's Dad?" Tim asked as he gave her a hug.

"At the clinic."

Of course he was. Even on a Saturday morning, even on the first day after his son came home to visit for the first time in two years.

"I'm sure he'd be happy if you went down there."

Tim let out his breath. "I'll go. What?" This as she put her hand on his arm.

"But not till you've had some breakfast. Or lunch." She gave him a sly look.

He supposed he deserved that. "Sorry. I overslept."

"How do scrambled eggs and toast sound?"

"That's great, Mom, but don't bother." He could have picked something up at Miller's, the local answer to McDonald's, on his way. Stan Miller made Egg McMuffins taste like a poor imitation of the real thing.

But she was already cracking brown eggs into the ceramic bowl he'd given her for Christmas how many years ago? Her back to him, she said, "You were out late last night. Did you have a good time?"

Tim felt like he was back in high school. He supposed he would until he left to go back to Seattle. Back home to Seattle, he told himself firmly. "Yes, I did. It was good to see the old crowd again."

"It's been a long time, I know." The words, "longer than it should have been" were left unsaid but understood by both of them.

Tim cast around for something, anything, to change the subject. "So, when did Jack finally get up the gumption to ask little Becky out?"

His mother brought his plate, the scrambled eggs steaming, and set it on the table. She was smiling all the way to her eyes now, Tim saw with relief. "From what I understand, it was the other way around."

Now that was news. "Do tell."

"Eat your eggs." The toast popped and Tim grabbed it, but kept his eyes on her. She actually chuckled. "The story goes that Becky got tired of waiting, almost a year after he came back home with his degree. He'd been teaching for six months when she finally walked right up to him and asked him what he was waiting for. They've been an item ever since."

Tim tried to imagine it. It was easier than he'd have suspected. "Her parents must have had kittens."

His mother sighed. "Jack is a good man, with a good job."

"You know that and I know that, but her parents can't possibly see it that way."

"No, they don't."

"Are they talking to her?"

"After a fashion."

"Are they even admitting he exists?"

She shook her head. "No. They've tried to matchmake for her with one of the boys in their church, but she wouldn't have anything to do with him. She almost lost her job over it, but Pastor Shellfield refused to let her go."

"I'd have thought he'd be the last person to stand up for her."

"Apparently he finds her secretarial skills indispensable." Avis frowned. "He ought to. He runs her ragged."

"I'm surprised she hasn't looked for another job."

"It's not easy in a community this size. Besides, she's not really that rebellious."

"Except when it comes to Jack," Tim commented, and finished off his eggs.

"Except when it comes to Jack." She took his plate before he could carry it to the sink himself. "Becky's parents always were the most reactionary of that congregation, anyway. Which is saying a fair amount."

Tim nodded. The Thorsteins had never made a secret of their Tea Party politics, but that wasn't what made them unusual, not here in rural Montana. Neither did their religion, not really, although they took it to much more of an extreme than even the others they shared their little fundamentalist church with.

No, it was how Mr. Thorstein treated his womenfolk. And how stiff-necked both of Becky's parents were. And how they'd refused to let Becky see the doctor and dentist until she'd gotten sick enough with complications from the chicken pox that Tim's father had called in child protective services all the way from Kalispell to intervene. They'd never forgiven Samuel for that interference, especially since the attention had also put an end to their poor excuse for home schooling her. Tim remembered her first day at school. She'd been like a frightened little fairy. But the frightened part hadn't lasted long.

His mother let out a puff of breath that wasn't quite a snort. "Sometimes I think they'd like to hide Becky in a closet."

"Except for matchmaking, I take it."

"Yes. They want grandchildren. But they definitely don't want Jack to be the father."

"What happened with the matchmaking?"

"Rebecca got up and walked out of the meal they'd invited the boy to. So far as I know, she hasn't been back to her parents' house since."

"Poor kid."

His mother nodded, then changed the subject again. Tim had the feeling she'd only been letting him off the hook temporarily.

She'd been working around the long way to what really mattered. His suspicion was confirmed with her seemingly-innocuous question. "How are things in Seattle?"

He had to be careful with this one. Leaning too hard either way would trap him. "They're fine. I'm glad the gap between my residency and the new job was such good timing, though."

"So are we. It would have been a shame for you to miss your father's party. The whole town's looking forward to it."

His father was about to turn seventy-five. He'd been the town's only doctor since long before Tim was born, when his parents had just about given up on having a child of their own. His father had been forty-five, his mother ten years younger, and they'd been married almost fifteen years.

Tim had grown up in a fish bowl, had spent hours in his father's office every week almost from the time he could walk, and had always known he wanted to be a doctor himself. It wasn't until he'd realized there was a whole wide world outside of Campbell that he'd understood a medical degree could be a ticket out of here instead of a reason to come back.

"I've been looking forward to it, too." His mother let that fib pass, but he could tell she knew it was one.

She pursed her lips. "I wish it was going to be his retirement party."

"It isn't?" Tim was genuinely surprised.

"He can't find anyone to take over his practice." She had her back to him again, washing the frying pan out.

Tim raised his voice slightly over the running water. "Has he tried?"

"Yes." She turned the water off and picked up a dishcloth.

"Are you sure?"

She blew out her breath, setting the now-dry frying pan down. "No."

"Do you want me to see what I can do?" There were avenues, through the state, through several medical organizations Tim knew of, hell, through the alumni association of the University of Washington, where he'd gotten his own degree.

She didn't look relieved, but she only said, "Yes, please."

"I'll be glad to."

"He's getting fragile, Tim. Go easy on him."

"He's about as fragile as a bulldozer, Mom."

His mother sighed. "He's changed." It was as close as she could get to saying, "I'm worried about him," and Tim knew it.

"I'll go over to the clinic for a while before I head out with Jack."

Now he did see relief in her expression. "Where are you and Jack going?"

"Just up to Bramlet Lake to fish for an hour or two." Tim had been surprised when Jack had suggested the outing last night. Tim had figured Jack would want to spend his first day home in two months getting caught up on life and spending time with his ladylove. But the escape had been too good to resist. Besides, he and Jack had a lot to catch up on, too. "Are you up for a trout dinner tonight?"

She smiled. "Of course. As long as you clean them."

Chapter 4

The clinic looked the same as it ever did, Tim thought as he parked the Prius in front of the little frame storefront. It was only six blocks from his parents' house, but he'd be leaving here straight for Jack's.

The building's proper name was the Grant County Medical Clinic, but nobody ever called it that, in spite of the black lettering on the big front window. It was always just "Dr. Samuel's office." It had been Dr. Samuel's office for forty-five years, ever since it first opened back in 1969.

The heavy curtains were drawn back now, indicating the doctor was in. Tim's father kept no set hours. He never had. He'd explained to Tim how injuries and illness waited for no one after he'd missed Tim's sixth birthday party because of an accident at the mill. Tim hadn't understood then. He did now. It was one of the many, many reasons why he wanted to work in a group practice.

He took a deep breath, squared his shoulders, and went inside.

"Well, look what the cat dragged in."

"Hello, Betty. Nice to see you, too." Tim had long ago learned not to take the bait his father's assistant handed out freely. Betty Real – pronounced Ree-al, like the money, she always explained proudly – had an RN degree that Tim half-suspected had come from a mail order diploma mill. But she was nothing if not reliable, and if her education lacked depth, her experience certainly did not.

"Your dad's in his office."

"Thanks." Aware of her gaze following him, Tim went past the single examining room and the storage closet, and knocked on the door at the end of the hall.

"Come in, come in." His father didn't look up from the paperwork on the scarred old oak desk that, so far as Tim knew, had come with the place.

His office hadn't changed otherwise, either. Still the same fake wood paneling, which always seemed ironic to Tim, given that Campbell's biggest employer was a lumber mill. Still the same old cockeyed blinds at the windows, and battered easy chair in the corner. Black and white asphalt tile on the floor. Still no computer for records, either.

Tim's mother had made several attempts to brighten the place up over the years, but Samuel had always brought everything back home, claiming her gewgaws distracted him. Maybe they did. Or maybe he just didn't want to waste the money on non-necessities. The clinic had never – would never – make anyone close to well-to-do. Which was another reason on Tim's long list of why he wanted to practice in Seattle rather than here. If he was ever to have a hope of paying off his student loans in a reasonable amount of time without scrimping and saving to the hilt, he needed to make some serious money.

At last his father glanced up. "Timothy!" He rose from his desk and came around, beaming.

Tim could feel himself smiling back, almost against his will. His father's grin was more infectious than the common cold. Dr. Samuel Swanson was wearing his usual uniform of flannel shirt, worn blue jeans, and boots, with his "I'm at work now" white lab coat over the top. He'd always been a slight man. Tim remembered the first time he'd been able to look down at the top of his father's head.

He seemed even smaller now. Slighter. His clothes hung off his body as if he'd been borrowing them from the closet of a sturdier man. His face was thinner, too. More lined. Unlike Tim's mother, who at sixty-five hadn't changed much at all since the last time he'd seen her except for a few worry lines on her face, Samuel suddenly seemed old. Well, he is, Tim thought resentfully. He's seventy-five, or he will be in a few weeks. He should have retired years ago.

"Hi, Dad," he said out loud. "Did you have an emergency this morning?" Tim knew full well that he didn't, or his mother would have said something.

"No, no. Just some paperwork. I was hoping you'd come by and rescue me from it." Samuel laughed, the sound almost brittle to Tim's ears. "Come look around. We've made some changes since the last time you were here."

Tim certainly hadn't seen anything new so far. Maybe they'd redone the examining room? "Sure, why not? I can't stay long, though. I'm going fishing with Jack later."

His father's face fell for a split second. If Tim hadn't been watching him so closely he'd have missed it altogether. "Of course. How is Jack?"

As Tim and his father checked out the examining room, unchanged in decades so far as Tim could tell, he realized his mother was right. Something was wrong with Samuel besides just age. And it was going to be Tim's job to diagnose the doctor.

* * *

He was still thinking about his father and the hour he'd spent at the clinic as he tramped up the trail ahead of Jack that afternoon when his friend's voice jerked him out of his reverie.

"So, what do you think of her?"

Tim tilted his head around to stare at Jack, almost losing his balance on the rocky trail. He'd wondered if Jack had an ulterior motive for this little excursion. Given that the man had just gotten back from two months out in the wilds of eastern Montana hunting for the dinosaur fossils that were his second vocation, Tim thought the last thing Jack would have wanted was a hike.

But they'd bounced in Jack's four-by-four over old logging roads to the trailhead, and gathered their gear for the hike up the mountain, through the larches dropping orange needles everywhere, their conversation nothing more profound than "You got that wagtail fly?" and "Wait a minute, I need my extra reel."

Who the hell was Jack talking about? "Her who? Tara?"

"I think we all know what you think of Tara, my friend." Jack laughed. "Especially after that little exhibition you two put on last night at the Red Dog."

Tim abruptly aimed himself up the hill again. Jack knew? The whole town would know by tonight, if they didn't already. "We didn't do anything," he muttered.

"What do you mean?" Jack exclaimed. "I thought she was going to reach across the table and throttle you when you asked her how much money she'd lost betting you wouldn't come home for your dad's party."

Tim relaxed. Nobody'd seen them in front of Tara's house. The small side street had been deserted. He knew that. "Who, then?"

"Rebecca. Who else would I be talking about?" Jack pushed past Tim, thumping him on the shoulder as he strode on.

"How was I supposed to know who? I can't read your mind." Tim caught up with Jack and thumped him back.

"What do you think of her?"

Tim considered. "She's Becky. I didn't pay a whole lot of attention."

"Too busy watching Tara?" Jack smirked.

Had Jack caught him at it? Denial was about his only choice now. "I wasn't watching Tara. I have better things to do."

"Pull my leg some other time." Jack snorted, then turned serious. "Did you ever explain to her about my cousin?"

Tim nearly tripped over a tree root. "What?"

Jack shrugged and strode on. "You know. Andrea. The one from North Dakota."

Andrea, Tim thought. The woman who'd resulted in Tara dumping him, and the last time he'd ever talked to her. Until last night.

"Hello?" Jack stopped in the middle of the trail and waited.

"What?" There was a reason Jack was his friend. Tim knew he'd remember what that reason was sooner or later.

"Did you tell her?" Jack demanded.

"No. She wouldn't let me get a word in edgewise, and the next thing I knew she was dating somebody else." A bald and tattooed librarian, of all people.

"So that's why she doesn't want anything to do with you."

Yeah, right, Tim thought. That's why she planted one on me that kept me awake all last night. Aloud, he said, "Jack, that was five years ago. I hardly think it matters now."

Jack shrugged. "Fine. So tell me what you think of Rebecca." He started up the trail again. Tim hurried to catch up.

He'd seen them acting all lovey-dovey last night, but surely Jack wasn't serious about her. "Why Becky?"

"Because I'm taking her to the Blacktail Mountain Inn tonight and I'm going to ask her to marry me."

This time Tim really did trip over a rock. "You're what?!?" He caught himself before he landed on his knees, and stared at his friend.

"You heard me." Jack thumped Tim again, harder than before. Tim rubbed his shoulder and readjusted the daypack straps. They were going to have to figure out a new way to do this male bonding thing before something got dislocated.

Then it hit him. "Becky?" Tim skidded to a stop. She'd grown up, but she was still just little Becky. Frankly, he hadn't paid attention to more than that.

Jack grinned. "She's hot, isn't she?"

"Hot?" Tim barely managed to keep the word from coming out of his mouth in a tone that would have gotten him far more than just a thump on the shoulder. "Yeah, if you say so, buddy."

Jack's face darkened. Wrong words. Tim backpedaled. Quickly. "Um, yeah, she's gorgeous, beautiful, all that."

Jack's frown vanished, and he laughed. "Yeah, I can tell you think so." He sobered. "It doesn't really matter what you or anyone else thinks. She's beautiful to me."

"So you're going to marry her." Tim couldn't help feeling skeptical. "If that's what you want, buddy." He couldn't imagine getting that serious about anyone, and hadn't been able to in years. Five years, to be precise. He jerked his thoughts away from that well-worn trail.

"Yeah. It's what I want. And I'm pretty damned sure it's what she wants, too. Lucky me." Jack grinned again. "You ought to try it sometime."

With who? "I'll pass. But thanks anyway."

"As long as Tara's turning you down, huh?"

Forgetting his resolution of moments ago, Tim thumped Jack. There, he thought as he watched Jack rub his shoulder. Now at least they were even. "That's got nothing to do with it."

"Sure, buddy. Whatever you say." Jack paused. "You'll be my best man, right?"

Tim grinned in spite of himself. "Sure. Anytime."

* * *

"Where are you taking me?" Rebecca asked Jack curiously the following evening.

Jack ran a hand through his hair, ruining the first decent haircut he'd had since June, then put his hand back on the steering wheel. "I told you. Kalispell."

"But where in Kalispell?" Rebecca jounced slightly on the four-by-four's well-worn passenger seat, and Jack let out a not-so-patient sigh. "Unless we're going up to Whitefish to socialize with the movie stars, we're way overdressed."

Maybe they were, he in a sport coat and tie, and she in a softly flowered dress, but he'd be damned if he was going to propose in his jeans. "You'll see."

"You know I hate it when you say that."

"I know you're going to ruin the surprise if you keep this up." Jack glanced over, knowing that pestering him was half the fun for Rebecca of any excitement he planned for her.

Arranging surprises for Rebecca had become one of the most singular joys in his life in the past two years. She enjoyed them so much. He knew it was because they'd been few and far between in the life she'd led up till he'd suddenly discovered her.

He knew that's how she thought of it, and Jack wasn't inclined to explain the truth. He'd watched Rebecca Thorstein grow up from a tiny golden seedling of a girl, to a slender straight wand of a woman. She glowed like a larch in autumn, he thought, surprising himself. Jack Rasmussen wasn't inclined to poetry.

He hadn't been inclined toward letting Becky Thorstein know how he'd felt about her all those years, either. She'd had to tell him. At least she'd waited until he'd finally established himself in respectable society in Campbell, the high school science teacher with a master's degree, who excavated, researched, and wrote respected paleontology articles in his spare time.

His belief in evolution put him beyond the pale with the tiny fundamentalist minority in Campbell, a situation he would have laughed off the way he'd laughed off his background from the poor side of town all those years ago. If it hadn't been for Rebecca Thorstein and her fundamentalist parents and her creationist church, he wouldn't have cared if anyone knew what his beliefs were. The school board did not kowtow to the minority, and he'd added to the Grant County School District's small stash of cachet by publishing in scientific journals.

He'd had it wondered to his face on more than one occasion why he'd come back to Campbell, when he could have gone on for his doctorate and taught at a university. But a university didn't have kids at a nice, early, impressionable age, ready to be inspired with the wonders of science. It didn't have the reassurance of home, his past notwithstanding. And, most important of all, it didn't have Rebecca.

Because of Rebecca, he was becoming extremely talented at holding his tongue. Sometimes, when they'd run into her parents on the street, he'd darned near bitten the thing off.

"Earth to Jack, Earth to Jack."

Jack mentally shook himself. "What?"

"I take it this means you're not going to tell me where we're going."

He grinned inwardly. Here we go again, he thought. "I did. Kalispell. And we're almost there."

"What were you thinking? You were frowning so." Rebecca slid a hand over his forehead, smoothing the lines away.

He brushed it away gently. "Watch out. I'm driving."

"You're so talkative tonight." She pouted a bit, but returned her hand to her lap.

He reached over and grasped it, bringing it to his knee, earning one of her quicksilver smiles. "I've got a lot on my mind."

"Such as?"

Such as trying to figure out the best way to get the ring that was currently burning a hole in his pocket transferred to her finger without making a fool of himself.

"Such as trying to figure out how to get you to quit pestering me to tell you something when it's obvious it'll ruin the surprise."

"Oh." Her face fell. She slipped her hand free, wrapping it with the other one, and suddenly became very interested in them as they lay stiffly in her lap.

Criminy. Now he'd done it. He often walked a fine line between teasing Rebecca and crushing her. Crushing her was hideously easy. He still marveled that she had any backbone left after the way she'd been brought up. "I'm sorry, Rebecca. I didn't mean it like that."

She straightened. He smiled encouragingly at her. "I know," she said softly.

"We're here, anyway." He turned off the highway onto a road that went steeply uphill just before they entered Kalispell. It wound into the dusk between evergreens and the barely-golden larches. Five minutes later he was pulling into a small parking lot in front of what looked like an overgrown ski chalet. A discreet sign next to the walkway said Blacktail Mountain Inn.

Jack killed the engine and turned to his passenger. Her eyes were huge and dark. He grinned. "Hungry?"

She simply watched him and nodded.

"Then let's go." He opened his door and climbed out.

Chapter 5

Elegant, Rebecca thought as Jack led her up the walk. Elegant and beautiful. And much too sophisticated for the likes of her. She could see the candlelight glowing through the windows, hear the soft classical music wafting out, smell the exotically delicious scents filling the room as Jack held the door open for her.

"This is lovely," she told Jack as the hostess led them to their table, past enormous windows overlooking the lights of Kalispell shimmering in the valley. The faint outline of the Mission Mountains rose to the east, black against the darkening sky.

Jack pulled out her chair, his expression mischievous. "Mike said you could get a good steak here."

Rebecca smiled at Jack's mention of the high school principal, a man known for his meat and potatoes attitude, and sat down. "A restaurant in Montana without steak would be against the law. But it seems a shame to go somewhere that smells as sophisticated as this and order steak. You could have gotten that in Campbell."

"There's something more sophisticated than a steak?" Jack inquired.

Rebecca laughed and picked up her menu. She still felt out of place, but she wouldn't be anywhere else right now for all the world.

* * *

The evening spun out magically. The food, decidedly fancier than a slab of grilled beef, was delicious. Jack hadn't been able to talk her into wine, but then he'd had never been able to talk Rebecca into spirits of any kind. Out of respect for her abstinence, he'd foregone anything himself, and found himself regretting the omission. He needed all the courage he could muster to do what he'd planned.

Finally, after the dessert plates that had held their slices of raspberry chocolate cheesecake were removed, Jack reached for Rebecca's hand. She let him take it, her expression curious.

"You're probably wondering why I asked you here tonight," he said, trying to joke off a little of his nervousness.

She smiled at him, the softness in her expression making him want to sigh. She was the only woman in the world who could make him feel that way. Turning her hand over under his palm, she wove her fingers through his. His heart skipped a beat. "I have to say the question has crossed my mind. But I knew you'd tell me when you got ready, and not a minute before."

She always knew when to trust him and when to tease. Jack marveled at it. "Is that okay? I mean, I wanted to do things right, and not just pop the question over peanuts at the Red Dog – Oh, hell." The curse word just made things worse. "Sorry. Sorry." Jack tried to let go of Rebecca's hand but found her slender fingers were suddenly capable of more strength than he'd figured on.

An eternity of seconds later, he risked a look at her face. The expression he saw there, half apprehension, half hope, caused the breath he'd been holding to go out of his lungs with a whoosh. Her fingers clenched tightly enough around his to make him wonder if they were going to go to sleep for lack of blood.

"I didn't mean to make an idiot of myself, either, but I guess it's too late now." He reached into his jacket pocket with his free hand. Pulled out a small black velvet box. Watched with satisfaction as Rebecca's eyes grew huge. Popped the lid with his thumb.

She let go and pulled her hand back. Jack watched her as Rebecca stared at her hands in her lap as if she was afraid they would do something she couldn't control. "Don't you want to see it?"

Slowly she raised her eyes to his. Nodded. Carefully Jack tugged the ring free from its black velvet nest and held it out so that she could see. The clear oval diamond in its classically simple gold setting winked in the candlelight like one in the field of stars outside.

Rebecca had lifted her left hand to her lips. Jack reached out across the small table and wrapped his fingers around her wrist, pulling it to him. She didn't resist.

The golden metal warmed as he slid the ring onto her finger, settling it past her knuckle. Feeling a bit foolish, he lifted her hand to his lips and kissed it. He'd never done anything like that before, but tonight it just seemed right. The same way getting all dressed up and driving to a fancy restaurant in Kalispell had felt right.

The way he suspected everything from here on in was going to feel right.

Jack looked up. Two enormous tears were sliding silently down Rebecca's pale cheeks. He was out of his chair and crouched by her side before he knew it. "Sweetheart, are you – I just assumed when you didn't stop me –"

"You really do love me." She sounded incredulous.

"Of course I do." Jack watched her quizzically. "You knew that, didn't you?"

The smile that slowly dawned on her face was a wonder to behold. "Yes. I guess I did. Oh, Jack!" Suddenly Rebecca flung herself into his arms, nearly toppling him over backward onto the floor. "I love you. I love you more than anything in the world."

The relief was like having a ten-ton boulder roll off his back. He stood, bringing her with him, and squeezed her slender frame in his arms. Tightly. Just as he planned on doing for the rest of his life. He could hear voices in the background, but he ignored them.

"I take it that's a yes?"

She giggled, her voice breathless. "If you'll ask me."

He chuckled into her hair, then pulled back to see more tears on her shining face. He reached out and wiped them gently away. "Rebecca? You're the one woman I know I can trust. I love you very much. Marry me? Please?"

"Forever," she said, and wrapped her arms around him again, raising her lips to his. The kiss was everything he'd always had with Rebecca, and more.

Jack wanted to forget where he was, and the fact that they were in a very public place, when a tap on his shoulder brought him around.

"The check, sir."

Jack straightened, hoped his face wasn't as red as it felt. "Thank you." He eyed the waiter, who was beaming. As were the three other waiters standing behind him, and the sea of faces of the people seated at the tables behind them. He gazed down at Rebecca, still clinging to his waist, his arm still tightly round her. He fished in his pocket for his wallet, started to hand his credit card to the waiter.

"No need, sir." Jack stared at him, puzzled, then looked down at the check. One word was written across it. "Congratulations."

"What's going on?"

"Another party has paid for your meal tonight, in honor of your engagement."

"Who?" said Jack, then felt a nudge from Rebecca. He glanced down at her.

"Just say thank you," she whispered.

He turned back to the waiter. "May we thank this person directly?"

"It's not necessary, sir."

Jack shrugged helplessly. "Then would you let them know we appreciate the gesture. Very much."

The waiter's grin widened. "I'd be glad to, sir."

As they strolled to the door, Rebecca squeezed Jack's hand. "I wonder who it was."

He had a suspicion, but he wasn't going to voice it till he'd had a chance to corner Tim. "Probably someone who was glad to see us and our ruckus leave the building."

"John Allen Rasmussen. What a terrible thing to say."

He grinned down at her. "But probably true." He pushed the door open for her, then followed her outside. When she would have gone on to his rig, he pulled her into his arms. "Now where were we?"

"In a public place, silly man."

Laughing, he followed her to the truck.

* * *

Tara was back behind her checkout desk at the library Monday morning when Rebecca came dashing in. It didn't overly concern her, as Rebecca dashed about on a regular basis. But this time, the light in her eyes had Tara grinning even before the door closed. As did the words that burst out of Rebecca's mouth loudly enough to get the attention of every one of the half dozen people in the building.

"He asked me!" Rebecca darted around the desk and flung her arms around her friend. "He finally asked me!"

Tara extricated herself and set the barcode wand down, then led the way the few steps back into her office. "Who asked you? And what did he ask?"

"Jack, silly! He took me into Kalispell to the Blacktail Mountain Inn last night, and he asked me to marry him!" Rebecca flung her arms around Tara again, and this time Tara returned the hug.

"Oh, sweetie, I'm so happy for you." Tara leaned back and got a good look at Rebecca's face. "Yep. I'm definitely supposed to be happy."

"Of course you are. I'm just about ready to explode. Look at my ring." This as she pulled her arm back and thrust her left hand at Tara. "Isn't it beautiful?"

The ring was lovely, and Tara found herself inexplicably close to tears as she admired it.

She cleared her throat. "It's gorgeous. Have you set a date yet?"

"Jack wants to do it yesterday." Rebecca giggled. "I think he's tired of waiting."

"I imagine he is."

"It's one of the things I love about him, though, that he was willing to wait for me. He understands how important it is to me to save myself until I'm married."

"I know, Rebecca. No one's faulting you. There's lots of times I wish I'd waited, too." Immediately Tara regretted the words.

Rebecca sobered. "Has he tried to talk to you at all?"

Tara strove for lightheartedness. "Who, Tim? What would he do? Drag me back to Seattle with him?"

"He did come home."

"For a visit."

"If Jack has his way, it'll be longer than that. He wants Tim to be his best man." Rebecca paused. "Which might make things a little awkward, considering what I wanted to ask you. Would you be my maid of honor?"

"Of course, Rebecca. I'd be glad to." Tara would do anything to ensure Rebecca's happiness, even if she had to strike a truce with Tim.

"But surely Tim will have to go back to Seattle sometime between now and the wedding?"

"I don't know." Rebecca grinned again. "It all depends on how soon yesterday can be."

* * *

"So Becky and Jack are getting married."

"So they are." And don't go getting ideas again, Dad, Tim thought as, by request, he accompanied his father to his office Monday morning. Drop him off, get out of there, go somewhere, anywhere else. Not that he had any plans or anywhere to go. Jack was working, and even if his other friends weren't, they didn't have time to drop their lives to keep Tim company. If he was in Seattle, he'd be working, too.

"And you're to be best man." Samuel unlocked the door and gestured Tim in as he turned on the lights.

"So I'm told." Tim shrugged and followed him. He had nothing else to do.

"A little bird told me Tara is going to be Becky's maid of honor."

Tim gave his father a sidelong glance. "I didn't know Becky'd had time to ask her yet."

"Asked and accepted. You two will have to behave yourselves. You don't want to ruin their wedding." Samuel chuckled.

Tim sighed. "We're adults now, Dad. I think we can manage to walk down an aisle together without killing each other or knocking the flowers over."

His father's eyes twinkled, always a bad sign, as Tim trailed him down the hall to his office. "Maybe you ought to try walking down that aisle for yourselves."

"Dad. Please don't start." The exasperation Tim couldn't keep out of his voice didn't slow his father down one bit.

"She's a lovely young woman. I know you were seeing each other when you were in college. A man can't help wanting to see his only child settle down." Samuel glanced up from the paperwork on his desk. "I just want you to be happy, son."

Tim wanted to roll his eyes. "I am happy." He was, dammit. He was finally done with his residency, he had a good job waiting when he got back from this trip, and his life was finally about to start. At last. All he had to do was convince his father to retire, then he could go back to Seattle, back home, and have at it. So what if calling Seattle home still felt odd? It wasn't as if he was ever going to call Campbell home again.

Samuel eyed him. Tim squirmed, feeling as if he was a bacteria under a microscope. One that needed a good antibiotic.

"Your mother invited Tara over to dinner tonight. She thought you might like the company."

Wonderful, Tim thought. He supposed Tara had accepted because she couldn't very well say no. Neither could he. So they'd spend the evening being polite and biting their tongues until they bled. Or not. Tim wondered if Tara had spent as much time thinking about that kiss as he had. This might be a good way to find out, and perhaps needle her a bit. That was always entertaining. "Great."

"You will be there," Samuel said, a hint of his old authority in his voice along with obvious pleasure that Tim hadn't argued about it. But he didn't sound fragile at all. Surely his mother was exaggerating just to get Tim to do something to push his father into retiring – and that was Samuel's choice, after all.

"Of course, Dad."

"Your mother didn't want me to tell you because she thought you'd find an excuse to go out."

"Dad, I'm not fifteen anymore. I'll be polite. Besides," well, maybe it wasn't a fib after all, "it'll be good to talk with Tara again. We didn't get to say much at the Red Dog Saturday night."

"It might be nice if you stopped at the library and walked her over." Of course it would be. His father, fragile? The man was still as much of a steamroller as he'd ever been.

"She knows the way."

"Timothy."

This time Tim did roll his eyes. "Okay. I'll stop by and walk her over."

Samuel, suddenly involved with a stack of charts, didn't answer. Tim shrugged and turned to go. Once he got back to the car, he could start making some phone calls. The sooner he managed to figure out what to do about his dad and the clinic, the sooner he could get out of here.

Back to where people treated him like the adult he was, instead of a miscreant teenager. And get started on his life.

"Son?" His father's voice pulled him back from the hallway.

Tim turned. "Yeah?"

"Come take a look at this x-ray." His father pointed at something on the film pinned to the fluorescent light panel on the wall. "It's so grand to have another doctor around to consult with."

Reluctantly, Tim went to peer over his father's shoulder. The x-ray was nothing exciting. A cracked rib. Probably a sports injury. But Tim gave his professional opinion, basked in his father's approval, and found himself somehow enjoying the whole process.

You need to get back to the real world, Swanson, he told himself sternly. Real challenges. Real excitement. Real options.

Soon, he promised himself. Very soon.

Chapter 6

The squat, square, county government building still looked the same as Tim remembered it as he strolled up to it late that afternoon, tan brick and mortar in a style that hadn't even been cutting edge in the fifties when it was built. The library occupied one corner on the ground floor, with wide uncurtained windows. Tim could remember countless winter afternoons spent gazing out those windows over the snow-covered grass out to the flagpole, wondering what the wide world was like.

His father, as Campbell's only doctor, hadn't felt comfortable leaving town for even a few days at a time. The sum total of Tim's travel experience up until he'd gone off to college had consisted of the occasional shopping trip with his mother to Spokane, three hours away, the twice-yearly overnight backpacking hikes into the Cabinet mountains with his boy scout troop, and one memorable week in Yellowstone National Park, again with the boy scouts, where he'd watched in awe as Old Faithful went off like a rocket.

The rest of his childhood he'd traveled in the library, visiting faraway lands and learning new cultures through the books that had opened his eyes. And forever dissatisfied him with the everyday world he'd lived with in Campbell.

He'd started studying college catalogs and counting the days his freshman year in high school.

In a way, he supposed, he could blame the library for chasing him away from the town. How could someone live here his entire life and not be curious about what lay beyond the endless miles of forest and river and mountain?

Apparently Tara could. Tim squared his shoulders and pushed the door open.

"Well, if it isn't prodigal Tim." Tara stood behind the counter, watching him as he came toward her.

Tim sighed. "I could kill Jack for calling me that."

She smirked. "You have to admit it fits. The first thought that went through my mind Friday night was wondering if your parents were going to kill the fatted calf for you."

Surprised at his own feelings of defensiveness, he replied, "It's not that bad."

Tara leaned forward. "How long has it been since you've been home? I've been back a year and a half, and you haven't been back since I got here."

Tim shrugged. "I don't know. A couple of years. I just finished my residency. It was hard to get away." Tim glanced around and couldn't help smiling at the familiarity of the library. "I love this place."

The expression on Tara's face softened. "Me, too."

"What happened to Miss Iris?" Miss, never Ms., Iris Mulholland had been even more of a town institution than his father was. She'd arrived at the brand-new library in 1955 in answer to an advertisement for a job as the town's first librarian. She'd been in her twenties, and she'd never left. No one had ever pried out of her where she'd come from or why. She'd run the library with a stern hand and an aversion to censorship that had brought her to loggerheads with the county council on more than one occasion, but they'd never been able to chase her away. Not that anyone had ever really tried. No one could have imagined the library without her.

Most people had loved her. Tim had adored her for the worlds she'd opened to him, and knew Tara had, too. Miss Iris was, Tara had once told him, the reason she'd chosen her own career, because she wanted to be able to change people's lives. Tim understood that one. Miss Iris had certainly changed his.

"She passed away. A year ago last January. Right over there, according to Rebecca." Tara pointed at the small print reference collection.

"Dropped in the harness, eh? She'd have wanted it that way, I bet. And you came home to fill her shoes."

Tara smiled wryly. "I hardly think that's what I'm doing."

"No, you're right," he told her.

She looked affronted. "I'm right? That's a first for you."

She didn't have to sound so surprised. "I haven't heard you hush me yet."

"She wasn't that bad."

"You say that now. I remember you complaining about her when we were in high school." Tim grinned reminiscently.

"She was so old-fashioned." Tara straightened, and Tim's gaze dropped, almost of its own accord, to her curvy figure. He brought his eyes back up quickly, but saw that he was too late. She'd seen him do it. Behind the laughter in her eyes was something he hadn't seen before. Nervousness? Worry? No, it couldn't be. Tara Hillerman didn't have a nervous bone in her body. And she hardly had anything to worry about. Unless it was about what happened Friday night. "I'm not."

Tim stared at her. If she could read his mind, he was in deep trouble. "Not what?"

"Old-fashioned." Tim mentally wiped his forehead at her reply. "You ought to take a look around. We've made some changes in the last year and a half."

"I want to." And he did. "It'll have to be quick, though. My parents are expecting us. Although I have to say I'm surprised you accepted the invitation."

Tara raised her eyebrows at him. "Your mother said your father had his heart set on it, and you know your father. He can be pretty persuasive."

Tim snorted. "He's a bully."

"He's a lovely old man." She obviously interpreted his skeptical expression correctly, because she burst out laughing. Tim joined in. When their laughter had run its course, she contradicted herself. "You're right. He's a bully. But a dear one."

"Yeah." May as well test his theory. "About Friday night..."

Tara jumped in quickly. "I didn't mean to take your head off in the Red Dog. It's just that nobody bothered to tell me you were going to be there, and I wasn't expecting you."

"Obviously. You never did tell me how much money you lost betting against my coming to visit." He leaned forward and put his hands on the counter. Just like Friday night, she scooted backward. Interesting. "But that's not what I was talking about. I was thinking about later, when I took you home."

"I meant to say thank you for the ride."

"You did, Tara. Trust me. You did." Tim watched with satisfaction as the storm clouds began to gather in her face.

"You don't have a gentlemanly bone in your body, do you?" Funny, that sounded more like hurt than indignation. Nah. He was imagining things.

"Not particularly." Not when he could have the rare satisfaction of watching Tara blush.

"I should have known better."

Tim chuckled. "True."

"So how fast is it going around town? If you told Jack, he'll tell Rebecca, and —"

His own hurt feelings were a surprise. "I didn't tell anyone, Tara. It's none of their business."

"Well, isn't that a relief." Her voice dripped sarcasm as she turned to fuss with the electronic gizmo sitting on the counter. Tim watched as her shoulders slumped. So much for keeping a civil tongue in his head for the evening. He wanted to strangle his father for sending him over here. Tara knew where the house was. She could make her own way there.

But he did want to look around while he was here. He was surprised how much he did. Surely she could ignore him if he ignored her.

He was halfway to the non-fiction section when she spoke again.

"Thank you." The sincerity of it caught him off guard.

He came back to the desk. "You're welcome. And I'm sorry if I hurt your feelings. I can't seem to help myself."

"I didn't do anything to stop you." She sounded genuinely regretful.

Maybe they could learn to be civil to each other. "Can we just forget it happened?"

"Really?" She stopped, then added, "Okay."

Tim decided to take another bull by the horns. "Jack asked me to be his best man."

"I'd heard." Tara set the gizmo down and started fussing with the shiny new computer jerry-rigged onto the old check-out desk. Miss Iris had not approved of computers, to the best of Tim's knowledge. This one and the half dozen of them he could see down at the end of the room were new additions, and long-overdue in his opinion.

"And you're going to be Rebecca's maid of honor."

She nodded.

"I figure we ought to practice a few civilized conversations before the wedding so we don't ruin it for them. Turns out I was more right than I thought."

Tara looked up and grinned. Tim's heart stuttered. He hadn't felt like that since, well, since Friday night. Damn, Swanson, he thought, you'd never forgive each other if you followed your gut on this one. Forget about it.

"And," he cleared his throat, "I figure we need to throw some kind of party for them. I planned on taking the guys out to the Red Dog one night and causing some mayhem for a bachelor party, and you could do the frou-frou wedding shower routine. But it might work better if we did it on the same night. What do you think?"

"Skip the frou-frou, Swanson, and I think you may be on to something."

"And here I thought you specialized in frou-frou. Sentiment. All that jazz."

"What do you mean?" Her voice held as much warning as curiosity.

"Wasn't that what having me drive you home Friday night was all about? Getting all sentimental and welcoming me back to Campbell?" Tim ignored the little warning bell in the back of his mind. "I don't know why you stopped when you did. I was just getting all warmed up. We could have had a proper welcoming home party."

He was prepared for a bit of anger. Derisive laughter, maybe. Ridicule at his expense, certainly. Nothing he'd said was any worse than what they'd flung at each other for years, and certainly her behavior had been asking for it. But he definitely didn't expect the stricken look Tara gave him.

"How could you?" she whispered.

"Tara?"

Her voice grew stronger, although she kept it low in deference to where they were. "Get out. Go away. I wouldn't kiss you again if you were the last man on earth."

It stung, far more than he wanted to admit.

"Fine. Then don't throw yourself at me again, okay?"

"Believe me, I won't." Tara turned on her heel and headed into her office.

Tim had to satisfy himself with stomping his way out of the library and letting the door slam behind him. It wasn't nearly enough.

So much for walking her to dinner at his folks' house. He wondered if she'd even bother to show up.

* * *

She could hardly let go and cry here. Not in her office. Not in her library. Not in her town. Someone would see her, try to be kind, and ask questions, and Tara didn't have any answers. Not that kind, anyway.

It was as if he'd read into her heart, figured out where it would hurt most, and arrowed straight there. Deadly accuracy, cruel wit. All aimed at her.

It would have been different if she could understand why they did this to each other. Tara knew full well that it wasn't a one-way street. They both practically expected the attacks; he'd probably figured the kiss Friday night was her way of ambushing him first.

And it might have been, or it might have been much more. She'd been avoiding even thinking about why she'd done it. At the time she hadn't needed a motive, because her inhibitions had been drowned in alcohol. He'd been there, almost as if she'd wished him there as she had been doing for years, safe in the knowledge that he never would be. She'd kissed him before she could stop herself.

He'd completely misinterpreted her motives, such as they were. Hadn't he?

Now she was supposed to go over to the Swansons' for dinner. She couldn't disappoint Samuel, who had been rather insistent that she show up, and Avis. Knowing Avis, she'd probably saved that fatted calf for tonight.

Why, oh, why couldn't Tim have done what everyone expected and stayed in Seattle?

* * *

Tim walked clear out past the train depot and back, delaying his return home as long as he dared, but being late for supper was a cardinal sin in his mother's eyes. And there wasn't any point in punishing her for what he'd done.

Not that he'd meant to do it in the first place. The words had just sort of slipped out. The way they always did when Tara was around. She was the dynamite, and he was the match. Always had been and always would be.

"Where's Tara?" Samuel's voice carried through the screen door and across the porch to where Tim was climbing the steps.

"She can't come. Something came up at the library."

"Really? No one told me."

Startled, Tim turned to see Tara rounding the maple tree at the corner behind him.

Tara smirked at him and added, "I wouldn't miss dinner tonight for the world."

Great, he thought. Just great. Out loud, he added, "Neither would I."

"Well, then," said Samuel, smiling genially as if nothing was wrong. "Come on in."

* * *

"So, Tara, how are things going at the library these days?"

Tara smiled stiffly at the elder Dr. Swanson, father of the man she'd once thought she was in love with and now cordially hated, as he passed her the butter-browned potatoes. She dragged her thoughts from Tim, sitting opposite her, and tried to concentrate on the conversation.

"They're going well. After a year and a half it finally feels like my library now instead of Miss Iris's. Some folks in town are a bit disappointed about that, and they've told me so, but lots of people have told me it's nice to see the library moving into the twenty-first century. The partnerships we've made with the county's IT department and the local internet service provider have made a huge difference, too."

She felt, rather than saw, Tim's curiosity, since she'd tried to avoid meeting his eyes from the minute they'd sat down to steaks that probably were from that fatted calf.

"It's wonderful to have instant access to information we used to have to wait days for from the state library. I notice you've begun sending patients over more often to learn about their diagnoses ever since Karen Silsand came in and got all that information on chronic fatigue syndrome a few months ago."

Samuel nodded, but gave Tara an odd look as he picked up his knife. "Oh. Yes."

"I try to make sure they're getting their information from reputable sources. But sometimes it's hard to make sure they don't go surfing off to just anywhere, thinking it's gospel. The kids with their school reports are even worse." Tara smiled over at Avis. "But then you know how kids are, with your volunteer work at the elementary school."

Avis smiled back, her eyes, Tara noticed, on Samuel. "I've had a little experience with them. Wouldn't you say so, Timothy?"

Tim nodded, his mouth full. He swallowed. "Whatever you say, Mom." He turned his attention back to his food, obviously trying not to discourage the conversation.

Not that his mother was going to let him, apparently. "Did Tara get a chance to show you what she's done with the library?"

He glanced up. "Um, no. We got to talking instead."

Avis nodded. "That's good. I imagine you two have a lot to catch up on."

"You could say that." His voice was curt.

Samuel turned to Tara. "Tim worked at the clinic with me today."

"So I heard. How was it, Tim?" Tara deliberately made her voice syrupy enough to pour over pancakes.

Tim glared at her. "It was fine. The day was fine. The library's fine. The clinic's fine. Everything's fine. All this sweetness and light is just fine and dandy." He pushed back his chair. "Tara, do you really want to keep up this charade?"

Tara smiled sweetly at him. "What charade are you referring to?"

Tim sighed heavily and stood up. "Look, I'm sure you're enjoying yourselves, but the company is giving me indigestion. Tara, it's been

an experience. Mom, great meal. Right now, I need to go for a walk."
Without waiting for an answer, he left the room. A moment later, the
front door closed, a bit more forcefully than necessary.

Tara shrugged uncomfortably, feeling more than a bit responsible.
Not that he hadn't deserved it, but his parents surely didn't. "I'm sorry.
I didn't mean to cause a ruckus. Tim and I are back to our old tricks,
I'm afraid. We started insulting each other the minute he showed up in
town, and haven't stopped since."

"I was hoping you two had grown out of that." Mrs. Swanson's
soft voice brought Tara's head around. "You were such good
playmates when you were children."

"Before we hit puberty, you mean."

"I suppose you could say that."

"You both need to get over it and get along," Samuel declared.

Tara stared at him curiously. "Why? He won't be in town long."

"He will if I have anything to say about it."

"Samuel." Mrs. Swanson's voice held a note of warning.

"Avis, you know he belongs here, as much as I do."

"You may think you know that, but I don't, and Timothy obviously
doesn't think so. And it is his decision."

Dr. Swanson's voice went stern, as it had when Tara was a little
girl. She suddenly realized that she hadn't heard that tone in his voice
in a very long time. "Only if he makes the right one."

The discussion was bouncing back and forth as if it was a ping-
pong match, as if it was one of many such matches played here over
and over for years. How long had Samuel been plotting to get Tim to
come home? How hard was it for Tim to try to get his father to let
him live his own life without hurting Samuel's feelings?

Tara couldn't believe she was actually feeling sorry for the poor
guy. It wasn't as if he deserved her sympathy. But she did. Her own
parents had encouraged her to spread her wings. They'd been happy
when she'd come home, but they hadn't pushed. She'd come home
because she'd wanted to.

Tim didn't want to come home. But he was having to fight his
father every step of the way over it. No wonder he was so impossible.

Tara looked up to see that both of Tim's parents were watching
her.

"If you two got along, Tara, he might be more inclined to come home where he belongs."

"Samuel —"

Tara squared her shoulders. "Dr. Swanson, I don't think —"

"Maybe you should, young lady."

Tara rose. "I think this is where I came in. Mrs. Swanson, dinner was lovely." She turned to Samuel and smiled grimly. "I've always known where Tim gets his stubborn streak from, Dr. Swanson. I appreciate your point of view, but I'm not in the market for a relationship right now, and if I was, it certainly wouldn't be with Tim. Thank you for thinking of me, though." She set down her napkin and walked out. As she strode toward the front door she heard Avis's voice.

"Samuel, when will you learn?"

And Samuel's laughter. The sound made Tara grind her teeth. "I don't think I'm the one who needs to be taught, Avis."

Chapter 7

Tim strode into the clinic the next afternoon with blood in his eye. He'd managed to stay out late enough the night before to avoid a confrontation with his father, although slipping out without running into him that morning hadn't been as easy. He'd put off coming in to the office as late as he could, knowing that his father was expecting him. And that he needed to do something. What, his mother hadn't been able to explain. Just something.

At this point, what Tim wanted to do was put Samuel in a straitjacket. He'd settle for persuading his father to retire, however. At seventy-five, he'd had a good run. Surely there was something left in his life that he'd never had the time to do. Sleep late in the mornings, if nothing else.

Tim tried to imagine his father living a life of leisure and came up completely blank.

Thomas Wolfe was right. You couldn't go home again. At least not if you had any sense whatsoever.

"Your father wants to see you." Betty scowled. "What did you say to him?"

Of course it was all his fault. It was always all his fault. "Me? I didn't say a thing. He's the one with the bug up his —"

"Humph."

Tim chuckled humorlessly. "He's trying to set me up with Tara."

"Humph." This time the sound could have been a laugh if Betty ever did such things.

"Yeah. I know. In his dreams." Tim took a deep breath. "Where is the old busybody?"

"In his office."

Tim walked down the hall and knocked on the door. Heard his father's muffled voice telling him to enter. Hesitated for a minute before resolutely shoving the door open.

"You wanted to see me?"

"I did. Where have you been all morning?"

"Out." Tim watched his father. "I don't work here."

"You said you were coming in today."

"I did. And here I am." Tim waited. Samuel fidgeted with a chart. "You wanted to talk with me about something?"

Samuel raised his head and looked Tim straight in the eye. Tim fought the urge to shift his feet. "Why were you so rude to Tara last night?"

Tim sighed, feeling about fifteen, then straightened. Obviously he was going to have to spell out some kind of non-interference policy with Samuel before he wound up wanting to thump him. Thumping Jack was one thing. Thumping a seventy-five-year-old man definitely fell over the line of rude – especially when the man in question was his father.

"I could tell you that she and I had an argument before we ever got to the house. I could tell you that what you saw has been our normal mode of communicating for as long as I can remember, except that you already know that as well as anyone else in town does. And I could tell you that I resent having to make nice in one of the most awkward situations I've been in for a long time. But none of it is your business.

"Who I see and when I see them is no one's business but mine. And I'd really appreciate it if you'd dump the matchmaking efforts."

There, Tim thought, that ought to do it.

Samuel's expression changed into the picture of penitence. "Sorry, son."

Let's see if I can find a puppy to kick for my next act, Tim thought, ducking his head guiltily. "It's okay, Dad. I didn't mean to jump down your throat." Samuel aimed his gaze back toward the tabletop, a little too quickly.

Tim came and sat down in the patient's chair opposite his father.

"I just want to see you happy," Samuel said, sounding wistful, but

Tim knew better, knew exactly how he was hiding the twinkle in his eye.

It was the perfect opening, but Tim so didn't want to take it. It was as much as asking for his father to bully him some more about staying. But he'd promised his mother he'd at least try.

"Have you given any more thought to retiring, Dad?"

Samuel's head came up with a jerk. "What's that got to do with anything?"

"You're seventy-five years old —"

"I know how old I am."

"Wouldn't you like to be able to travel? I'd love to have you and Mom come to see me in Seattle. To have the chance to do some things for yourself?"

Samuel gestured out the window at the town in general. "And who is going to take care of them?"

Tim sighed. Here we go, he thought. "Have you even tried to find anyone? Besides me, that is?"

Samuel stared down at his desk.

"You haven't, have you?"

"No." Samuel said it so softly that Tim almost didn't hear him.

"If I can find someone willing to take over your practice, will you at least consider retirement?"

A long pause, then, "Your mother put you up to this, didn't she?"

Tim shrugged helplessly. "Yes, she did. And now that I look at you, I understand why she did it. Dad, you're not young anymore."

"I know."

"It's okay to let go. Really, it is."

"I know."

"Will you at least think about it? For Mom's sake?"

Samuel let out a gusty breath, but at last he nodded.

Tim stood, relief coasting through him. "Good. I'll make some calls tomorrow."

"It won't be that easy."

Tim stopped on his way to the door. "I'll find someone. No one's indispensable."

His father's next words, uttered just as Tim closed the door, were nearly inaudible. "Maybe not. But love is."

* * *

"I hope you enjoy the new book, Mrs. Hanson."

"Oh, I always look forward to a new Stephanie Plum book, Tara. Besides, I've been waiting and waiting to find out who was behind that door."

Tara smiled mischievously. "I can tell you if you like."

The plump, gray-haired woman clutched the book to her ample chest. "Don't you dare."

Tara chuckled as Mrs. Hanson made her way to the door. She was a frequent patron and one of the library's most ardent supporters, which, much to Tara's pleasure, included supporting Tara's modernization plan. But Tara's mood changed altogether when she saw who was being a gentleman and holding the door.

Mrs. Hanson beamed up at him. "Thank you, Timothy. We're so glad you've come home."

Tim smiled, although even from the desk Tara could see the exasperation in his eyes. "You're welcome." He turned, letting the door close behind him, shaking his head. She supposed she couldn't blame him, but he could go be exasperated anywhere but here so far as Tara was concerned. "What are you doing here?"

He strode up to the desk. "Last time I checked, this was a public library. Maybe I'm here to get a book."

Of course he was. Rattled, Tara told him the only thing she could think of, but even she knew it was merely a diversion. "You're no longer a resident of this county. We don't issue library cards to non-residents."

He burst out laughing. "Good grief, Tara. Who are you, the library police?"

"And what if I am?" Feeling ridiculous, she asked, "What were you looking for?"

But he was shaking his head. "Who. The right word is who. And I'm looking for you."

"I don't have anything to say to you." She turned to the computer, only to be stopped by his hand on her arm.

"I just want your opinion on something."

Sure he did. "Since when does my opinion mean anything to you?"

"Since you know this town better than a lot of people." Tim paused and glanced over his shoulder at the teenager who'd suddenly materialized behind him. "Look, can we go in your office and talk about this?"

Tara sighed. "Give me a minute." She turned to the young man. "Hi, Jeff."

As she checked out the stack of books, making small talk with another of her regular patrons, Tara watched Tim out of the corner of her eye. He leaned casually on the corner of the counter, the tension in his posture barely visible. As soon as she was done, Tara put the bell out on the counter and waved Tim back to her office.

"Can we make this quick? I've got work to do."

"I'll do my best." But he didn't say anything more. Oddly enough, she'd swear he was fidgeting, even though he didn't move.

Deliberately Tara sat behind the desk she'd inherited from Miss Iris, wanting her authority. Tim perched awkwardly on a corner of the big oak monstrosity, knocking some papers askew.

"Do you mind?" She glared at him.

"What? Oh." This as she gestured him to a chair. "What's the matter? Don't like me looming over you?"

"Not particularly. Now, what is this very important issue you want my opinion on?"

Tim settled himself into the chair. Now the expression on his face made her want to fidget. He looked worried, of all things.

"I'm sorry about last night. I should have known my dad was going to try to play matchmaker with a sledgehammer."

Tara stared at him, then found her voice. "I'm sorry, too. I shouldn't have accepted the invitation, or at least I should have warned you."

"You knew?" He leaned forward.

Tara shrugged. "He's been buttonholing me about you ever since I came home. It's no secret that he thinks I'm the reason you won't come back to Campbell to stay. I should have told you, is all."

Tim snorted. "It would have been nice."

"Hasn't he been after you, too?"

"I haven't talked with him much in the last year or so. When I call, I usually end up talking with Mom, and she's always the one who calls me. She didn't say a word, but then I wouldn't have expected her to."

Tara leaned back in her chair. "No. I guess not." She watched as Tim seemed to relax a bit as well. "But that doesn't mean I forgive you for what you said here yesterday."

"That's okay. I probably don't deserve to be forgiven anyway."

"What?" Tara stared at him.

He shrugged, an embarrassed expression on his face. Tara opened her mouth to quiz him on it, but he spoke first. "Never mind. That's not what I came here to ask you about, anyway."

She didn't want to change the subject, but she let him do it, anyway. "That's right. You wanted my opinion about something, didn't you?"

Tim nodded.

"Fire away. I have plenty of opinions. Whether they're the kind you want to hear or not is another story altogether."

Tim took a deep breath. "Do you hear anything about my dad?"

Tara shot him a surprised glance. "What do you mean?"

"Or about the clinic?"

Tara cast about, then decided to settle on the innocuous until she knew what Tim was aiming at. "Lots. People have always appreciated having him here. It's nice not to have to drive to Kalispell for every little thing. It's reassuring to know he's here in case of an emergency, and to be treated by someone who knows you. But you know that. Everyone here has always felt that way." She cocked her head. "What are you driving at?"

"Have there been any problems? Anyone unhappy with the treatment he's been given?"

Tara was taken aback. "I'm not the first person who'd be told about things like that —"

He interrupted her, much to her annoyance. "The library's not gossip central anymore?"

"I try to discourage that sort of thing."

Tim stared at her. "Why?"

"This is a library, not a coffee klatch."

"So? It's one of the centers of the community. What's the difference?"

Tara sighed. She'd been fighting this attitude ever since she'd arrived. It hadn't helped that she'd been the object of everyone's attention for coming back home after she'd claimed she never would. If Tara wanted to be honest with herself, which she did, her own position in the gossip mill was one of the reasons she'd tried to squelch the chatter in the one place she could do so to begin with. "Look. Miss Iris meant well. But her, er, curiosity was sort of embarrassing."

Tim chuckled. "Yeah, it was." His humor didn't last long, though. "So what you're telling me is that you don't want to have an opinion?"

"I guess so."

Tim rose.

"But I would like to know why you're asking."

Tim turned from where he already had his hand on the door. "I'm asking because my mother's worried. My dad's seventy-five years old, and shows no sign of wanting to retire. She doesn't like him going off and getting into dangerous situations."

"He's a doctor, not a skydiver."

"Doctors get into trouble, too, especially in a place like this, so close to the wilderness. Mom says he still insists on going out with the search-and-rescue teams, even though she's asked him over and over not to."

Tara hadn't thought of it that way. "Have you talked with him?"

Tim leaned on the doorknob. "Yeah. He thinks he's invincible." His eyes bored into hers. "No one's invincible, Tara."

"No. I guess not." She twirled the pencil she'd absentmindedly picked up. "And you're the one who's going to have to tell him, aren't you?"

"Yeah."

Something in his tone made her wonder. "You've already tried, haven't you? I bet that went over like a lead balloon."

He looked positively defeated. "Yeah."

She couldn't help feeling sorry for him. In spite of the fact that he'd been a jerk last night. "Well, at least it all makes sense now."

"What do you mean?"

"The matchmaking." She couldn't help smiling when his face went blank. "He's trying to make you want to stay. You're the only doctor he wants to have replace him."

"You think I don't know that?"

"Would you? Stay, I mean? If it meant that you could get your dad to retire?"

Tim grimaced. "It's not going to come to that, I hope."

Tim was dreaming if he thought that was the case. Or at least that's what Samuel would believe, and Tara was betting on the elder Dr. Swanson having the last word. She did feel sorry for Tim. But that didn't mean she was going to play the part Samuel was trying to put her into. Thank goodness Samuel wasn't her father. "I wouldn't count on it. Your dad is one of the most determined people I know."

"And I inherited that determination."

"Good for you."

He shoveled a hand through that beach-boy blond hair. She really did feel for him. And honestly, not all of it was simply feeling sorry for him. Just because she didn't have any intention of, good grief, marrying him, didn't mean her memories of Friday night, vague and fuzzy as they were, hadn't made her wonder if the reality could possibly have been as good as what she did remember. Besides, she'd never seen poor Tim so off kilter before. Not even when she'd dumped him five years ago. Being off kilter looked good on him.

Tim eyed Tara as she stood and came around the desk, grasping the doorknob as if it was his salvation. Slowly she walked to the window that let her observe the checkout desk, and slowly she lowered the blind, closing them into the privacy of her office.

"Tara? What are you trying to prove?"

"Nothing. If you're not interested, nothing at all." She stepped closer.

"And if I am?"

Tara stopped dead in front of him, the warning bells clanging for a moment. She decided to ignore them. "Are you?"

"Interested? Tara, I've always been interested."

"Me, too." There, she thought, that startled him.

"That doesn't mean it isn't suicidal," he said ruefully.

The imp in Tara chortled. "But what a way to go, right?" She reached up and touched her lips softly to his. He made a throttled sound and pulled back. Cleared his throat. Twice.

"You don't want this. I'm not staying in this town."

Tara shoved him hard enough to make the door bang when he hit it. "Tim, you are so full of yourself. I wouldn't want you to stay even if you had your heart set on it."

Tim twisted the knob and shoved the door open. "Then what the hell was that for?"

"It certainly wasn't a marriage proposal. Your head is the size of Mt. Rushmore."

"Fine. Whatever. Sorry I bothered you." Tim dodged around the checkout desk and aimed toward the door. He was gone before she could say anything else.

But she wasn't alone. Tara drew a deep breath. "May I help you?"

"I'm sorry to trouble you, dear." That wasn't a smirk on Mrs. Joiner's face. She was far too kind a person to smirk at anyone. She held out her library card.

"Oh, yes. I'm sorry." Mechanically Tara picked up the barcode wand and scanned it. She began checking out the small mountain of books.

"He's a handsome young fellow, isn't he?"

"Who?"

No, it wasn't a smirk. Tara refused to let it be a smirk. "Your Timothy."

"He's not my Timothy, but, yes, I suppose he is." Tara cast around for something, anything, to change the subject. Books. "So, it's to be Japanese history this week?"

Mrs. Joiner was reading her way around the world these days. She chuckled, but much to Tara's relief she let her off the hook. "Yes. After reading about the Mongols, I want to know more about the only nation that managed to repulse them."

Thankfully, Mrs. Joiner was one of the folks who'd bought into Tara's conviction that the library was not gossip central, as Tim had put it.

After she was gone with her pile of Japanese history books, Tara went back into her office and sank onto the edge of the desk. She wanted to put her head in her hands.

So. He'd been home what? Four days? And he'd already kicked her down twice. Okay, Tara thought. That's it.

It wouldn't be much longer till he was gone. He'd be on the road the morning after Samuel's party. Tara was willing to bet good money on it. Or – maybe not, considering the sum she'd lost betting he wouldn't show up in the first place. But still. She could endure anything for a couple more weeks. Right?

Tara raised her closed fist and rested it against her heart. Right where it ached.

Anything.

Chapter 8

"Now this won't hurt a bit."

Why did Dr. Samuel always have to lie about these things? If he thought he was doing her a favor, he wasn't, but Rebecca suspected his words were more part of the procedure than anything else. Get out the needles, lie about them to try to make people feel better. Oh, he meant well, but for someone like her, it just made things worse. Of course, for someone like her, *everything* about getting shots or having blood drawn just made it worse. It wasn't rational of her, but she couldn't help it, and she knew exactly why she hated it. Thank you, Mother and Father, she thought. Thank you so much for making going to the doctor feel like visiting the boogeyman.

Rebecca took a deep breath and held her arm out stiffly, the sleeve of her cotton blouse rolled past the elbow. She stared up at Jack, who stood beside her, knowing that her terror was plain on her face.

He squeezed her other hand, but he spoke to Dr. Samuel. "She's not a little kid screaming at the sight of a needle."

"I'm not?" She felt like one. Rebecca wound her fingers with Jack's. They were warm and strong, but he was supposed to be protecting her from bad things, not pushing her into them.

"It's okay, babe, I'll protect you from the big mean doctor." But he wasn't. Rebecca knew it was a stupid question, but why wasn't he? Jack gazed lovingly down at her, just as Dr. Samuel inserted the needle into her vein.

"I wasn't a big mean doctor even when you were a little girl, was I now?" Dr. Samuel's voice was soothing, easy, meant to calm her. He'd been dealing with her fear of needles since she was eight years old, in his own clumsy way, and he'd been the one who'd suggested Jack's presence while this blood sample was drawn, mentioning that the support might do her good.

Right now Rebecca was absolutely sure Jack's presence had not been a wonderful idea. Flaking out in front of her fiancé over a blood test, especially the one she had to have so they could apply for their marriage license, didn't seem tailor-made to build trust. Then again, neither did the fact that *he* didn't have to have a blood test to get the license. That was about as unfair as things got, in her opinion.

Rebecca tried to answer Dr. Samuel, but couldn't quite find her voice. She was too busy trying, unsuccessfully, not to let her eyes wander to the vial filling with the dark red liquid. Her parents had always told her that letting the doctor put a needle in her was against God's law. They believed modern medicine was against God's law. Then again, she'd probably have died from the complications of chicken pox when she was eight if child protective services hadn't insisted that her parents allow Dr. Samuel to take care of her. But their wrongheaded opinions hadn't helped her own natural squeamishness one bit. Right now Rebecca wished with all her heart that she shared her parents' beliefs, if only to get out of this awful blood test.

"You're doing great, honey." Jack squeezed her fingers reassuringly. "He's almost done."

"No," Dr. Samuel replied. Rebecca's gaze jerked up to him, stricken. He pulled the needle out of her arm and swabbed the spot with antiseptic. "We're all done. You just sit here for a minute while I get you a band-aid."

Rebecca relaxed in relief. Jack grinned down at her and ruffled her hair with his free hand. If he said anything even remotely related to "I told you so" right now, she was going to have to call off the engagement. But fortunately, he didn't. Instead he let go of her hand and wrapped his arm around her shoulders. Rebecca leaned into the comfort of it. The worst was over. Now they could get married.

Well, not quite yet. Not until the blood came back from wherever Dr. Samuel had to send it so it could be tested. Rebecca wondered how long that would take – she was champing at the bit as much as Jack was, she thought, which made her smile in spite of everything – and opened her mouth to ask.

But Dr. Samuel was still speaking. "Now, we're going to run an anemia test on this blood, too, Rebecca, along with the rubella test. You haven't had one in a while."

"Okay." The vampire had his blood. She might as well let him do everything he wanted with it so he wouldn't want to draw more.

"Anemia?" Jack asked.

"I used to be iron-deficient. I'm not anymore."

Samuel chimed in. "She tested anemic in high school. I've been trying to get her to come in to have it checked occasionally ever since."

"I'll make sure she comes in regularly from now on." Jack's voice was firm. Possessive. Normally she would have reveled in that, but –

"I take my iron pills." Rebecca knew she was dangerously close to whining, but she couldn't help it.

"It's just a blood test, Becky."

She glared at both of them. "Just a blood test. Right."

"Aw, c'mon," Jack wheedled. "You're not going to be a chicken about it, are you?"

"Maybe," she replied defiantly.

Jack grinned and lifted her down from the examining table. Bussed her full on the lips, right in front of Dr. Samuel. Rebecca could feel herself blushing from head to toe. She took a swipe at Jack, missing when he ducked.

"Children." The reproach in Dr. Samuel's voice was spoiled by his benevolent smile. "No roughhousing in my office."

Jack slung his arm around her again, effectively preventing another assault. Rebecca couldn't decide whether it annoyed or pleased her. "Let's go get some lunch." He chuckled. "You need to get your strength back."

She attempted another swipe at him, connecting with the hard pectoral muscles she so admired, and doing nothing but hurting her hand. He laughed again.

"Oh, you!" she told him.

They left the office together, stopping to say hello to Tim, who was on his way in. His presence in the clinic was beginning to feel

more and more normal, Rebecca thought as Tim and Jack discussed
a hike they'd like to take over the weekend if the weather didn't turn.
Rebecca wondered if Tim would be more sympathetic about her fear
of needles than Dr. Samuel was. Probably not.

Anyway, the ordeal was over. Now that it was, Rebecca was more
than sure it was worth it.

* * *

Two hours after Tim arrived at the clinic, all hell broke loose.

The call came in from the mill in the middle of the afternoon.
There'd been an accident. No, Betty said, her face pale, the caller
wasn't sure how bad the injuries were. Just that it was her neighbor's
son Mark, and they needed help right away.

Tim and Samuel were both out the door, bags in hand, before she
finished speaking.

As soon as they arrived at the mill he knew it wasn't good.
Mark Thronson lay sprawled on the concrete floor, a knot of people
surrounding him. They parted when they saw Tim and Samuel
coming. Blood was everywhere. Tim knelt down, conscious of the
crowd watching and of his father next to him. One of the big saw
blades had left Mark's leg sliced open down to the bone. The wound
gaped open a good eight inches along his right thigh. Bill Wiggins, the
foreman, had had the presence of mind to squeeze the edges of the
wound together and apply pressure, but it wasn't doing much good.
At Tim's signal, he lifted his hands and backed away, and Tim began
the work of treating the wound, a spare eye on his patient's face.
Mark was shivering, drifting in and out of consciousness.

Tim should have been used to this. After all, he'd gone through
a rotation in the emergency room during med school. Somehow,
though, he'd never longed for his tidy internist's office in Seattle,
around the corner from one of the best hospitals in the country, so
badly before. He'd never dealt with something like this without decent
backup.

His father was calm and collected, as if he dealt with injuries like
this every day. But even he didn't, although Tim knew he'd treated
his share of mill accidents. It wasn't as if the management weren't as
safety conscious as it was possible to be in an environment like this.
After all, it was money out of their pockets when the L&I inspectors

showed up. It was just that a lumber mill was an inherently dangerous place, no matter how safety conscious anyone could be.

Tim heard a mutter of, "so much for the 'no accidents' bonus this year" from somewhere behind him, and someone else shushing the speaker. As much as he understood the frustration, it was a good policy. Nothing like a little financial incentive to keep people watching out for each other.

Somehow Tim found himself doing the bulk of the work of stabilizing Mark and dealing with the wound. He'd gotten the bleeding stopped and a pressure bandage applied, when he looked up to see his father's face. His father looked, was that pleased with him? underneath the concern for their patient. Tim shook his head warningly, and his father's expression went back to straight concern.

But he didn't have time to think about his father right now. His patient – when the hell had Mark, who'd been in his class in high school, become Tim's patient? – his patient's eyes were open.

"Hey, Tim. Glad you're here." Mark's voice was weak, but coherent.

Tim ignored the greeting. "How are you feeling?"

"Can't feel my leg." Fear seeped through Mark's woozy expression.

"That's because I gave you a shot to numb it. I'm glad it's working. Your leg's going to be just fine." And it would, eventually, but it was going to take a while. And it would never be quite the same, depending on how well the severed nerves healed. But Mark didn't need to know that right now.

"Oh." The word held a world of relief. Mark's eyes rolled back and his eyelids fell shut again.

The medevac helicopter from the hospital a hundred and twenty miles away in Kalispell took forever, or so it seemed, but it finally arrived, wings beating the air above the asphalt parking lot outside the mill. Mark's wife – Mark had married Patsy Wilmer? Tim thought, amused in spite of himself, remembering how they'd hated each other in high school – came running up just as the paramedics were loading her husband onto the helicopter, and she scrambled aboard with him. Tim wondered, briefly, if they had children, then had his question answered by Samuel, who reassured Patsy just before the chopper door was closed that he'd make sure someone took care of the girls.

It was late afternoon before they made it back to the clinic, only to have to deal with questions from the media – Campbell's lone radio station and the weekly newspaper – and what felt like half the town.

The uproar died down eventually. Samuel offered the loan of a spare shirt, to replace the bloodstained one Tim was wearing.

"Now you see one of the main reasons this town needs a doctor." Samuel took out a shirt for himself.

Tim wished his father would quit accusing him of assuming something he'd never denied. "How frequently does something like that happen?"

Samuel pulled his own shirt off. He'd lost weight, Tim noted. Weight he couldn't spare. "Not as often as it could, thank God, but often enough." His father fumbled with his shirt buttons, then straightened to look Tim in the eye. It was all Tim could do to keep from looking away. "What happened to Mark could have been fatal. He was lucky he didn't bleed out, with the blade hitting the artery the way it did."

Tim couldn't deny the truth of what his father had just said. "I take it you've seen other accidents at the mill that would have been fatal if you hadn't been available?"

"A few."

"More than a few."

Samuel was silent for a moment. "Yes. More than a few. Do you remember what happened to Jack's stepfather?"

"Vaguely." Tim thought about it, recognized the euphemism Samuel was using. Jack hadn't had a father, step or otherwise. His mother hadn't seen fit to make any of her relationships that permanent. "He was drunk at the time, though, wasn't he?"

Samuel's voice grew sharp. "Yes, he was. That didn't make him any less injured."

Tim couldn't deny that, either.

"Why doesn't the mill have a doctor of its own?" Even that would only solve part of the problem, but it would be a start.

"The mill doesn't have enough employees for OSHA to require that the company keep one on the premises. From what I understand, when the union went after them about it as well as a number of other complaints a few years ago, they were more or less told that the site was marginally profitable as it was, and if the company had to add that much cost to the mill's overhead, it would make more sense for them to shut the site down than to keep it running. The mill is the lifeblood of this town, Timothy. Without it, Campbell wouldn't survive."

Tim drew back. His first thought was, maybe it's for the best. But just because he didn't want to live here didn't mean everyone else would be happy to be forced to leave. Some families in town had been here for generations. Some of the kids he'd gone to school with were descended from the original settlers back in the 1880s, when a small gold strike had been made in the neighborhood and Campbell had sprung up around it.

He didn't have the right to make that decision for anyone here, either, even if they were crazy enough to want to stay. "No. Of course not." Tim paused. He had to start looking for someone with an M.D. who was crazy enough to want to live here. "Do you mind if I use your office phone again?"

Samuel's lips quirked. "Going recruiting?"

Tim sighed. "Someone has to."

* * *

Not that his efforts were getting him anywhere. Tim set the phone down two hours later and propped his feet up on his father's desk, his little gray book in one hand as he absentmindedly ruffled its pages with the other.

He'd tried a couple of connections through his alma mater, the University of Washington medical school, and had gotten Campbell on what he'd been assured was a rather long waiting list of rural communities in similar situations. The UW was the only medical school in the Pacific Northwest, and it pulled in students from half a dozen states, including Alaska, but many of them never went back after graduation. Like me, he couldn't help thinking. How many of them are like me?

He'd then called several of his colleagues who'd more or less laughed at him when he had broached the subject.

"If you're so worried, old man, why don't you stay?" had been the most blunt response he'd gotten so far. He was going to have to have to do something about Gary Wilson when he got back. Just because he'd grown up in the city didn't mean he had to be rude about something he didn't understand.

Tim glanced at his watch guiltily. It was after seven. His mother was undoubtedly furious with him for not showing up at home for dinner by now.

Too late to call the state medical board in Helena tonight, too, but he suspected they were going to give him the same runaround he'd gotten from the UW. Montana was a big state, and almost completely rural. Oh, he'd call in the morning. He wasn't going to leave a stone unturned. But he wasn't expecting much, if anything, from them.

He didn't want to go after the mill, but now it didn't seem that he had much choice. He had to explore every option. Somehow he was going to have to convince the mill's management that the need to provide medical care for their employees was not a good reason to shut the mill down. He wasn't all that sure his powers of persuasion were up to the task, but he had to try. Tomorrow. First thing in the morning.

Tim's stomach growled. He frowned. He'd done all he could for the moment. He'd start again tomorrow.

Tonight he was going to go out for dinner, even if there wasn't much to choose from. Only one sit-down choice, if he didn't want to drive the fifteen miles up the Yaak Road to the Red Dog, although he was tempted, if only to get out of town, even just that far. He'd have been more tempted if he'd been willing to eat peanuts and beer for supper, which was about all he'd have to choose from there. The only other option was the Campbell Café here in town. He wondered if the menu was still the same as it had been all his life. Still, it was better than going home just now.

Tim picked up the phone one more time and dialed his parents' house, an apology to his mother ready on his lips. The phone rang through to the answering machine. Odd, he thought. He left a message and set the receiver down.

He'd apologize to his mother after supper. Right now he needed food. Grabbing his jacket, Tim headed out the door.

Chapter 9

Tara stared at the three eggs and one slightly green hunk of cheese, the sole contents of her refrigerator, trying to will something else to appear. She needed to go grocery shopping, but she'd been late leaving the library tonight, her preparations for the board meeting the following day having been sidetracked by thoughts of Tim. Her bright yellow kitchen clock read 7:18 pm, so she'd missed her chance until tomorrow.

She shook herself and closed the fridge door. Staring into it wasn't getting her anywhere. Neither was her little house's utter silence. She kept imagining the sound of Tim's steps on her front stoop.

Dinner sounded wonderful, Tara thought tiredly, as long as someone else was doing the cooking. After calling Rebecca and getting her voice mail, she shrugged her shoulders and headed out. Somebody was bound to be around the Campbell Café to chat with over dinner. At the very least, Mae, the owner, would be good for a word or two.

But when she pushed open the door, a dozen voices greeted her. Tara could feel the tension streaming away from her as she approached the row of tables shoved together down the middle of the restaurant's one dining area. People scooted left and right to make space for her next to Rebecca and Jack, who were sitting next to each other – very next to, as a matter of fact. If Rebecca had been any closer to her fiancé, she'd be sitting in his lap.

As Tara seated herself, she realized the gathering could have been Friday night at the Red Dog all over again. Tara wondered why no one had called her. Or maybe they had. It wasn't as if she'd been paying attention to her messages at the library or even glanced at the voice mail on her home phone.

In the flurry of greetings and congratulations – she hadn't seen Jack since he'd asked Rebecca to marry him – Tara didn't notice who was sitting next to her on the other side until she'd given Mae her order. Handing the menu back, she settled herself into her chair, saw, and almost leaped right back out of it.

"Hi, Tara." Tim's rich tenor slid over her, through her, making her want to shiver, despite his commonplace words.

"Tim." Before he could say anything else to disrupt her equilibrium, she turned away. Rebecca and Jack were no help, wrapped up in each other as they were. Tara gazed rather desperately up and down the row of faces, looking anywhere, everywhere, except at the man beside her. She should have known he'd be here tonight. If she hadn't already ordered, she'd have left. Gone home and made an omelet or something. But it would be rude, and besides, Tara wanted that fried chicken in the worst way. She'd get Mae to make it up to go.

But before she could get back up to go catch Mae, Tim's large, firm hand came down on her arm. Tara could feel the warmth from it through the fabric of her blouse. It was about all she could do to keep from searching out the rest of that warmth. Determinedly, she tried to shake it off, but she knew, even as he lifted it, that it wasn't her effort that had made him remove it.

His voice was soft now, pitched below the babble of conversation going on around them. "Am I making you uncomfortable? Would you like me to leave?"

She wanted him to leave the café, Campbell, and Montana, in that order, and in as expedient a manner as possible. But she looked down at the half-eaten meal of meatloaf and mashed potatoes sitting in front of him. "No. Finish your supper. I'll go."

"Look, Tara, I'm sorry."

"For what?"

For some unfathomable reason that appeared to startle him. Tara was uncomfortably aware that they were beginning to attract attention. After a moment's baffled silence, he answered, "I don't know."

"Then why on earth are you apologizing?" Her voice was louder than she'd meant it to be. Heads swiveled around.

"Hell if I know." He pushed his chair back.

It was all Tara could do to put her hand on his arm. Tim stared down at it as if it was going to bite him. "Eat your supper," she snapped. "I'll go."

"No, you won't." He glared her down. She removed her hand. He scooted his chair back to the table.

"Then you won't, either." She'd be darned if he was going to do her a favor.

"Fine."

"Fine."

Tim deliberately turned away and shoved a forkful of meatloaf into his mouth. Mae, grinning, set Tara's meal down in front of her.

Her face hotter than the freshly-fried chicken, Tara picked up her drumstick and took a bite.

It seemed forever before the chatter started back up – a full ten seconds – but at last it did, the multilayered conversation of a crowd of people who have known each other all their lives. It rippled over and around her. The population at the row of tables ebbed and flowed, friends of all ages stopping by for a few minutes or a meal.

Tim had apparently decided to ignore her completely, exactly what she wanted from him for once. Within minutes he was deep into a discussion of something or other with Alan Vanderhof, seated on his other side. Tara decided that she wasn't going to let him ruin her evening and dug into her food and the conversation.

She looked up as the door opened yet again and Dr. and Mrs. Swanson entered the café. He nodded innocuously enough at her as he seated his wife, but he looked pleased. Just because I'm sitting next to him, Tara thought, doesn't mean a darned thing.

They went to the other end of the table, thank goodness, and she nodded back. The last thing she needed right now was more matchmaking. Tara couldn't help wondering, as she watched that sweet man chatting with Mae about tonight's special, why Tim couldn't have been more like him – or maybe that was the problem.

Tara smiled at Penny Soderberg, seated next to her husband and her little daughter Kathy across the table, and answered a question about the annual library card drive at the elementary school where Penny worked as secretary. A nice, normal conversation, with a nice normal person, in the café of her hometown. Not Tim's. Not anymore.

Campbell was home. These were the people she knew and loved. *This* was the reason she'd come back a year and a half ago.

A little while later, Tim got up and left. Tara said a polite good-night, as did everyone else, and relaxed still further as the door swung closed behind him.

She rose to leave a while after that, feeling like herself again. But she knew the affection in the voices telling her good-night belied the curiosity that followed her out the door.

* * *

The second the café door closed behind Tara, the comments began. Rebecca knew they would. She was simply glad the bunch of busybodies waited until the two of them were gone.

"It's a shame," Dr. Samuel said.

"A crying shame," chimed in Cindy from across the table. Rebecca gave her a pleading look, but she just grinned.

"Putting those two in the same room ought to be outlawed." What did Alan Soderberg care about how Tim and Tara got along? The man just liked to stir up trouble.

"Yup." That was Dr. Samuel again. Rebecca could see his wife trying to shut him up, but Avis wasn't having any luck whatsoever. He was deliberately stirring things up, and wasn't about to be stopped. "I wonder which one of 'em caused the fight this time?"

"I bet it was Tara."

"Jack!" Rebecca leaned up to whisper in his ear. "Stop that! You're as bad as Dr. Samuel." But he just grinned back down at her. She had to say something. Defend her friend, who wasn't there to defend herself. She raised her voice. "No, it wasn't."

Alan Vanderhof laughed. "I thought he was going to take her head off."

"Her head? It was his that almost —" Jack made a slicing motion across his neck.

"Hush," Rebecca said. "You're not helping." But now Jack was laughing, too.

"Says who?"

"Cindy!" What had Tara done to *her*? Rebecca glared at their erstwhile friend. "How could you?" But Cindy only shrugged and giggled.

"Does it matter?" Dr. Samuel's voice cut across the chatter.

Rebecca took a deep breath and answered through the last of the laughter. "No. I'd just like them to get along, for their own sakes. But making fun of them behind their backs isn't helping."

Dr. Samuel smiled at her down the length of the table. Ignoring the important part of what she'd just said, he replied, "You and me both. The problem is they're both so in love with each other that they can't see straight."

The whole room rocked with laughter all over again.

Rebecca started to get up, fully intending to go strangle Dr. Samuel, but Jack held onto her. Rather than make a scene, she stayed put and fumed. Oh, but she'd have plenty to say to both him and Dr. Samuel, the first chance she got.

Avis apparently had plenty to say, too, not that Dr. Samuel was paying the least bit of attention to her no-doubt sensible words. Obviously he was just waiting until the noise calmed down a bit before pitching his voice across the crowd. "I propose to point it out to them."

"You trying to get yourself killed?" Jack called out, and the laughter broke out again.

Rebecca leaned over, not far, just so her mouth was close to Jack's ear. "I mean it. Hush. Don't rile him up worse than he already is."

Jack merely shook his head at her. The man simply wouldn't see reason.

Samuel waited again. He was a patient man. In some ways. "Who's willing to help me?" he asked the room at large, once he could make himself heard.

"You're out of your mind," Alan said.

"Crazy as a loon," added Jack.

"At least half a sandwich short of a picnic," Cindy commented, still giggling.

The situation was completely out of hand. Rebecca sighed, knowing that the rock was rolling down the hill now and there was no way she could stop it. The only thing she could do now was get involved and try to keep it from crushing Tara. Rebecca wasn't going to say this was all Dr. Samuel's fault. Tim's father meant well, but there were things he didn't know. Reasons why Tara fought her attraction to Tim that had nothing to do with the present and everything to do with the past. Tim wasn't going to stay in Campbell. Tara wasn't going to leave, with him or without him.

Rebecca let out another sigh. The things she did for her friend. But if she didn't, who knew what would happen? "I'll help."

Samuel grinned at her. "Good girl." Avis scowled at her for some reason Rebecca couldn't fathom. She shrugged back helplessly.

Jack intercepted Samuel's grin, tightening the arm he had around Rebecca's shoulders, and returned it with one of his own. "Me, too. I've got a vested interest in seeing they don't ruin our wedding. What's your idea, Dr. Samuel?"

Dr. Samuel chuckled. "Well, this is sort of what I had in mind..."

* * *

"What do you mean, Campbell's already in the program?"

Tim leaned back on his headrest in the Prius the next morning, his cell phone at his ear. It was the only way he could think of to get anywhere with his search for a doctor without his mother interrupting him at home or his father bugging him at the clinic.

There weren't many places down in the bottom of a river valley in the middle of nowhere where he could actually get reception on his smart phone. Even the one company that provided land line service in Campbell hadn't deemed it profitable to build a tower in town. About the only way he could get any bars at all was to go clear out to the dam five miles northeast of town and pick up on the signal from the tower the Army Corps of Engineers maintained there.

The voice from Helena was prattling on about – "What?" Tim interrupted the woman's seemingly endless monologue. "We've already been sent two doctors? No, we haven't."

The voice started up again. Tim stared blankly out at the enormous spillway below, dry at the moment, and interrupted the officious woman again. "I can tell you neither one of them is here. Campbell has no doctor except for my father, Samuel Swanson, who is about to turn seventy-five in a week and has no business still practicing."

The woman started droning again, and he turned to look in the other direction at the seemingly endless length of Lake Canusa, stretching long and narrow between its canyon walls.

He'd been asked a question. "No, he's healthy. For his age."

And another. "Yes, he seems to be holding things down. For now." Tim emphasized the last two words.

"No, he doesn't feel like he can't handle the situation – but, ma'am, he's not in a position to be doing the kinds of things a doctor in a remote place like Campbell winds up doing."

The voice began droning again. Tim shifted again, staring downstream to where the road turned to round a bend in the valley before reaching Campbell, which was why he couldn't get any reception down there, and waited for the woman to run down. Apparently he wasn't going to get anything accomplished until she finished her spiel.

At last she stopped speaking, after she'd very firmly told him, several times, that after striking out twice the town didn't deserve a third chance. She didn't phrase it that way, but that was what she meant. He was not going to take no for an answer, however. Not on this subject, and not from some clerk. "Fine. Who do I need to speak to in order to get us back on the list?"

Well, that got her out of her practiced spiel, he thought at the silence on the line. He was surprised she wasn't used to someone refusing to take no for an answer, but he certainly wasn't going to give up that easily. He could almost hear her shaking her head, but at last she agreed to put him back on the list. At the bottom. It was better than nothing, he thought wearily. Not to mention the condition she placed on the concession. "I will do my best to find out what happened to the other two doctors, and when I do, I will let you know. Thank you."

Sighing heavily, he ended the call and glanced at the time on his phone. His father would be in his office. Where else? Tim thought sarcastically, and headed back down to town.

* * *

"So where are they?"

Samuel sighed. "I have no idea. The first one stayed all of two weeks before she politely told me this was not the kind of job she'd been looking for, and that she'd had a better offer elsewhere. She was talented, but I don't think she'd ever been to a small town before. The other doctor assigned to us after she left never showed up."

"I reported both incidents to the state medical office, but it's been a year since Dr. Winger left. They pretty much told me when I reported the last one missing that we'd used up our quota."

"When were you going to tell me this?" Tim demanded.

Samuel smiled. "It doesn't matter."

Tim wanted to tear his hair out. "It doesn't matter? You've had and lost two doctors, and you say it doesn't matter?"

"It doesn't change the situation. Campbell needs a doctor, and as long as you won't stay I'm the only one they've got."

"So even though Campbell needs a doctor, you gave up because they told you our 'quota' is up?" Tim began to pace across the small room. "I talked the state people into putting us back on their list, by the way. This morning. At the bottom, but it's better than nothing. And I'm not giving up on finding someone else, either."

Samuel shrugged. "A lot of other little towns in Montana need doctors worse than we do. They don't have a doctor at all, let alone two." Samuel brightened. "Could you see our patients this afternoon? Your mother needs me at home."

Tim eyed him. "What for?"

"I have no idea. You know how your mother gets."

Tim couldn't argue with that. But it wasn't like his mother to pull his father away from his work. Or for his father to let her. They can now because you're here, Tim thought. Well, it was the least he could do. For now.

"Sure, Dad. Go on and see what Mother wants."

"Thanks, son. It's good to be able to leave my patients in capable hands." Tim rolled his eyes as his father left the office. If he didn't find someone, anyone, with an M.D. to come and take over his father's practice, he would never get out of here.

And why was he starting to think that way? Because after Mark Thronson's accident Tim was beginning to see just how badly Campbell needed a doctor. And why his father couldn't just walk away and leave the town without one.

His father was right, but not in the way that he'd meant it. Campbell had always been barely big enough to keep one doctor busy;

the only reason it did that much was the fact that it was a hundred and twenty miles to the hospital in Kalispell. The clinic was only open when it needed to be as it was.

He could remember the countless times his dad had come home after a half day at work, with plenty of time to take Tim fishing or hiking. He'd felt like one lucky kid, especially as most of his friends' fathers worked for the mill and not only put in their eight hours come rain or shine, but were generally too tired for fun when they did get home.

He, on the other hand, had had the run of the woods with a father who enjoyed spending time with him. It had been a pretty idyllic childhood, when he cared to think back on it. One he'd been fortunate to have. If he'd been planning on small-town life any time soon himself, he could do worse than being the G.P. in Campbell.

But he wasn't. He wasn't Tara. And where had that thought come from? Why had she come back?

Tim went out to the reception area. "I guess I'm your doctor for the day," he told Betty.

"That's what your dad said." She sounded as grumpy as ever, but she handed him the first chart willingly enough. Little Petey Silsand was running a temperature and throwing up. Sounds like a virus, Tim thought. Real challenging.

He shook his head. And headed into the examining room.

Chapter 10

His father came back in the middle of the afternoon. Tim started to follow him to the office to find out what it was his mother had wanted, then heard the front door creak open and Jack, of all people, talking to Betty. What was he doing here? Abruptly Tim turned and headed back toward the waiting room.

"Hey, Tim. What's up?"

"I was about to ask you the same thing." Jack looked fine, although he was leaning rather hard on the edge of Betty's desk. "Are you all right?"

"Fell off the back of my rig and banged up my ankle." Jack looked sheepish.

"Well, get off of it at the very least. Want me to take a look at it?" Tim went to help him toward the examining room, but Jack resisted him. "Come on. I'm not going to put you in a cast or anything." Tim seriously doubted it was broken, since he was walking on it, albeit gimpily.

"Where's your dad?"

Good grief, Tim thought. "I have an M.D., too, you know. I can show it to you, if you want. Come on."

But as Tim was trying to maneuver his stubborn friend back toward the examining room, Samuel came out of the office.

"There you are," Jack said to Samuel, his relief as inexplicable to Tim as it was palpable. "I twisted my damned ankle."

"Well, come on then, and I'll take a look at it." Samuel glanced over at Tim as if he'd just seen him. "Give me a hand, would you?"

"Sure. Whatever." But after they'd maneuvered Jack into the examining room and onto the table, no mean feat when the patient suddenly refused to put his weight on one foot, Samuel dismissed Tim as if he was a first year med student.

Fine, Tim thought. No skin off my nose.

Tim was just about to close the door behind him when Samuel said, "It's too bad about Tara." Criminy, here we go again, Tim thought, then wondered why Samuel was bringing her up this time. As if it was any of Jack's business. Was she sick? Why hadn't anyone said so?

"Shh," Jack said.

"Oh, he's long gone. Told me he was going somewhere."

No, I didn't, Tim thought indignantly.

"Yeah, well, it is too bad about Tara. She's been moping around ever since Tim showed up at the Red Dog Friday night."

Tim, who'd been just about to head toward the waiting room to see if anyone else had come in off the street needing his help, stopped dead. So that's what Tara's behavior looked like from the outside? Jack could be so clueless.

"She's never gotten over him, has she?"

Good grief, would his father never give up? Tim wondered what he and Tara would have to do to get the point across. Apparently fighting over dinner twice, once in public, wasn't enough to demonstrate that Tara wasn't moping. She was pissed. She'd told him how many times now that she couldn't wait till he went back to Seattle? That this wasn't his home anymore?

Honestly, that attitude of hers was beginning to bug him. Just because he wasn't living here anymore didn't mean that this wouldn't always be his hometown. That he didn't care. If he didn't care he'd have walked away by now. From his dad, who probably would insist on seeing patients until he dropped dead in the examining room whether Tim found a new doctor or not, from everyone who insisted on staying out here in the middle of nowhere when they could move to a place with a real life, real amenities, a real hospital and a movie theater and shopping mall, not to mention everything else. A place with cell phone reception, for crying out loud. From Tara, who for some godforsaken reason decided to come back and immure herself here for the rest of her life. Why? Tim knew he shouldn't care, or even wonder, why, but he did. But not gotten over him? In his father's dreams.

But Jack's response made Tim's mouth drop open. "Rebecca says she hasn't ever gotten over him." Was he serious? And he had the gall to actually sound sympathetic. Whose friend *are* you? Tim wondered angrily. But there was something else in Jack's voice, something Tim couldn't quite put a finger on. "And she ought to know. Rebecca says Tara has been trying to get up the courage to tell him how she feels ever since he came home, but she's afraid he'll laugh at her."

How she felt? She hated him, plain and simple, in spite of their attraction. She didn't need to tell him that. He already knew. And wait a minute. Tara had never had a problem telling anyone anything. Tim supposed he could see Becky, newly-engaged and all that, wanting her friend to be in love, too, but if she believed Tara was in love with him she was far more into wishful thinking than he'd have believed anyone could be. And yeah, Jack had just gotten engaged, too, but his friend – friend, hah, Tim thought. The last thing a friend would do is encourage his father's delusion.

"He probably would. Tim's cynical that way." Or maybe it was the other way around. But Jack had never had any delusions. He'd never been able to afford them. It took a few seconds after that bombshell for the insult to sink in. Cynical, my –, he thought indignantly .

Tim put his hand on the doorknob, then yanked it back as if it were red hot when Jack spoke again. "She's so in love with him she can't see straight."

Tim nearly fell over his own feet. In love with him? What kind of crack were they *smoking*?

"It's a crying shame is what it is. She's a nice girl, and Avis has said more than once she'd love to have her as a daughter-in-law." His father sounded aggrieved. Of course he did. But there was a thread of – something else – in his voice. He wasn't just yanking Tim's chain. He doesn't know I'm out here, Tim thought. He's being honest. "I do hate to say this about my own son, but I have to say she's probably too good for him."

Tim sagged against the wall. He'd always thought his father was proud of him. He'd certainly said so often enough, when Tim had been high school valedictorian, when he'd gotten the scholarship to the University of Washington, when he'd graduated from the pre-med program at the top of his class, all through medical school and his residency. His father had even sounded pleased about Tim's new practice when he'd called a couple of months ago, eager to share his latest triumph with the parents who'd always supported him. He'd been pleased. Tim had been thoroughly convinced his father had been pleased at the time. Or had Tim only heard what he'd wanted to hear?

If I did, Tim thought wearily, I learned how to do it from the best.

He'd thought the conversation was over, but Jack was speaking again. Tim wasn't sure just how much more he could take. "It would help if she could forget about him. I know you've been glad to see him, but it would have been better for her if he'd never showed up." Tim was really beginning to wish he hadn't. Or was he? He'd enjoyed seeing old friends, and he'd wanted to see how his father was doing, and – hell, he admitted, in some ways he'd even enjoyed fighting with Tara. He wondered what it would be like not to be fighting with Tara. It had been too damned long...

He wouldn't mind more kisses, either. But he couldn't stay. It would ruin all his best-laid plans. If Tara did love him, maybe she would come back to Seattle with him. That's what they'd planned, back in college, the two of them together, conquering the big city.

For a moment, just a moment, Tim allowed himself to think about what could have been, without that big, stupid misunderstanding about Jack's cousin. It had been like a really bad romantic comedy, only without the happy ending. The kind where if the couple would just talk to each other, there wouldn't be a misunderstanding at all. He had to at least try to explain –

"He'll be gone soon." No, I won't, Tim thought. Not till Tara is willing to come back with me. "It's been all I could do to talk him into staying long enough to help me out."

"Much as I've enjoyed seeing him again, I hope so. Tara's been a good friend to Rebecca and I hate to see her hurt." A pause. "Thanks, doc. That feels a lot better."

"You're quite welcome, son. Try to keep your weight off it as much as you can. I've got a cane I can lend you."

"Thanks. I'll do that."

The sound of the door opening had Tim scuttling down the hallway. Tim fought the urge to punch Jack at the sight of the lazy grin on his friend's face.

"Hey, Tim. What's up?"

Tim cleared his throat as he followed Jack to the waiting room. "Nothing. It's slower than pond scum around here."

Jack laughed. "Glad to hear it. I'd hate to see the emergency it would take to keep you busy."

"Yeah, I guess." Tim hadn't thought about it quite that way. It wasn't that he wished illness or injury on the good people of Campbell. It was just that he needed more of a challenge. And he couldn't get it here. Was that such a crime? "Was it just a sprain?"

"Yeah. Later, buddy."

"Later."

Tim watched his friend limp, with the aid of the loaner cane, out the door.

His father was in an obnoxiously good mood the rest of the afternoon, for a man who was so disappointed in his son. But Tim was too preoccupied with his own thoughts and plans to care. He had a second chance with Tara, and he wasn't going to blow it this time. When he went back to Seattle, he wasn't going alone.

* * *

But first he had to have a plan. Somehow Tim didn't think simply barging over to Tara's house and proclaiming his feelings for her was going to get him anywhere. She wouldn't believe him, and he wouldn't blame her.

But by midnight he still didn't have one, and it was beginning to worry him. Tim lay flat on his back, arms over his head, in his childhood room with the anatomy charts and travel posters on the walls, staring without seeing. Tara? She really loved him? The same Tara Hillerman who'd had nothing but scathing words – and two inexplicable kisses she definitely didn't want to talk about – for him since he'd driven into town?

Tim knew better than to believe his father on the subject, no matter how much he wanted to. But Jack said so, too. Jack was Tim's best friend from way back. Tim respected him. Knew him to be honorable. Knew what he'd gone through to become the respectable

citizen and teacher he was. Why would Jack agree with Samuel unless
he knew it to be true?

But Tara?

Tim hadn't been able to think of anything, or anyone else, all
afternoon. The concept opened a whole new world. And certainly
explained why she'd gotten tipsy and kissed him the night of his arrival.
The fact that she'd needed dutch courage in order to do it struck him
as sweet.

She still loved him, in spite of everything. Oh, Tara, Tim thought,
his body tightening. She'd been the love of his life, even if he'd spent
the last five years denying it. She'd given him her love and her trust.
As he'd given her his.

He could remember the night they'd lost their virginity together
like it was yesterday. The sweetness of her as he'd wrapped her in his
arms and promised her forever. The warmth of her body under his.
The heat of it all. And the sweet peace he'd felt afterward, buoyed by
the very rightness of what they'd done.

He'd never felt anything like it since. Never found a woman who
made him feel the way Tara had, as if he was both her knight in shining
armor and her very human lover and she couldn't make up her mind
which she wanted most. He'd just about quit trying to find someone
who would.

Tara still loved him. After all this time. Tim couldn't believe it.
He still had a chance with the love of his life.

He was going to take that chance and run with it. Maybe he
wouldn't have to spend his life alone after all. Maybe he could spend it
with the woman who'd ruined him for everyone else.

He would show her that he was still in love with her, too.

The enormous grin on his face matched the lightness in his heart
as Tim finally fell asleep, as he had every night since long before he'd
come home, to dream of Tara. Only this time, he swore, the dreams
were going to come true.

* * *

Tara pushed the clinic door open. The waiting room was deserted.
"Is anyone here?" Maybe Dr. Swanson – both Dr. Swansons – and
Betty had gone out to lunch. The clinic's waiting room was always left
unlocked, in case there was an emergency, Dr. Samuel always said, and,

for the same reason, a cupboard filled with basic medical supplies sat in one corner. It only seemed normal since many folks in town still didn't lock their own doors, but at least he did lock the door to the hallway leading to the examining rooms, office, and storeroom.

She called again. Nobody home, apparently. She'd pick up her prescription later.

She was just about to head back out the door when the hall door opened and Tim peered out. Oh, great, Tara thought. Not now. He looked good in khakis and a button-down shirt, his white coat as natural a part of him as the rest of his clothing. The quintessential young urban doctor. He could have just stepped off the set of *Grey's Anatomy*.

"Hi, Tara. Can I help you?" The door opened the rest of the way and Tim walked out, offering a hand to her.

Tara stepped back. Urban, maybe, but she suspected he looked like he belonged here more than he ever had in Seattle. She suspected it was the hiking boots on his feet. "I was looking for your father. Or Betty."

"Sorry. They're out to lunch. I'm holding down the fort." Tim smiled.

It was the weirdest smile she'd ever seen. He looked positively goofy. Like he'd been sampling the Prozac. Or, Tara thought, panicked, like he was about to go postal on her.

"Would you like to sit down, wait for them?" He pulled up a chair, swiped a hand across it, offered it to her. When she made no move toward it, he straightened and approached her again. Tara backed up again, then stopped. She wasn't going to let him get her up against the door, but if she took more than two more steps, that was exactly where he'd have her. What was wrong with him?

"Or is there something I can do for you?"

Yes, Tara thought. Tell me what ambush that devious little mind of yours is planning right now, and let me get out of here before you launch it. "Nothing, thank you."

"Are you sure? It wouldn't be any trouble at all. "

The words just slipped out. "How do you know?" He couldn't back her against the door if she opened it first. "I'll come by again later. I need to get back to work now."

"Were you, by any chance, looking for this?" Tim picked up a piece of paper from Betty's desk and waved it at her. "It's got your name on it."

She reached out and snatched the scrap from his hand. She should have looked there first, drat it. Before she ever let him know she was here. "Yes. Thank you." Now she could get out of here.

But Tim beat her to the door, not in any sort of hurry at all, leaning his hand oh-so-casually on the jamb, and Tara stopped, trapped again. Maybe if she just kept going, he'd get out of her way. She took a deep breath and stepped forward, only to let it out in a whoosh at his next words.

"Interesting prescription you're picking up there."

"My prescriptions are no one's business but my own."

"And your doctor's."

"You're not my doctor. Your father is." Although if Tim stayed and Dr. Samuel retired, Tim would be her doctor. Over my dead body, Tara thought. She'd drive a hundred and twenty miles to Kalispell first.

"True."

She blustered on. "My prescriptions are certainly no business of yours. And if you don't mind, I need to get back to the library."

Tim's lazy smile was the last straw. Tara pushed at him. It was like pushing against a brick wall. His smile grew warmer. "How would you like to go out to dinner with me?"

Tara's knees suddenly went weak. "What?" It came out as a squeak.

"Dinner. You know. Good food, maybe a bottle of wine. I thought it might be nice to get out of town for a few hours."

"Out of town?" Cripes, she sounded like a parrot.

Tim chuckled. "I thought we might go into Kalispell." Right. Four hours round trip in that little rice burner of his. Not on her life. Tara wished she could get the door open, but that was hard to do when it opened inward and he was leaning against it.

Then he lost the smile. The intense expression on his face as he watched her was almost worse. Tara brought her hands up in self-defense, but somehow they settled on his chest instead. The white cotton of his lab coat was smooth under her hands. His body warmth radiated out, warming them.

"I've missed your company, Tara." She could have sworn he almost sounded as if he was wheedling her to go with him. As if he really wanted to spend time with her. But why? They could barely tolerate each other's company at the best of times, and at the worst –

Tara shook her head mutely at him. He reached out and gently caressed her cheek. She swallowed. "C'mon. It could be fun," he told her.

She supposed it could. The same way Chinese water torture could be fun. What was wrong with him?

Apparently the only way she was going to get out of here was to answer him. To tell him he was out of his mind. That he needed to see a psychiatrist, preferably one in Seattle. She meant to say a solid, firm no. The word was on the tip of her tongue, but somehow what came out of her mouth was a breathy, "Okay."

Tim beamed, which to her eyes just proved that he was a nutcase. She certainly felt like one. "I'll pick you up at five-thirty." But at last he stood back from the door and she could get the heck out of here.

Tara sidestepped, pulled the door open, and slipped out before she could betray herself any further.

She was going to regret this.

Chapter 11

"Well, here's one thing I'm not going to wear." Tara yanked the gray dress out of her bedroom closet, just to get it out of the way.

"Why not? You'd look lovely in it." Rebecca sounded amused, which was extremely annoying just now.

The gray silk dress was the prettiest thing Tara owned, but that didn't mean it could work miracles. Lovely was never a term she was going to use to describe herself, nor did she want anyone else to do so. She wasn't a girly girl and hadn't been one in a very long time. She did not miss that part of herself, not one little bit.

But she wasn't going to get into that discussion with Rebecca right now. What mattered was what she was or wasn't going to wear tonight, not who she was. "Rebecca, that's the main reason I can't wear it. I don't want to encourage him, for crying out loud."

Tara flung the dress down on her bed, on top of half a dozen other outfits she'd found fault with. "Where's the phone? I'm calling him up and canceling. I can't believe I told him I'd go in the first place."

Rebecca, curled up in the bentwood rocker that graced a corner of Tara's old-fashioned white-eyelet and four-poster bedroom, waved the cordless phone in question and yanked it back quickly when Tara made a grab for it. "I've confiscated it. You're not backing out and you know it. That's the coward's way out."

Tara tried another feint, scowling when it didn't net her the phone. "No, it would be the most intelligent thing I've ever done. Driving two

101

hours into Kalispell with a madman would be horrifically stupid." She turned to make yet another raid on her closet.

Rebecca's voice was far too gentle and reasonable for Tara's mood. Why she'd decided to ask her friend for help with this disaster was beyond her right now. "Then why did you tell him yes in the first place?"

Tara whirled, another outfit in her hand ready to join the pile of clothes on her bed. "I have absolutely no idea how I could have been that monumentally stupid. Don't you think I've been asking myself that for the last three hours?"

"Do you want to know what I think?" Rebecca asked.

Tara wasn't sure if she was being rhetorical, but thought she'd better answer, anyway. "Not particularly."

Rebecca went on anyway, in that annoyingly reasonable and calm voice of hers. "I think you said yes because you wanted to. I think you're nervous. And I think it's sweet."

Tara glared at her erstwhile friend as she uncurled herself and stood up. "And," Rebecca added, "I think we'd better make a decision here, considering that Tim's going to be picking you up in twenty minutes."

She strolled over to the bed and plucked the gray dress from the pile of clothes. "Good. You didn't wrinkle it." She shook it out and stroked the fabric. "It's so soft. Like touching water."

The pearl gray silk was a remnant of Tara's cosmopolitan life in Portland. The simple shirtwaist fastened up the front with delicate silver buttons, the fabric shimmering in the last daylight coming through the window.

"I can't remember the last time I put that dress on." Actually, she could. She'd worn it to a work function at Wilmer Brothers the night before she'd resigned her position to come home to Campbell. Much as she loved the dress, which was why she hadn't jettisoned it the way she'd dumped most of her business wardrobe, at the time it had been just one more symbol of a long list of reasons why she hadn't been happy working in a big city corporate library. Why she belonged back home. "It probably doesn't even fit anymore."

A hint of impatience entered Rebecca's otherwise calm voice. "Then why is it in your closet? You won't know if it still fits until you put it on."

Tara tried one last objection. "It's way too dressy. Can you think of anywhere in Kalispell where I wouldn't be completely overdressed in that?"

Rebecca smiled, a dreamy expression on her face. "Yes, I can. The Blacktail Mountain Inn."

Tara snorted. "As if he'd take me there."

Rebecca raised an eyebrow. "But if he did, you'd want to be dressed for it, wouldn't you?"

"You're hopeless. *I'm* hopeless." Tara sighed, but dropped the dress over her head, fastened the soft belt around her waist, let the full skirt flirt with her stockinged knees. It did still fit, which was gratifying. Almost too perfectly. She'd forgotten how the silk felt, so smooth against her skin. How it clung and flared in all the right places. It did make her feel pretty. Girly, for crying out loud. Tara didn't want to feel girly. Not tonight. She wouldn't say not ever, but not for a good long time, anyway.

Rebecca was looking ridiculously pleased with her. Might as well indulge her friend, this one time. The opportunity certainly wasn't going to happen again any time soon.

So Tara let Rebecca fuss with her hair, and poke through her jewelry box. But she cringed as she saw the locket her friend picked out.

Tim had given her that locket. A very long time ago.

"No, Rebecca, not that one."

"Why not?" Rebecca cocked an eye at her, but Tara couldn't begin to explain. "It's the same metal as the buttons, and it's beautiful." Before Tara could stop her, Rebecca reached over and fastened the fine chain around her neck. "There. It's perfect."

I can take it off after she leaves, Tara told herself, then reached a hand up to feel the locket as it dangled above the hint of cleavage exposed by her collar open – against her better judgment – to the third button. And when she went to the bathroom to – again against her better judgment – apply some makeup, the locket gleamed against her skin. She knew, darn it, that she wasn't going to take it off. Even at the risk of Tim ridiculing her for wearing it.

A dab of blush, a bit of gloss and mascara, a few drops of perfume, and Tara was at her girliest, whether she wanted to be or not. As she stared at herself in the bathroom mirror, she couldn't help thinking, this is who Tim would want me to be. And that was not who she wanted to be. Not anymore.

She sighed, let Rebecca give her one last going over, saw her friend out, and sat down in her living room to wait for her doom.

* * *

"You're *what*?!" Tim's bellowing voice carried down the hall to the waiting room. It was a quarter to six. He was supposed to have picked Tara up fifteen minutes ago. Instead he was having yet another insane argument with his father. Who no doubt would have cried uncle quite happily if only he'd known where his son was headed for the evening. Not that Tim had any intention of fueling that particular fire again.

Samuel's calm voice brought him up short. "I'm going out with the search and rescue team."

Tim wanted to tear his hair out. "Why?"

Samuel stared blankly at him, as if the answer was patently obvious. Which to him it was, Tim thought. Just not to anyone else. "Why? Because I'm needed. There's a very good possibility that one of those hikers is badly injured. I'm not going to be climbing the mountain. I'll let the pros handle that."

"That's big of you." Tim shook his head. "No. You're just going to hike in seven miles to where they've set up base camp in the pouring rain, which may very well be snow by the time you get there because of the altitude. You won't pay a bit of attention to yourself, and you'll probably come home exhausted with a bad case of pneumonia. I remember what it was like when I used to go out on these expeditions with you."

"Timothy." The tone of Samuel's voice had Tim searching his father's face. "Someone has to go. They need a doctor. And I'm it."

"And you wonder why I'm so adamant about you giving up your practice."

"Would you leave them without a doctor?"

Tim sighed. He was so tired of hearing that question. It was his father's trump card and would be till Tim either came home or Samuel dropped in the harness. Tim glanced around the waiting room, wishing that something would jump out and rescue him. And capitulated. "No, dad. I'll go. If you'll promise me one thing."

"What's that, son?"

"Promise me you'll retire. Soon."

Samuel nodded briskly. "As soon as you find me a replacement."

"Dammit, Dad..."

A yellow-slickered man stuck his head into the office. "You ready to go, Dr. Samuel?"

Tim turned to him. "You'll have to put up with me instead. Let me make a quick phone call."

The man beamed. So did Samuel, who said, "Go on, then. And good luck."

* * *

The phone rang just after Tara began to wonder if Tim's invitation had been just another way to play dirty. Rebecca had left twenty minutes before, and she'd spent the remaining time pacing grooves into the hardwood floor of her living room.

At the shrill chirp of the phone, she scrambled madly to find it. Six rings later, she unearthed it from the mountain of clothes on her bed.

"Tim?"

His voice on the other end of the line sounded frustrated. "I'm going to have to postpone our date."

That was relief she felt, wasn't it? Yes, it was, Tara reassured herself. Not disappointment. "What happened?"

"I've got to go out with a search and rescue team. Some idiot hiker fell off a cliff in the Cabinets."

"Oh." The weather being what it was, he was likely to run into snow up in the mountains. She'd done that herself a few times, hiking on the end of the season. He was going to be cold and miserable up there. She should be glad about it, but she wasn't. "Is there anything I can do?"

"No, but thanks for asking." His voice had changed. Lightened, somehow. "I've got to go. I'll call you when I get back."

Almost against her will, she told him, "Be careful."

Tim chuckled. "Of course."

She snorted. Idiot, she thought. "There's no of course about it."

"I know." Now he sounded as if he meant it.

She might hate him all day long, but she wouldn't wish what he was about to do on her worst enemy. "As long as you do."

They exchanged good-byes. Tara slowly brought the receiver down to her lap and tapped the button to sever the connection. Went to the couch and plopped down.

So much for the date from hell. It was just as well. They'd have been fighting before they got out of town.

So why was she disappointed? Oh, not in Tim. He had to go, or his father would have insisted on going. And he was obviously needed, or the team wouldn't have asked for the doctor in the first place.

Tim's first priority would always have to be the injured or ill. It was part and parcel of being a small-town doctor, and she did have to say one thing about him. He wasn't happy about being here. He wasn't happy about his father's refusal to retire unless he stayed. But he did have his priorities straight. She wouldn't have respected him if he didn't. And she did.

The funny thing was, she could have sworn she'd heard an undercurrent of excitement in his voice about going out on this search and rescue. Tara was beginning to suspect something she was quite sure Tim was trying very hard to ignore.

And I should know, she told herself. Dr. Samuel, you're right. Not about your idiotic matchmaking attempts. But about Tim.

* * *

Tim *was* cold and miserable. The rain had turned to sleet, then snow, over an hour ago, and the flakes seemed to be making a beeline straight for his neck, no matter how many times he readjusted the collar of his Gore-Tex jacket. His boots threatened to slide out from under him with every step, the trail glassy with pine needles under the thin coat of ice. The straps of his pack pulled with all the force of gravity down the mountainside behind him. The sky was charcoal gray, the almost full moon just about completely obliterated by thick clouds. Tim thought about his quiet, clean, urban office back in Seattle and sighed as he wiped the sweat off his forehead.

Thirty degrees out and he was sweating. He could remember the time when a hike like this had been an enjoyable weekend outing, but then he'd never done it on a forced march in the middle of the night before.

At least the company was encouraging. Jokes and the occasional grin aimed his way made his exhaustion at least tolerable, if not ignorable. Anyone who did this for a living wouldn't have to worry about staying in shape. And it was way more interesting than the weights he lifted at the gym in Seattle.

You're not going to enjoy this, Tim thought grimly. No one in his right mind would actually find himself admiring the lacy snowflakes falling on his navy blue parka and dissolving, ever so slowly, as he set one foot in front of the other on the trampled gray trail. No sane person would breathe the sharp moist air and let the freshness of it fill his aching lungs with the almost tangible flavor of snow. No one who valued his intelligence would find himself listening to the banter of the volunteer search and rescue team, wondering what it would be like to do this on a regular basis.

No one, especially him, would feel the challenge of it wake up a part of his soul he thought he'd buried; the part that had earned his way to becoming an Eagle Scout, that had skied and hiked and kayaked till he'd known the Cabinet Mountains Wilderness as if it was his own backyard. He wasn't going to let this ridiculous rescue mission wake up the homesickness he'd banished three days after he'd left for college.

Abruptly he realized that they'd reached the spot at the foot of the talus slope where they were going to set up base camp. The young man whose rescue the team was about to attempt lay roughly two-thirds of the way up the slope. He'd been there since this afternoon.

Yesterday afternoon. Tim scrabbled in his coat pocket for his otherwise useless smart phone to check the time and noted it was well past midnight. Around him, the bustle of the team doubled as they prepared to make the rescue at first light. Tim shrugged off his pack and started making preparations of his own.

* * *

The hiker wasn't a local. His name was Mack, according to the panicked companion they'd left back at the ambulance with a twisted ankle – incurred, of course, while rushing back down the trail to sound the alarm. Mack's injuries weren't life-threatening, but that was about the only good thing Tim had to say about his condition. Hiking across a talus slope, its loose rocks and pebbles covered with a slick coating of ice, had definitely not been his best move.

The lump on the back of his head was bad enough that Tim was concerned about a possible skull fracture, but making certain one way or the other would have to wait until his patient was airlifted to the hospital in Kalispell and close proximity to an x-ray machine. The young man was decidedly concussed, too. Under his ripped clothing were any number of contusions and bruises. And one wrist was swollen.

Tim went about his work, now glad of the supplies in the pack which had been digging into his shoulder blades all the way up here. His father kept it ready to hand at all times in case of emergency, but Tim had gone through it after Mark Thronson's accident and added a few items in addition to replenishing others, and now he was grateful for the foresight.

The snow continued to pelt unheeded down his neck as he did everything he could to make sure his patient would arrive at the helicopter seven miles back down the trail without further damage. Just to be positive, he strode alongside the litter, keeping an eye on his patient as the team relayed the young man down the trail. He supervised the transfer to the helicopter.

And he rode with his patient to Kalispell, to watch over him until he could safely be handed over, with briefing, to the emergency room doctors at Flathead County General.

It wasn't until Mack had been carried off that Tim walked back outside and stared around blankly. It was still snowing, but down out of the mountains it wasn't sticking to anything but the grass and trees. If he'd been in the mood to appreciate it, he'd have said it was pretty, but he was so tired he was weaving on his feet. He also hadn't given a single bit of consideration as to how he was to get back to Campbell without a car.

"Hey, you."

Tim turned, to see Tara walking toward him. "Wow, am I glad to see you. I was wondering how I was going to get home." He ignored the quirk of her lips on his choice of words. Campbell would always be home, no matter where he lived, and he knew she understood. "But what are you doing here?"

She grimaced. "Your dad sent me." She took his arm and got him moving, he assumed toward her rig. "Brad radioed back to the clinic while you were dealing with your patient, and your dad called me."

"Of course he did. Sorry about that."

"Don't apologize."

They'd reached her rig, a bright blue Jeep. When Tim tried to go around to the driver's side, Tara laughed and took him by the arm. "Not on your life. You don't need another helicopter ride this morning."

He let her bundle him into the passenger seat. It felt so good to just sit down, to lean his head against the seat back, to close his eyes.

"Hey, don't go to sleep on me just yet. When's the last time you ate?"

He couldn't remember. "Yesterday's lunch, I think."

"That's what I thought. Let's stop and get you some breakfast before we head back."

He didn't have to answer. His stomach did it for him.

Tara laughed again.

Chapter 12

Tara pulled off of Kalispell's main drag into the 4Bs restaurant, which served breakfast twenty-four hours a day, and managed to bundle Tim back out of her rig and inside. He didn't protest. He simply leaned right into the high back of the booth in exactly the same posture he'd had in the Jeep and closed his eyes again in spite of the rattle of dishes and the sound of voices all around them. When the waitress came, Tara made small talk with her and ordered for both of them on autopilot.

Tara couldn't stop watching him. He certainly didn't look like a big city doctor right now. He looked absolutely exhausted, and not because he'd gone soft in Seattle, either. Even Tara had to admit that. His blond hair was damp in spite of the knit cap he'd yanked off in the car, and molded to his head as if plastered there. His cheeks and nose were as red as Santa Claus's suit.

Against her will, Tara almost felt sorry for him. She was sure this wasn't what he'd bargained for when he'd come home for his dad's birthday. And, much as she hated to do it, she had to give him credit. His father might be bullying him for all he was worth, but Tim didn't have to be here taking it.

He opened his eyes when the food came. The pancakes, eggs, and sausage she'd ordered for him appeared to be enough of a prompt to his empty stomach that they outweighed his exhaustion, at least long enough for him to inhale them. Tara smiled at the waitress as she topped his coffee mug up for the third time, too.

For a moment Tara thought he was going to pick the plate up and lick it clean as well, but at last he leaned back again and said, "This wasn't what I'd had in mind for our first meal out together."

"What, you don't like the 4Bs?" The Montana chain restaurant was about as classic a diner as diners came, with a long counter, dark wood paneling, and plenty of metal-edged Formica. Truckers liked it, but it was the locals who kept it in business.

"I haven't eaten in one since I left Campbell." He looked as if he were confessing some great sin. "They don't have them in Seattle."

"I know."

"If it weren't for the Campbell Café, I'd say they make the best pancakes I've ever had."

The waitress came by with the check. Tara watched Tim fumble in his pockets and come up empty. "I didn't think I was going to need my wallet up on the mountain." He gave her a sheepish look as she pulled her own wallet out of her purse. "This wasn't what I had in mind for our first date, either."

Tara stared at him. "I wasn't planning on going out on a date with you."

He looked baffled, although she wasn't sure that wasn't simply from being half-asleep. "What do you call what we were going to do last night?"

She knew exactly what she'd been calling it. "Insanity."

He looked like he was trying to figure out how to answer that when a yawn almost cracked his face in two. Tara abruptly decided that it wasn't any fun to kick him when he was already down.

"Come on, let's get you home."

Thankfully, as she'd figured he would, he slept the entire way, propped between the seat back and the passenger door, her emergency blanket draped over his unconscious form. If she didn't know better, Tara thought, she'd have sworn she'd hit him over the head with a mallet.

He didn't snore, just snuffled quietly a few times. Except for the one time he spoke in his sleep, just as they passed by Lake Thompson, almost halfway back to Campbell. Just one word. Her name. In a tone she'd never have recognized out of him. A tone that made her heart clench. He sounded lonesome. And wistful, for crying out loud. The man had no business sounding wistful. Not when he was saying her name.

"I know you're not staying," Tara told him firmly. "Besides, we hate each other." She just wished he was listening to her.

* * *

"You've got to say something about my cousin, or this isn't going to work."

That same morning, Rebecca stared across the corner table at Jack as her hotcakes cooled. At this hour on a Sunday the Campbell Café was practically empty, and they didn't have to worry about being overheard.

"What does your cousin have to do with this?" she demanded.

Jack let out a deep breath. "Oh, come on. Don't you remember?"

Rebecca didn't remember the incident in question firsthand because she hadn't been there. The whole disaster had gone down in Seattle just before Tara and Jack graduated from the University of Washington, Tara with her master's degree in library science and Jack with his in science education. Tim had still been in the middle of medical school. Rebecca, of course, was home in Campbell, still being a good girl by her parents' standards, which did not include a college education. Her firsthand memories of those years were full of envy and disappointment.

But she might as well have been on the spot, given that she'd heard more about the whole traumatic incident than she'd ever wanted to know. She'd heard Jack's version of Tim's side, with the pure, Jack-added dollops of guilt and frustration at having ruined his friend's love life. She'd heard Tara's side. Several times. She'd never tried to explain Tim's side of the kafoffle to Tara herself before, not because she didn't care, but because she'd always been convinced that she wasn't the one Tara needed to hear it from. Maybe that had been a mistake. Rebecca guessed she'd find out today, one way or the other, and hoped she wouldn't lose her best friend in the process.

But she hadn't realized Jack was still hung up about the whole thing. Or that he still felt responsible for breaking Tim and Tara up. Jack sounded as if their current problem had brought back memories he didn't want to remember. "Tim said he never told her who she was, and knowing Tara she's probably still hung up on the whole thing."

"Jack, that was five years ago," Rebecca protested. "In the first place, I'm sure she's forgotten all about it." Well, no, Rebecca knew Tara hadn't, but it was a side issue, and fooling Tara was going to be hard enough without trying to bring up that sore point. "In the second place —"

Jack interrupted her, a sure sign he wasn't going to let this go. "Right. Would you ever forget the fight that broke you up with the love of your life?"

Rebecca reached out a hand and clasped Jack's where it was resting on the table. "I hope I never have to find out, love of my life."

Jack tried to retrieve his hand. Rebecca hung on. "Okay, okay, don't get sentimental on me," he complained.

She let go and forked up another bite of pancakes. The last thing she wanted to be doing was eating cold pancakes. She set the fork back down. "The real problem is that there's no way I can bring Andrea up without Tara getting suspicious. Tim's just going to have to work that out with her himself. It's going to be hard enough to pull this off without her radar pinging as it is."

Jack looked a lot more confident in her than she was in herself. "I'm sure you and Cindy will manage. After all, you've got a lot at stake here."

"You mean Tim's got a lot at stake." Rebecca picked up her milk instead. At least it was *supposed* to be cold.

Jack nodded. "And Tara."

Rebecca sighed and capitulated. "And Tara. And us. Dr. Samuel was right. It would be awful if they ended up fighting at the wedding."

Jack chuckled. "Knowing Tim and Tara, it won't matter if they've fallen ass-end over teakettle. They'll still find something to squabble about."

She really did wish she could get used to Jack's occasional use of coarse language. She knew he only let the occasional expression slip when he was around her now because he was comfortable around her. She should be glad he was comfortable around her. And she was. But it still made her uncomfortable. And why? Because her parents disapproved of coarse language. Along with everything else about Jack. Rebecca grinned at him, her expression deliberate for more than one reason. "And that's why we love them."

"We do?" Jack's expression was wide-eyed and innocent. Rebecca aimed the syrup at him. He put up his hands. "Okay, okay. We do."

* * *

The library was quiet on Monday afternoon. On a brilliant fall day like this one, with last night's storm over and the first snow in town threatening like imminent doom any day now, most people who didn't have to be inside probably weren't. Even the usual after-school crowd was smaller than usual, and now only one or two kids were parked back by the computers in the children's area.

Tara grabbed a book truck from the back room and loaded it with recent returns. She was short one shelver who'd had to go into Kalispell for an orthodontist appointment. She had the other shelver busy with the picture books, but someone had to catch up on the load.

She put the bell with its small sign on the desk and pulled the book truck back toward the non-fiction. A couple of cartloads ought to do it, but she certainly hadn't envisioned getting a Masters degree in library science only to end up shelving books again.

Tara straightened, put her hands to the small of her back, and looked around the small Grant County District Library with pride. Who was she kidding? Shelving books in Campbell beat out the fancy research questions she'd fielded at that stuffy corporate library in Portland any day. This was her town, and her library. Her responsibility and her joy. She wouldn't give it up no matter how many books she ended up shelving.

She dropped a hand on the cart and pulled it down the aisle,

Half an hour later, she'd almost emptied the truck and was about to head back to the workroom to reload it when she heard the door open. She stopped to listen for a moment, but the bell didn't ring. She shrugged and went on with her work.

* * *

"Where is she? I don't see her." Cindy's whisper sounded like a gunshot in the quiet room to Rebecca's straining ears.

"Shhhhh..." Rebecca gestured, her finger raised to her lips. "She's here. She's got to be here. The library doesn't close for another hour."

"Wait. She's got the bell up."

"Is there something I can do for you ladies?" A voice came from behind them. Not Tara's, thank goodness. This one belonged to one of the high school kids Tara hired part time in the afternoons, a black-haired, bespectacled young man who hadn't quite yet filled out his breadth to match the height that had put him on the Campbell High basketball team in spite of his bookishness.

Cindy giggled. Rebecca glared at her, earning a curious stare from their would-be assistant. "No, Pete, but thanks, anyway."

"If you're looking for Ms. Hillerman, I think she's shelving in the nonfiction." He reached for the bell.

Before he could ring it and ruin everything, Rebecca said hastily, "No, we just came in to get something to read, but thanks."

"Okay. Let me know if you need anything." He shrugged and headed back toward the children's section, pulling his loaded cart behind him.

As soon as Pete had folded his lanky self back in front of the picture books and hopefully out of earshot, Cindy giggled again. Rebecca was beginning to wonder if her friend was going to be able to contain herself enough for them to pull this off. "Behave," she whispered.

Cindy grinned unrepentantly. "That was close."

There was no help for it. With a sense of impending doom, Rebecca strolled, carefully casual, back toward the nonfiction, Cindy close behind her. The squeaking of a book truck, its wheels needing lubrication, brought them both to a complete halt.

The squeaking stopped. Rebecca held her finger to her lips. That sent Cindy into another fit of the giggles. Heaven knew why. No, she knew why. She hadn't meant to mimic the late, beloved Miss Iris. The gesture had just come out that way. Finally Cindy managed to get hold of herself, although she was red in the face when she lifted her head again.

The soft squeak of the book truck on the worn asphalt tile floor and occasional mutters of Tara shelving and tidying books were finally all there was to be heard over the pounding of Rebecca's heart.

Rebecca nodded. Cindy took a deep breath. "It's too bad about Tim," she said clearly. And almost too loudly. Rebecca held her breath.

The squeaking abruptly stopped. She let it back out again in a whoosh. Cindy was grinning like a fool. Here goes, Rebecca thought. "It sure is."

* * *

Two aisles over, Tara froze, just as she'd been about to call out to see if they needed any help.

What was the matter with Tim now? He'd been fine – still exhausted but otherwise okay – when she'd dropped him off at his parents' house yesterday noon. Before she could say anything, Rebecca started speaking again.

"He didn't want to come back to Campbell in the first place."

Tara breathed. Oh, she thought in relief. Just old news.

"His father needs him."

"But he didn't even know Tara was here, or I bet he wouldn't have."

She certainly hoped she wouldn't have kept him from visiting his parents. She was more than sure she wouldn't have, too. Watching Tim over the last few days had made her realize he wasn't who she'd thought he was. But it didn't mean she – Tara stared at the book in her hand and set it back down on the cart.

Rebecca commented, "Jack says it really hit him broadside, seeing her again." This was incredibly out of character for Rebecca, who despised the gossip Campbell thrived on, mostly because of what it had done to her Jack. But she was seeing romance everywhere she went these days, ever since Jack proposed to her. So Tara supposed she could understand. Maybe. She'd read Rebecca the riot act later, and they'd laugh about it, and Tara would set her straight.

"He's been moping around ever since he got here." Right, Cindy, Tara thought. And you know this how? "Poor guy. Nothing like unrequited love to bring a man to his knees." Okay. That was over the line. Cindy was out of her ever-loving mind. Tara opened her mouth.

"He's loved her for years," Rebecca agreed. And Tara closed her mouth again, the breath knocked right out of her. "You should have seen him when they were in college. When she threw him over, Jack thought Tim was going drop out of medical school and run off. Heaven knows to where."

Tara froze again, stunned. Drop out of medical school? Over her? Becoming a doctor had been his lifelong dream.

"Jack felt responsible, too," Rebecca added. "Since he was the one who'd asked Tim to show his cousin around."

"Jack's *cousin?*" Tara whispered, the words barely a puff of air between her lips.

"Andrea's a pretty girl, but Tara should have known Tim wouldn't cheat on her."

Tara's hand came up to her lips. It couldn't be true. Tim *had* cheated on her. It was the cornerstone of her entire life, her entire reason for being, since she'd seen him with the blonde. She'd latched onto Hans just to get even, not that Tim hadn't known, the big lummox. He'd told her so when he said good-bye to her at graduation. He'd been positively sweet about it, just adding to her guilt. She'd escaped Seattle right after graduate school only to discover she couldn't run away from her own feelings. She was home living in *Campbell* because of Tim and the blonde, for crying out loud.

The blonde who was Jack's cousin, apparently. Visiting Seattle, no doubt, and Tim was doing Jack a favor.

And he hadn't been cheating on her.

"Oh, my God," Tara whispered.

Rebecca said sadly, "But it's always been hard for Tara to give anyone the benefit of the doubt."

And she'd thought Rebecca was her *friend*. Tara charged down the aisle again to give both of them a piece of her mind, then stopped at Cindy's next words.

"What's Tim going to do?"

Rebecca sounded as if she'd lost her last friend. Well, she just might have, Tara thought. "Nothing, as far as I can tell. They were supposed to go out Saturday night, but I guess Tara gave him the cold shoulder. I bet she was glad when he had to cancel on her to go rescue that hiker. Jack said he was pretty depressed this afternoon." He hadn't been the last time *Tara*'d seen him. Either Rebecca was imagining things, or – "He'll probably just go back to Seattle."

"It's sad."

"Really sad."

Silence.

"I guess the book I was looking for is out."

Tara took a deep breath and called out. "I can check for you on the computer, if you like."

And wasn't that the oddest noise? They sounded as if they were both choking. At last, Rebecca said, in a strangled voice, "Okay. Thanks."

Tara stuck her head around the end of the shelves. "What's the title?"

Rebecca stared at her as if her mind had suddenly gone blank. Cindy piped up, "Um, *Men Are From Mars, Women Are From Venus?*"

Recovering herself with great difficulty, Tara shook her head. Cindy had an evil sense of humor, and it was out in full force just now. As if nothing at all was out of the ordinary, she said, "Come on. You're in the wrong section. These are the six hundreds. The book you want is in the one hundreds." As calmly as if her heart wasn't pounding its way out of her chest, Tara led the way to the correct shelf, where the book was innocently waiting.

She grabbed it and strode to the checkout desk, Rebecca and Cindy trailing behind her. Cindy produced a library card. Rebecca just stood there looking miserable. As well she ought to, given the conversation she'd just had, Tara thought, and glared at her erstwhile friend. Rebecca was refusing to meet her eyes. She'd deal with Rebecca and her sudden penchant for gossip later, when she wasn't at her place of work. Because she suspected she wouldn't be acting very professionally when she did.

But what if what Rebecca had said was true? Tara took a deep breath and handed the book to Cindy. "Here you go."

"Thank you," Cindy chirped, and dragged Rebecca out the door.

* * *

"You think she believed us?" Rebecca asked breathlessly as soon as they were around the corner, out of sight of the library's windows. She felt like a hot air balloon let loose from its tethers. She knew she shouldn't be feeling this way, that she should be feeling horrible about misleading her friend – although "misleading'" was probably not the right term. Forcing Tara to face the truth was more like it. Tim did love Tara. And Tara loved Tim right back, and she knew Rebecca knew it. Just because Tara was too stubborn to admit it didn't mean it wasn't true. But Rebecca simply hadn't realized how darned *ridiculous* the whole situation was going to be.

"Who knows?" But Cindy sounded far more amused than anything else. Laughing at the situation was one thing. But she shouldn't be laughing at her friend.

Then Rebecca caught sight of the self-help volume in Cindy's hand. "I can't believe you asked her for *that* book!"

Cindy stared down at it and snorted. "I couldn't think of anything else. Did you see her *face* when I asked for it?"

"I know." Rebecca couldn't help it. The laughter burst out of her, which set Cindy off, too.

"Poor Tim, my foot," Cindy managed to gasp out at last.

Rebecca stopped short of her car, parked along the street, sober once more, suddenly feeling as if she'd set an avalanche in motion. "He'd better not hurt her again. Because if he does, he's going to have to answer to me."

Chapter 13

Tim? Still in love with her? Tara sank onto the chair in her office, her professional duties forgotten. Tim? The man who'd abandoned her for five years without a backward glance, who'd never even tried to explain the blonde... Not that she'd given him a chance to. She'd been too insecure to even begin to listen.

Jack's cousin. The blonde was Jack's *cousin.* Come to think of it, Tara vaguely remembered Jack talking about someone coming to visit – family from North Dakota, if she remembered correctly – the week before the fateful day when she hadn't given Tim a chance to explain...

Oh, Tim. I'm so sorry.

She'd been so sure he'd been cheating on her, but it wasn't his fault. He'd been loving and attentive, and everything a girl in love could have wanted. But she'd been so insecure, so sure of how a man like him couldn't possibly love a girl like her.

How he could truly mean it when he said that he preferred his hometown sweetheart to all those beautiful, smart college girls.

Tara knew she hadn't given him a chance.

It was hard to give someone a chance when all she could do was compare herself, from the backwoods of Montana, to all those city girls, with their city fashions and their city confidence and their city tastes. Oh, she'd tried to fit in, to learn how to be like them, but she'd never felt like she had. She had made friends among her fellow small town transplants, but never with the city girls who intimidated her so.

Then she'd only made things worse by taking that corporate job in Portland. She still didn't know why they'd hired her. She'd really never fit in there, either, and she'd always felt like she'd been faking it. Faking it was no way to live a life. She'd had three years of unhappily trying to be someone she wasn't, checking the job listings on the Pacific Northwest Library Association website every week, telling herself that she wasn't leaving her good job, that she was just curious about what was out there. Then the opportunity had jumped out at her as if it were written in neon lights, "Wanted: Library director, Grant County District Library, Campbell, Montana."

And she'd come home. She'd thought she was happy, and she was happy here, but something was still missing. Tim. She hadn't realized just how much she wanted him to be part of her life again until he'd come home.

But he still loved her, according to Rebecca. Oh, Tara knew Rebecca had staged the whole conversation. Cindy's giggles had been a dead giveaway, and besides, Tara knew full well that Rebecca's own head-over-heels state made her want a happily-ever-after for everyone around her.

But that wasn't the point. The point was Tim hadn't cheated on her after all. And he might still love her, in spite of what she'd done to him when he'd given her the merest slip of an excuse. Which, of course, he hadn't. She'd just seen it that way because she didn't know any other way to keep him from breaking her heart.

Tim pined for her, just as she did for him. He'd asked her out last Saturday, not because he was bored in Campbell and wanted to liven up his weekend by giving her a hard time, but because he genuinely wanted her company.

As she wanted him. His company, his intelligence, his kisses... His world-class butt and his world-class temper.

"Hey, Ms. Hillerman, you want me to finish that truck you left in the nonfiction?"

Tara's gaze shot up, and she felt herself coloring. She managed a self-deprecating smile. "If you wouldn't mind, Pete, that would be great."

"Sure. Mr. Framingham has a reference question."

"Thanks. I'm coming."

As Tara headed back out to the front desk, she raised her hands to her hot cheeks.

Tim still loved her. Who'd ever have thought she'd be that lucky again?

Now all she had to do was convince him he wanted to stay in Campbell with her.

* * *

First things had to come first. She had to let him know he had another reason to stay. Tara spent the rest of that afternoon plotting and planning, and most of the evening, as well. These things had to be accomplished with a certain amount of finesse, especially when her – their – future was at stake. And when crow was going to be the major item on her menu.

When she strolled into the clinic Tuesday morning before the library opened, it was with the most casual of demeanors, and her heart in her throat.

"Hello, Betty. How are you on this fine fall morning?"

Betty Real glanced up from the teetering stack of charts – and was that a laptop? – on her desk. It looked as if every file folder in the clinic had suddenly decided to roost there. "Young Dr. Timothy finally convinced his dad computers aren't the invention of the devil, and that all the patient records won't vanish into thin air if they're digitized. I'll be darned if I know how he did it. But now –" she gestured down the hall toward the two examining rooms "– they've both got the idea that dumping all the scutwork on me is all they have to do to make it happen." She pointed at the sleek little laptop, perched among the stacks like some sort of alien being. "Dr. Timothy thinks part of the reason we can't attract a new doctor is because we're not in the modern age." She snorted.

"Where did it come from?" Tara asked.

"Tim brought it in. About time, if you ask me." Betty, like most of the residents of Campbell who didn't work at the mill, kept body and soul together by means of more than one job. When she wasn't playing dogsbody for Dr. Samuel, she was one of the three part-time employees who kept Campbell's lone, community-owned internet service provider up and running. She'd been complaining at Dr. Samuel for years about his old-fashioned ways.

Tara pursed her lips, trying not to smile. So, was this Tim giving Dr. Samuel an ultimatum, or Dr. Samuel adding yet another bribe to get Tim to stay in Campbell?

Either way... Tara shook herself. She had a reason for being here.

Betty added, "Dr. Timothy's worse than his father for just expecting things to happen. Spoiled by the big city, I guess."

This time Tara did smile, at the comment and at Betty's moniker for Tim, which sounded very much as if she'd decided he was going to stay, too. "Is he?"

Betty scowled. "If I'd known just how little help he was going to be, I'd've told the boy to stay in Seattle."

Tara's smile dimmed just a bit. Yes, there was that. She still wasn't sure how even "twue wuv" was going to fix that little issue. Big issue. Gigantic problem. "Is Tim here?"

"Who's looking for me?"

Tara turned to see the object of her search striding down the hallway, white coattails flapping over flannel, jeans, and boots, stethoscope around his neck. Her heart flipped over. How on earth had she ever thought she was going to be able to live the rest of her life without this man? How were they going to work this out?

Restraining herself, with difficulty, from flinging herself into his arms and begging forgiveness, Tara gave him her brightest smile, noting in satisfaction when he blinked.

"Good morning, Tim."

"Hello, Tara. Not feeling well?" A line of concern appeared between his eyebrows.

Tara hastily disabused him. "What? Oh, no. I came to see you, if you have a minute."

"Sure. For you, I have as many minutes as you need." He waited. Tara waited.

She gave up first. "Is there somewhere we can talk?"

Tim glanced over at Betty, who threw up her hands and said, "Don't ask me. I'm too busy stuck doing data entry all day to keep an eye on you."

"Which is much appreciated," Tim told her. Betty did look mollified. More than mollified, actually. Good. Betty wasn't going to be the last tipping point – that was Tara's job – but she could hinder the process more than necessary.

Tara watched Tim as he considered their options. "Dad's with a patient. I guess we could use his office." He sounded dubious about that idea, to Tara's ear, at least.

She cleared her throat. "I'd rather he not walk in on us."

Tim grinned, and it was her turn to blink. Oh, she had it bad. She had to convince him to stay. She had to.

"Really? Well, the only other option is the storage room." He eyed her. "Would that be private enough for you?"

She felt herself redden. "Sure. I'd just like a minute alone with you, if you don't mind."

* * *

No, Tim didn't mind being alone with her. Not one little bit. He'd like to know what the heck was going on, but he didn't mind time alone with Tara. Even in the storage room.

"Come on," he said, very much aware of Betty's amused gaze following them down the hall. He opened the door to the storage room, more of a big windowless closet, actually, with boxes stacked on bare metal shelves to the ceiling on three walls. He flipped the switch for the bare bulb hanging above them. There wasn't much room. Barely enough for the two of them to maintain a civil distance.

For him to keep his hands off of her.

Tim closed the door behind him and turned to Tara. "Now what was it you wanted to talk about —"

The rest of what he'd been about to say was gone. Just like that. Swallowed by Tara's warm mouth. And Tara's warm body.

Tim's brain completely scrambled, just like it had the night he'd come home. Oh, Tara, was all he could think. Please don't let this be a hit and run again. He wrapped his arms around her and hung on.

She was devouring him. This wasn't a simple, gentle kiss, and it wasn't slow and easy. It was lips and teeth and tongue, and heads tilting this way and that. It wasn't like he remembered the night he'd come home at all. It was better. But it wasn't enough.

Her hands slid through his hair, pulling him more tightly to her. As if he was going to try to get away. Little did she know. Still it wasn't enough.

Tim yanked her up until they were plastered together. And it wasn't enough. Nothing was going to be enough except being naked in bed together. Every night. Forever.

Frantic, he pulled his mouth away from hers to taste her neck. Slid his hands under the light, fluffy sweater she wore to wrap them tightly around her waist. Tara's skin was so much softer than the sweater, so much smoother and sleeker. And so hot she felt like she was running a fever. He wanted to lift that sweater up and over her head in the worst way, but he still didn't know why she'd suddenly decided to kiss him again. He loved her, but the last he knew, she still hated him. He lifted his head. Loosened his hold.

Put a hand on her chest – on top of the sweater, dammit – when she reached for the buttons on the plaid shirt under his white coat. His own voice sounded odd to him as he asked her, "Not that I'm complaining, but what's going on here?"

She blushed and dropped her gaze. He raised his hand from her chest and lifted her chin. "I, I just –"

Gathering her in his arms, he held her closely, feeling her rapid heartbeat match his. Nothing had ever felt so right, but he just couldn't take this sudden outpouring at face value. It mattered too much. He thought about the first time Tara had kissed him lately and the idiotic words slipped out before he could stop them. "You haven't been drinking, have you?"

She leaned back and stared up at him. "It's nine o'clock in the morning, Tim!"

She had a point. Besides, he'd have been able to taste liquor on her, and he was so glad he hadn't. But he still didn't trust this. Or her. "You aren't being carried away by old times?"

"No." The confusion in her eyes cleared up into affectionate amusement. And something else. Tim caught his breath. He hadn't seen Tara look at him like that – well, since before the blonde disaster.

"I'm not drunk, Tim. And I'm not reminiscing." She hesitated, which was so unlike her it tugged at his heart. "Would you like to come over to dinner tonight?"

All right. Now he was officially in an alternate universe. But it was a universe he liked, very, very much. After what had just happened, he supposed he shouldn't be surprised by anything, but he couldn't help asking. "Is that why you came into my office and ravished me? To ask me to dinner?"

Tara grinned. He couldn't help grinning back. "I thought you might be more likely to accept if I gave you a bit of an appetizer, so to speak."

No. Surprise wasn't half of what he was feeling right now. He cleared his throat. "An, um, appetizer?"

"Maybe."

He had to know if she was setting him up for a fall again. "Tara, what's going on here?"

"Why don't you come over tonight and find out?" He choked at her words. She finger-combed the hair that he'd just enjoyed mussing, and tugged her sweater back into place. "You might want to fasten your shirt before we go out."

She turned toward the door. Tim reached for his buttons. She glanced over her shoulder at him.

"Tonight?"

"Sure." How could he refuse? "What time?"

"Oh, about seven?"

"I'll be there." Tim watched her wicked little behind swish through the doorway, waited a few futile minutes to give his body a chance to cool down, and followed her.

* * *

Tara left work the moment the library closed that afternoon at five. She made two stops on her way home, then whirled into action.

Her menu was going to be simple. Roast beef and vegetables, green salad, and an apple pie from the Campbell Café's bakery. Tara figured she'd play it safe. Men around here liked their beef. She assumed Tim's palate had grown more sophisticated in Seattle, but she didn't feel confident enough to try anything elaborate. The wine she'd purchased on her lunch hour would take off any rough edges.

Once the roast was in the oven, she pulled out the good dishes and glassware she'd accumulated in Portland, and a thick crimson tablecloth, and arranged them on the little dining table in the corner of her living room, then added matching candles in brass holders. Tara debated if it was cool enough for a fire in the fireplace, decided she wanted one even if it wasn't, and laid logs, kindling, and paper, ready for a match.

She blanched as she noted the time. She needed to get ready herself.

She was headed for her bedroom when the doorbell rang. If that was Tim here at a quarter past six she was going to draw and quarter him. She strode back to the door and flung it open.

"Hey, you!" Rebecca stepped in.

Tara let out her breath. "Hey, yourself."

"Jack's got some school thing going on tonight and I wondered if you'd like to go get some dinner at the café." Rebecca sniffed appreciatively and sauntered over to the table. "But I guess not. Smells good. Looks like you're having company."

Tara squirmed under Rebecca's teasing gaze. "I am."

Rebecca smiled innocently. "May I ask who?"

Rebecca was going to find out sooner or later, Tara thought resignedly. Might as well get the recriminations over with. "Tim."

"Oh, Tim." Rebecca's tone reeked of innocuous interest, but Tara knew better.

"Yeah. And I hate to be a wet blanket, but he's going to be here in less than an hour, and I've got things to do."

"That's okay." Rebecca strolled to the door. "Have fun." She left. The expression on her face as she'd opened the door was extremely self-satisfied, Tara thought, and would have to be dealt with. Later. She had work to do.

First, she took a long, warm shower and applied some sweet-scented lotion, then she dried her hair and swept the loose red-brown locks back from her face with a pair of combs. A small amount of makeup, judiciously applied, came next. Then she went into her bedroom and gazed at the gray silk dress. Well, it was the most sophisticated thing she owned.

And she desperately wanted to look sophisticated tonight. She wanted Tim to see that she could be more than just a Campbell girl, from the back of beyond in Montana. She wanted to be someone he would be proud to be seen with. Someone he could take places and not feel like he had to show her which fork to use.

Someone like all those city women she was sure he'd been dating for the last five years. She was so lucky one of them hadn't snatched him up. Tara's hands, so determinedly steady with blow-dryer and mascara wand, suddenly shook.

Sure, Tim may have told Jack that he'd missed her, but Tara knew that whatever Rebecca'd heard from Jack had been built up in Rebecca's love-soaked brain to the point of no return. Tara knew, in spite of her initial reactions to the staged conversation, that Rebecca, as well-meaning as she was, was quite capable of blowing anything into a grand love affair.

Still, Tara knew she wasn't going to let this chance slip her by. She still couldn't believe she'd let it slip by for five years without seeing the truth.

If Rebecca wanted to take the credit when Tim and Tara became an item again, Tara was willing to let her have it. She, Tara, would have Tim.

Stepping to the bed, Tara let her robe slide off her shoulders and picked up the first bit of lacy lingerie.

Chapter 14

Tim pulled the Prius up to the curb in front of Tara's home, killed the engine, and looked at his watch for the seventeenth time since he'd left his parents' house, five minutes before.

It still said 6:55 p.m. Close enough, Tim thought, and leaned over to pick up the flowers he'd bought on his way back to his parents' house from the clinic. Tara liked roses. He'd had a sudden strong memory in the flower shop of Tara's positive reactions to the rose corsage he'd bought for their high school prom, ten years ago. These blooms filled the car with their fragrance just the way those had.

He climbed out of the car and headed up the walk to her door. Standing on her porch, where he'd recently had his first Tara-kiss in five years, he hesitated, took a deep breath, and rang the doorbell. Reached up, straightened his collar. Waited.

It seemed like forever, even though it was only a moment or two, before the door swung open and she stood before him.

She looked beautiful. He wasn't quite sure what she'd done to enhance her eyes so, but he could have told her it wasn't necessary. Her clothing was more sophisticated than anything he'd ever seen her in, too, including her high school prom dress. The gray silk flowed over her like water, the color making her hair and skin glow. He hadn't known she could look quite like that, and he found himself feeling slightly intimidated, oddly enough, which was ridiculous.

Not that he didn't appreciate the packaging, but it wasn't the packaging that had him hoping she'd decided she cared for him the way he cared for her. It wasn't the packaging that made his blood pulse warmly through his veins, anticipating the promise she'd made him that morning.

She could have worn a potato sack and it wouldn't have made any difference. However, Tim did know better than to say so.

"You look great." Glad he'd thought to buy the flowers, because they gave him something to do while he was feeling so awkward, he held them out to her.

Tara smiled. "That's a nice hello." She took the roses, buried her face in their peach-colored glory, then moved back to let him in. Tim stepped through the doorway and followed her from the darkness outside into the warmly lit living room.

He could smell something delicious cooking, hear the soft strains of Enya floating out of the stereo, feel the warmth of the fire she had going in the coolness of the autumn evening. Could see the intimate table in the corner that she'd set for the two of them, candles glowing against the shadows.

Over it all, he was aware of Tara, her elusive fragrance, the silky shine of her hair, her light, rapid breathing as she watched him. He wanted more. To touch, to taste, to feel her against him. Unconsciously he reached out.

Tara stepped back. "I'll just put these in water and go get supper."

Tim caught himself. You've got all evening, Swanson, he thought. Don't rush things. He smiled easily, and followed her into the kitchen. "Is there anything I can do?"

She gestured. "You could open the wine."

The bottle lay on the counter next to a corkscrew. Tim picked the bottle up and peeled the foil off the top, then applied the corkscrew. When it was out, he sniffed the cork, then looked at the label and drew back, surprised. "You've got good taste in wine."

"I hope so." Tara lifted the roast from the pan onto a platter, then started arranging the vegetables around it. "Rosauer's has come up in the world a bit in the last few years, but I really don't know what I'm doing when it comes to wine other than red goes with beef, which is what we're having tonight."

"You bought this in town?" The last time he'd been to Campbell's lone grocery store and its wine and beer section, the most sophisticated alcohol they'd carried was by those Gallo fellows down in California.

Tara looked positively smug. "You don't have to sound so incredulous. Campbell's changed in the last few years."

In more ways than he'd realized. "How?"

She went to the refrigerator and pulled out a bowl of salad. "The tourists. We don't just get the fishermen and the hunters anymore, although even there we're getting a higher class group ever since they improved Route 2. Lots of people come through here on their way to Glacier National Park, or up to Canada, and since we're just about the only place to buy anything for miles around, they stop here. Ask often enough, and the grocery store will carry prosciutto and French wine. Even old Amos will keep the odd surge protector and modem cord in with the hammers and snow shovels."

"Betty was telling me about the hardware store's new computer department, but I'm still not sure I believe her. Amazing." Tim picked up two stemmed glasses and the bottle and carried them out to the table. Tara followed with the platter. "That looks good."

"It's nothing fancy." She set the platter down.

Tim caught her by the elbow before she could go back in the kitchen. "It doesn't have to be fancy." He gave her a meaningful look.

The expression in her eyes was fathomless. Tim watched her stroll back to the kitchen, then poured the wine and sat down.

A moment later she returned with the bowl of salad and a basket of rolls, and seated herself.

Tim watched her surreptitiously as he forked a slice of beef. She seemed strangely unsure of herself, completely unlike this morning when she'd come onto him like a blowtorch. Right now she was utterly different from the self-assured Tara he'd always known and liked, even when she was baiting him, or teasing him, or giving him the worst of hard times.

She glanced up at him ever so briefly, their gazes catching, before she concentrated on her food again. She was avoiding meeting his eyes, he realized, for no reason he could understand. Her fork slipped out of her hand once, chiming musically against the plate.

When they'd both taken the edge off their hunger, Tim decided it was time to find out why on earth she was so nervous all of a sudden.

But, as usual, Tara beat him to the punch. She raised her head and looked him straight in the eye for the first time since they'd sat down.

"I want to apologize."

Tim stared at her. "For what?" She'd better not be apologizing for this morning. That interlude in the storage closet had been the highlight of his day.

"For slapping you."

"What?" She hadn't slapped him. Not that night after the Red Dog, not when he'd stood her up, not when she'd come to rescue him in Kalispell, and certainly not this morning. Tara was nothing if not a pacifist, which made her something of an anomaly in this town where hunting season was an annual rite, and fistfights at the Red Dog a semi-regular occurrence.

She looked sheepish. "It was a long time ago, but I imagine you remember. You came to my room one evening while we were in grad school. We had a date. And I, uh, misinterpreted something you'd done, and slapped you – right across the cheek." She must have seen the sudden memories in his face. "You do remember."

He remembered. He was flabbergasted. And he couldn't help being a little suspicious. "Why now?"

She took a deep breath. "Because I didn't know that I'd misinterpreted anything until yesterday."

Tim didn't know whether to be relieved or worried. Or angry, for that matter. But she'd completely taken the wind out of his sails, and taken the evening in a direction he'd really rather not have gone. "Who told you?" he demanded.

Why wouldn't she meet his eyes? "About the blonde I saw you with being Jack's cousin Andrea from North Dakota? The one you were showing around campus at his request?" Tara sighed. "Does it matter?"

Angry. He was angry enough to send his blood pressure sky high. "Hell, yes, it matters. I want to know who you trust more than you do me."

Tara gave him a stricken look. "I trust you, Tim."

"Sure you do." Tim pushed himself back from the table. He had to get out of here before he did or said something he'd regret later. So that was why she'd wanted him here this evening. To get that off

134

her chest? He hoped she felt better, because he sure the hell didn't. "Thanks for dinner."

"Wait." Tara reached over and laid a hand on his wrist.

He couldn't think of a single reason why he should. "What for?"

She actually had the gall to sound sad. "There were a lot of reasons I didn't want to believe you then. None of them having anything to do with whether I trusted you or not."

Sure there were. "Such as?"

Tara let go of him. She picked up her napkin and twisted the cloth.

She wasn't going to play him anymore. "See you later." He rose.

But before he'd taken one step toward the door, she said plaintively, "Can't you wait just a minute?"

Tim didn't turn to look at her. He didn't want to look at her. Those big gray eyes of hers were more than capable of softening him up, and he didn't want to be softened. "Tell me why I should."

"You're not going to take my word for it, are you?" She sounded close to tears. Which was totally unlike her.

But he wasn't going to turn around, dammit. "I don't see why I should. You didn't want to take my word for it five years ago."

"I was afraid to."

That did make him turn around, when almost nothing else would have. Tara, afraid of what? "Come again?"

Tara set down the napkin, picked up her wineglass. Took a long sip. Grimaced. Either she really didn't care much for alcohol in spite of that night at the Red Dog, or she was genuinely upset, because she'd picked a brilliant Pinot Noir. Not that it mattered now. She set the glass down.

"There's not an easy way to say this." She picked up the napkin and tortured it again. Tim silently watched her long slim fingers wrap around the red cloth.

"It's just that Seattle's the big city, and the university was such a huge place. So many people. I never felt at home there. I never felt like I belonged. I always felt like such a hick, like I should have been barefoot, with holes in my overalls."

She had to be joking. "You sure had everybody fooled," he told her.

"That's what it felt like, too. Like I was fooling everybody, like any little slip would have had everyone laughing at me."

"Even me?" He was offended all over again.

"No, not you." Tara gave him a wry glance and dropped the napkin. "When I was with you was the only time I felt like I fit in. You knew where I'd come from, you'd come from the same place, and I felt like you understood.

"But you seemed to fit in so easily. You made friends, and the girls all went after you –"

Tim hoped he wasn't blushing. "No, they didn't."

Now it was her turn to look like she didn't believe him. "Yes, they did. Almost every girl I met wanted to know if we were a couple, or if you were fair game. I just knew sooner or later one of them wasn't going to care if you were available or not, and I'd lose you to one of those sophisticated city women.

"Then when I saw you with Andrea, well, I assumed the worst. All I was trying to do was keep you from breaking my heart." Tara finally looked up at him, her expression completely open to him. For the first time in a very long time, Tim realized, and he didn't like what he saw there, not one bit. Tara had no business feeling so terrible about herself. She was, she was – "Unfortunately, I think I did that for myself."

Tim walked slowly and deliberately around the table, coming to a halt in front of her. He held out his hand.

Tara stared up at him, her gray eyes glistening, her expression wary and hopeful. Slowly she reached out and put her hand in his.

"That," said Tim, his hand tightening on hers, "is the most ridiculous reason you possibly could have concocted for dumping me. I love you, Tara. I loved you when you poured paint in my hair in kindergarten, when you argued that the sky only looked blue on the debate team in seventh grade, and when you spilled your soda all over my tux at the prom." One good tug on her hand, and she was in his arms again, exactly where she should have been for the last six years. "I didn't want any of those city girls. I wanted my childhood sweetheart. The girl I've admired and respected all my life, even when I wanted to strangle her. The woman who knows all my faults –"

Tara interrupted, her voice muffled in his shirtfront. "You can say that again."

"– And loves me in spite of them." Tim paused, his arms tightening around her. "You do still love me, don't you?"

Slowly Tara lifted her head, until her lips were a scant inch from his. "I do love you, Tim. With all my heart." She grinned, that expression the exact one he wanted to see, the one that showed she knew the only thing that mattered to either of them, that she loved him, that she knew he loved her. Her eyes still bright with tears, she asked the question he most wanted to hear. "So, are you going to kiss me, or what?"

Chapter 15

It was as simple as that. Tara could feel five years of loneliness and supposed betrayal drifting away as if they'd never been. All she could feel now was the rightness of it all. The simple strength of his arms around her, the soothing heat of his lips on hers, the way her whole world changed when he told her he loved her again.

It was a miracle. A class-A, first-water miracle. And the best part was that Tim seemed to think so, too. She'd thought his kisses passionate before. Now they stole her breath.

When he pulled away she followed him, leaning forward, slipping her hands through his hair to bring him back. He smiled, and slowly brought his hands up to hold her face. Tara closed her eyes, only to feel gossamer kisses on her eyelids, her cheekbones, the tip of her nose. Soft kisses. Torturous kisses. Tempting kisses, as he nipped her chin and tilted her head back to gain access to the pulse beating at the base of her throat.

His hand slipped to the back of her neck. Tara arched toward him and heard someone moan.

Oh, god, it was her. She froze.

It had been an awfully long time. What if he was disappointed? What if he laughed at her?

They were a long way from the two naïve college kids who'd lost their virginity together all those years ago. Now he had a basis for comparison, while she – well, she didn't.

Tim tilted his head back and stared at her. "What's the matter, Tara?"

She had trouble getting the words out. "Nothing. Just more nerves, I guess."

"You don't have anything to be nervous about." Tim reached out and tugged lightly on a strand of her hair. "Just come back here and let me kiss you some more."

His hand slipped from hair to neck and pulled her back to him. "You're beautiful tonight. Edible. Delectable. You don't want me starving, do you?"

Well, when he put it like that... Tara surrendered to his warm mouth, open on hers.

* * *

Having her in his arms was just as he'd remembered it, only better. He was older, wiser he hoped, and Tara had matured into a sexiness that took his breath away. She still moved as if this was all new to her, and it triggered emotions of wonder and joy that Tim had forgotten to associate with sex for a long time.

Not that he'd been sleeping around. At first he'd tried to forget Tara with other women, which had been a stupid and utter waste of time. He'd never been able – or wanted – to sustain a long-term relationship with anyone but her. Without love and intimacy, sex had been a relief and nothing more, a relief he'd stopped pursuing when? Longer ago than he wanted to think about, anyway.

And now, to have the one woman who'd spoiled him for all time in his arms again, her tentative ardor so like five years ago when she'd swept him under, was firing him like he'd never been before.

It was like coming home, where he belonged.

"Tim?"

"Yeah?" He smiled down at her as he tugged the lacy bra strap down her shoulder. Tara tried to turn her head away from him, so he couldn't see her face. He leaned down and nudged it back with his lips.

"Maybe it's been a long time."

Surely she didn't mean – curiosity warred with the lust coursing through him. "How long?"

Tara blushed crimson, but answered him. "Like five years?"

That brought him to a complete halt. "You mean you haven't, since –"

"I tried, Tim."

"What do you mean, you tried?"

She was blushing furiously. It charmed him. As if everything else wasn't. "I just couldn't."

"Because you love me?"

She hesitated. "Because they weren't you."

Tim wanted to pick Tara up and carry her off. Certain that she would make hash of any such chauvinistic reactions, he only kissed the tip of her nose.

"Guess we've got some lost time to make up for."

Deliberately he went back to the bra strap. But slowly this time. There was too much at stake now to rush through anything. The ivory strap whispered down her lightly freckled arm and over her hand. Tim slowly reached for the other strap, watching her face, seeing the bits of excitement, the wisps of nerves, chase across her expression.

It was almost as if they were losing their virginity together all over again. But not quite. It was better. He remembered what she liked, what made her lose control. Still holding her gaze, he slipped the second strap out of the way, unhooked the clasp, grasped the whole business, and threw it over the side of the bed. Then he bent his head to her pink-tipped breasts. They were just begging for his attention.

He reveled in her gasp as he touched her nipple with his lips. Listened to her breath catch as he ran his tongue over the tightly-furled nub. Heard with great satisfaction her long silky moan as he settled down to suckle the sweetness that was Tara.

"Oh, God." Tara's hands helplessly reached up and kneaded his scalp. "Timothy..."

He lifted his head for a moment, perused the shocked pleasure on her face, and bent again to savor her. When her hands began to roam down his back, he switched his attention to her other breast, and let his own hands begin exploring.

It was so much better than the first time. And he'd held that first time in his heart as the best thing that had ever happened to him. That he'd never be able to have again. But here he was.

This time, though, he wasn't a fumbling kid. He'd insinuate himself past all her defenses, even as she clenched the muscles in her thighs when he ran his hand down her hip.

Nervousness was one thing, but – "You know I wouldn't hurt you for the world, don't you?"

She smiled shakily and brought his face back up for another long, deep kiss. "I know. I think."

"I'm sure of it."

"I'm glad one of us is."

Tim reached down between them, to find her slick and wanting. She writhed when he brushed her lightly with his fingertips, moaned again when he found the tight knot of nerves, and, when he caressed her there, slid her hands down to his buttocks, underneath his briefs, and tugged. Hard. He could feel the erotic bite of her nails.

Thought fled before sensation. His briefs vanished, kicked to the floor, as did her panties, the last vestiges of any physical barrier between them. Tara slid a hand around and grasped him.

"Now," she gasped, her voice urgent. "Please. Now." She guided him home. And, God help him, that's exactly where he was. Home. Pumping and driving, his hands clamped on her shoulders as tightly as she clenched him, surrounding him, holding him. Her legs locked tightly around his waist, his body covering hers as she writhed and bucked beneath him.

Then she shuddered, over and over, holding him, releasing him, caressing him as only Tara could. Her arms fell limply away.

Tim reared back, plunged deeply one final time, and followed her into the darkness.

* * *

"I've waited five years for this. I thought I was going to have to wait forever, " Tim told her. Tara snuggled under his arm, wrapped tightly around her, as they lay back, their breaths slowing. "I'm not letting you get away this time."

"Okay." She slung a leg across him to show him she agreed.

"We'll figure out the logistics," he went on with a deplorable ability to form complete sentences after what they'd just done. "It can't be that hard. We're both grown-ups. We can compromise somehow."

"Okay." His dad was going to be so pleased. Not nearly as pleased as she was, but still.

"I want you in my life. On a permanent basis."

Her heart sang. "Okay."

"Geez, you're agreeable." He sounded positively disgusted with her.

Tara tilted her head back as well as she could considering his death grip on her and gazed at him. She had him exactly where she wanted him. Where she wanted to keep him. "Keep talking like that, Dr. Timothy, and you may end up telling your friends the impossible's happened."

He snorted. "What? That I've fallen in love? It's already happened. Let 'em laugh. I can't stop 'em."

She couldn't help the smirk that spread across her face. "I don't know about you, but where I come from, the kinds of things you're saying mean marriage."

Tim watched her. Tara wondered if he realized exactly how tightly he had his arm wrapped around her, as if he thought she was going to try to escape him now. Ha. He was going to have a heck of a time escaping her. She shrugged, playing along, as he said, "I know. You're not scared?"

"Petrified." Tara couldn't help tilting her head to kiss him. "Terrified. Scared out of my wits."

His grin quite ruined his supposedly-disgusted expression. "I guess that means we have to find you a ring."

"You guess right." She took a deep breath. "Everybody's going to just love this."

He squeezed even harder. She squeaked, and he loosened his grip. Slightly. "What's the matter? Don't you think we can take them on?"

"With you, I can take on anything," Tara told him, and kissed him again.

They were already halfway to fulfilling the promise of those kisses for the second time that evening when the phone rang. Tara tried to stop him, but Tim reached for it, anyway. She supposed it was an ingrained habit, being on call no matter what, but no one was going to call him for an emergency at her number. Not yet, anyway.

"Hello?" He listened for a second. "Yeah, it's me," then mouthed, "Becky," in Tara's direction.

"Give me that!" Tara grabbed for the phone.

Tim snorted with laughter and sat up, holding the phone so that Tara couldn't get to it, then replied to something Rebecca said. "In a manner of speaking." Paused again. "What advice?" Tim swung his legs off the bed and aimed toward the door, Tara hot on his heels. "Depends on what you wouldn't do."

"Timothy Swanson!" Tara made another grab for the phone. Tim neatly eluded her. "Talk to you later, Becky." Tim turned to where Tara stood naked three feet behind him, planning her next move. He waved the phone at her. "Did you want this?"

"I'm going to kill you," she told him.

He grinned. "Before or after you marry me?"

Oh, he was asking for it... "After. I want your rice burner."

She jumped him.

* * *

"Congratulations!" Dr. Samuel ushered Jack and Rebecca into his office.

"Thanks again, Doc," Jack said, sounding as puzzled as Rebecca felt. Dr. Samuel had already congratulated them on their engagement when they'd come in for the blood test. "You are coming to the wedding, aren't you?"

"I wouldn't miss it for the world. But I hope it's soon." Dr. Samuel reached over and chucked Rebecca on the chin. "Before you start showing. Your parents aren't going to be happy with you as it is."

"Uh, showing? Showing what?" Rebecca stared at him, utterly baffled. Behind her, Jack made a throttled sound.

"You don't need to play coy with me, young woman," Dr. Samuel chided her.

"I don't know what you mean." She'd never felt so confused in her life.

"I mean the baby. You're about a month and a half along, but I'm sure you knew that already." He smiled at her gently, as if he hadn't just lied through his teeth.

Rebecca's jaw dropped. "A baby? As in pregnant?"

"Great. So who's the father, Becky?" Jack's voice had Rebecca's head swinging around sharply.

"Jack, I don't know what he's talking about! I can't be pregnant —"

"Now, young lady, accidents happen to the best of us..." She swung around to stare at Dr. Samuel again.

"Accidents?" Jack spat out the word. "I don't think so." Before she could say something, anything, to him, he was gone, the thuds of his booted feet fading down the hallway. She heard Tim's voice, and Betty's, and something that sounded like a bear's growl, then a door slammed. Silence fell.

Rebecca sank into a chair and finally found her voice. "Dr. Samuel, I can't be pregnant. I've never had sex."

* * *

"Dad?" Tim stuck his head around the door of the office. "What happened?" So far as he knew, Becky and Jack had only come in to pick up the results of the blood test so they could go apply for their marriage license this afternoon.

Then Jack had stormed out, completely ignoring Tim's attempts to get his attention, then, a few minutes later, Rebecca had left in tears without saying a word, and not to follow her fiancé.

His father was sitting in his office chair, looking like the world had fallen in on him. Now more than a bit concerned, Tim entered the room, closing the door behind him. "Are you all right, Dad?"

His father looked up and smiled weakly, but his mind was obviously still elsewhere. "Oh, hello, Tim."

Tim grasped for patience. "What happened just now? I saw Jack tear out of here like a madman, then Becky, too." He watched his father, concern edging over into genuine worry. The last thing the old man needed was his patients giving him a hard time.

His father hesitated for a seeming eternity, then said quietly, "Becky's pregnant. I thought it would be good news, so I sprang it on them together. Young folks these days don't ever seem to wait for marriage anymore."

His father's words blew the thick atmosphere up like a land mine. "Pregnant? But Jack told me Becky wanted to wait until they got married." He didn't add Jack's opinion on the subject. Jack's impatience wasn't any of Dr. Samuel's business. Especially given the way Tim had spent last night with Tara.

"Apparently that's what Jack thought, too." Dr. Samuel shook his head, looking weary. Tim wished he'd been there, but, no, he'd been in the examining room giving Mark Thronson, who'd come home from the hospital in Kalispell a couple of days ago, the first of his follow-up exams. The gash on his leg was healing nicely, thank God.

But wait a minute. "The baby isn't his?"

"That's what he says." Samuel stood and paced for a moment, then perched on a corner of his desk and rubbed his gray head. "I'd never have expected anything like this from little Becky Thorstein. Her parents will be so ashamed."

Yeah, they would be. Idiots. They'd never taught her anything of any use whatsoever. Not that she didn't deserve it, if she was cheating on Jack. But Tim couldn't picture it. It just didn't compute. But then he hadn't seen Becky for several years until just recently. A lot could have changed in several years. "That's the least of her worries now, Dad."

"Oh, I don't know. I rather think the church won't see their way to keeping her employed, either."

"You're probably right. But I just can't believe – *Becky*?"

" I feel rather sorrier for Jack. Poor fellow. He's had his heart set on her since they were children."

Tim knew he had. Jack had been protective of Becky from the moment he'd met her, on the playground her first day at public school. She'd been eight. He and Jack, and Tara, had been eleven. Tim could still remember the poleaxed expression on his best friend's face when he'd first spotted Becky. And Jack's muttered, "She looks like an angel or something," promptly followed by red-faced embarrassment and a shove that had almost knocked Tim over when Tim had busted out laughing at him.

Jack had always treated Becky like an angel. "I can't believe it."

"Maybe the father will step forward." Samuel glanced up from where he'd been staring at his hands as if he expected to sprout another finger.

"Maybe." Tim doubted it, because if anyone else was serious about Becky he'd have claimed her that night at the Red Dog. Speaking of which, he'd bet good money that was where his friend was now. "I'm going to go find Jack before he does something stupid."

"Go ahead, son. I'll manage here."

He'd have to. "Thanks."

"If there's anything I can do..." Dr. Samuel sounded almost apologetic. Well, it wasn't anything he'd done. He'd just been the messenger.

"It wasn't your fault, Dad." How could it be?

"Somehow that doesn't seem to help," his father said sadly.

"I know."

"If I can help —" his father reiterated.

"You'll be the first to know." Tim headed out the door, letting it close behind him.

* * *

"You're what?" Tara sat stunned in one of the visitor chairs in her office, her arm around a copiously weeping Rebecca in the other.

"Pregnant. Or at least that's what the test says." Rebecca sniffled, and reached for another tissue. Tara steadied the box in her lap as Rebecca pulled one loose.

"But I thought you were saving yourself."

"I am!" Rebecca wailed.

Tara tried to make sense of the situation and gave up. There was no sense to be made of it, so it had to be nonsense. "Rebecca, I know we all believe in divine intervention, but the last virgin birth was two thousand years ago."

Rebecca shot to her feet. "You don't believe me, either, do you? Jack didn't, and Doctor Samuel didn't, and —"

"Of course I believe you, sweetie." With some difficulty, Tara tugged her best friend back down to the chair.

She wasn't weeping any more. Her face was red with anger. "I'm not pregnant. I know I'm not pregnant. I can't be pregnant unless all those stories we used to believe about toilet seats when we were kids are true. That's as close as I've been to anyone. Including Jack. You've got to believe me. Someone has to." Her voice trailed off into desolation. "I can't believe Jack doesn't believe me. He of all people ought to know."

Tara thought she understood why Jack didn't believe her. Not that he had the right to hurt Rebecca like that, no matter what his mother did to him. Now Tara was angry, too, because she did believe Rebecca, for what it was worth. Something was seriously screwy here. Whatever had happened, whatever the stupid test said, nothing was grounds for ruining her best friend's life like this. "What did the test say?"

Rebecca hesitated. "I, I don't know, exactly."

She'd been astonished before. Now Tara was dumbfounded. "What do you mean, you don't know? Didn't you even look at it?"

"It was a lie. I didn't want to look at a lie. Besides, Jack just stormed out, and, and he −" The tears were threatening again.

"He didn't even look at it, either?" Men, Tara thought. Damn them all. They just jumped to conclusions and didn't pay attention and didn't listen.

"No." Rebecca took a deep breath. "You weren't there. It was awful. You know how jealous Jack is. He scared me."

Tara couldn't help herself. "He didn't hit you, did he?"

Rebecca straightened. At last. Tara'd been wondering what happened to her friend's normally sturdy spine. "Jack's never hit me." She sounded reproachful. "I'm not stupid. If he'd ever even come close I'd never have agreed to marry him."

Well, that was a relief. "Good girl." But it didn't explain − oh, she didn't need explanations, and if Rebecca thought about it she wouldn't need them, either. It was the worst thing that could have happened. Trust was a big thing with Jack, and Tara understood why, what with his mother and all, but he had no right to just − disbelieve Rebecca like that. No matter who his mother had been. Jack wasn't the only one with a bad history when it came to trust. Rebecca'd been fighting that one all her life, too. Tara was so angry for her friend she could spit. Dr. Samuel, she thought, what have you done now? With an effort, Tara brought her attention back to the woman trying so hard to master her emotions in the chair next to her.

"But he was so mad that he scared me, a little bit."

"I'm sure he was. But he'll calm down once we figure out what happened." He damned well better calm down, and fast. "There's got to have been some mistake." Tara squeezed Rebecca's shoulders again, and was rewarded with a tiny damp smile. "I'll go over to the clinic and see if Tim will let me get a look at the results. You just stay here and get yourself together."

"Thanks, Tara."

"What are friends for?" Smiling at her best friend, Tara let herself out.

Chapter 16

"Pregnant." Jack spat to the room at large. He slugged back a shot of whiskey, beer apparently being inadequate to his purpose this afternoon. Tim supposed he couldn't blame him. "She's" – the expletive was crude and succinct, and described the normal way the process happened – "pregnant."

Tim had been on the money the first time. He'd found Jack's 4x4 in the Red Dog's parking lot and his best friend inside, more plowed than he should have been able to manage in such a short time. But at least he could see Jack's keys hanging on the rack behind the bar. Those hooks were where your car keys went if the bartender decided he wasn't going to be responsible for you wrapping your rig around a tree on your way back to town. Tim nodded gratefully at Charlie. Charlie's shrug back at him was eloquent.

Tim plunked himself down on a barstool, asked for a soda, then turned to Jack, who was staring at him blearily as if he couldn't quite figure out where Tim had come from. "You're sure you're not the father?"

Jack's words weren't slurred as they should have been, but quite clear. "Yeah, I'm sure. She told me she wanted to wait till our wedding night, and like a fool I humored her. Look where it got me."

"You've never –" Tim gestured "– with her?"

"Nope." Jack looked up from his empty glass and waved at Charlie for more. "I thought I was in love."

Tim couldn't help it. A chuckle escaped him. Jack glared at him. "What's so funny?"

Tim quickly sobered his expression. His friend was dead serious. "That's not usually how things work when you fall in love."

At least it hadn't in his and Tara's case. The previous night had been all he could have wished for. Affection and friendship and a shared history, and the best sex he'd ever had. Tim felt his pulse skip a beat at the memory, and quickly turned his attention back to his friend.

"Yeah, well, I wanted everything to be perfect for us, and I thought if that's what she wanted, I could wait. Funny how she couldn't." His tone was so bitter Tim winced. Charlie came back with the whiskey, filled Jack's glass, and took the bottle away again. Jack tilted his head and tossed the liquor back again, then gestured at Charlie, who ignored him. Thank God for small favors.

Tim was starting to get a little worried about how many brain cells Jack was killing over this. "Hey, maybe you want to slow down with that a little."

Jack stared him straight in the eye. "I don't think so."

Tim raised his hands, palms out. "Okay, buddy. Whatever you say." And resigned himself to waiting through the long afternoon so he could make sure he got his best friend home safely.

"Besides, you oughta be wanting to celebrate. You don't hafta get along with Tara anymore." Now the man's words were slurred. As if discussing Becky was the one thing that kept him sober. He leered at Tim. In his less than sober state, he came across looking like a sideswiped owl. "At least not on my account."

"Thanks. I'll take that under advisement."

"She's more trouble 'n' she's worth, if you ask me. Just like all women. Just because your dad thinks you ought to be married off —" Jack grinned hugely, apparently finally forgetting his own troubles in the whiskey. Or maybe he'd killed off enough brain cells to accomplish the task permanently. Tim sincerely hoped so. "Connin' us into foolin' you, too. What is it about this town that ever'body's got to be married off?"

And that was the final confirmation of what Tim had realized not long after that stupid overheard conversation last week. He was almost overpowered by a sudden urge to make everything right for Jack the way Jack had made everything right for him even if it hadn't really been his intention at the time. Dr. Samuel had been dead serious, but to Jack it had all been a joke.

The amazing part was that his joke had changed Tim's life, but now was definitely not the time to thank Jack for it. Instead he only replied, "I don't know, buddy. I just don't know."

* * *

"Why won't you let me look at it?" Tara glared at Dr. Samuel, who glared right back at her and didn't budge. She didn't know where Tim was – probably with Jack, wherever his stupid hide was – but he'd have let her see it. Dr. Samuel, on the other hand, was being a bullheaded idiot about it.

"Because it's not yours to look at." Dr. Samuel leaned back in his chair and folded his arms.

Tara wanted to strangle the man. Didn't he realize he was destroying lives here? "I'm here because Rebecca asked me to look at it."

If he didn't quit sounding so patient she wasn't going to be responsible for her actions. "Then you'll need to bring Rebecca here with you. She needs to come in so I can examine her, anyway. She should have been in when she first missed her period."

"But she didn't." Tara was a hundred per cent sure on that one, even if Rebecca was far too modest to discuss something like that, even with her best friend.

Dr. Samuel's expression changed, to the familiar epitome of the caring doctor. "She told you that? Then she definitely needs to come in. Please tell her so for me."

They'd gotten completely off the track. Tara sighed and began again. "There's been a mistake."

Dr. Samuel frowned. "There certainly has, young lady, and you're not making it any better."

Now she was down to pleading. Rebecca would have done the same for her. "She's my friend, Doctor Samuel. My best friend. I know as well as I know myself that she's not pregnant. There has to have been some mistake."

But Dr. Samuel was shaking his head. "The results were clear. I'm just sorry for young Rasmussen. A nice young man like that, to find out his fiancée's cheating on him..."

So much for pleading. It was time to rip his head off. "So Rebecca's automatically at fault?"

"She's the one who got herself in a family way, Tara. I'm having a hard time believing it, too, and I don't like it any better than you do yourself. I helped bring her into the world, and I've watched her grow up into what I thought was a fine young woman. You don't think I don't wish this hadn't happened?"

It was time and past time to go find Tim. Tara didn't bother to keep the sarcasm out of her voice. She wasn't sure she'd have managed it even if she'd tried. "I'm sure she appreciates your point of view, but you're ruining her life for no reason, and it's not fair. Where's Tim?"

"He went off to find Jack, who I imagine is out getting drunk. Not that I blame the young man." Samuel tilted his chair toward the shelves behind him. "Now where did I put that book?"

Clearly dismissed, Tara stalked from the room.

Tim would help her. He had to.

* * *

Tim was in the process of pouring Jack into the passenger seat of the Prius when Tara peeled her Jeep into the grassy parking area at the Red Dog.

Tim sighed. He'd hoped he wouldn't have to deal with her until later.

She climbed out of her rig, slammed the door, and looked them both up and down with disgust. "Been drowning Jack's sorrows?"

"In a manner of speaking." Tim turned to shove Jack's foot the rest of the way in and shut the door, the sound of snoring already audible through the closed window.

"Rebecca's pretty upset, too," she told him.

Tim snorted. "I imagine she is."

"You don't understand!"

Tim leaned back against the car and watched her. Bed wasn't the only place she was passionate, and he appreciated that, but just not right now. "I don't understand what? He thinks Becky lied to him. Of course he'd be furious."

Tara came closer and planted her hands on her hips. Tim had had his own hands there just that morning... With difficulty, he jerked himself back to the present.

"Don't call her Becky like she's some stupid little girl. Her name's Rebecca. And she didn't lie to him. The woman's been saving herself for marriage. She made a big deal out of it. All her friends knew. From what I understand, Jack wasn't real happy about it, but it was important to her. She wouldn't have goofed it up at this late date."

"It was important to him that she didn't sleep with someone else while they were engaged, either, but the test says she's pregnant.

"Even the good people of Campbell aren't likely to believe it was immaculate conception. And Jack's been in eastern Montana for the last two months, digging dinosaur bones. Kind of hard for him to knock her up long distance."

"You've seen the test results?"

Tim hesitated. "Well, no, but Dad has, and he's got no reason to lie."

"No deliberate reason."

That got Tim's back up. What came next spilled out before he could stop himself, whether he was a hundred per cent sure or not. "Why can't you just accept that your little friend Becky isn't as pure as you thought she was? Or are you regretting that you didn't make a big issue out of it yourself?"

* * *

The slap stung her hand and left a red mark on his face before she knew she'd done it. Tara stepped back, staring at her palm, waiting for his reaction, shocked when all he said was, "Hell of a swing you've got there."

"Is that a compliment?"

"Oh, it is. Trust me." Tim reached up to rub his cheek.

"Lots of experience with getting slapped?"

"Just the one you apologized for last night. It was plenty."

Tara rubbed her reddened palm against her jeans. He would bring that up. He'd turned and walked away without a word then. She wondered what he'd do this go around.

"Look, I was out of line."

An apology? Tara shook her head to clear it. She had to be imagining things.

He took her hand and rubbed it gently. "I don't regret our first night together, or last night. I do regret how long it took us to get back together, and I don't intend to lose you again.

155

"But according to the test results at least, Rebecca's pregnant, and there's no way Jack could have done the deed. Maybe Rebecca is so upset because she couldn't live up to her own standards, and now she's going to have to pay the price."

Tara stared at him, feeling a bit sideswiped. By a Mack truck. "With who? Rebecca and Jack have been all over each other – exclusively – for at least the last year and a half. Unless Jack's lying – for reasons that absolutely escape me at the moment – and they met somewhere so he could do the deed himself, there couldn't have been anyone else."

"You don't know for sure, Tara. Not even in Campbell."

"Yeah, I do. I'd be willing to bet my life on it."

"Really?" Tim's smile had Tara pulling her hand loose and backing off a step. "Your life?"

"Yes. My life." Tara watched him warily. "It's a figure of speech."

"Is that all it is?" Tim's smile widened. "Or do you want to place a real bet?"

"What on earth are you talking about?"

"We could solve our logistical problems in one fell swoop. If you're right, and this whole mess is some sort of mistake, I'll move back home and live with you here in Campbell." He paused. "If she really is pregnant, you come back to Seattle with me." He stuck out his hand. "What do you say?"

Tara swallowed twice before she recovered her voice. "I say, Timothy Swanson, that you're out of your ever-loving little mind. Didn't anybody ever tell you not to bet something you couldn't afford to lose?" She reached out, took his hand this time, and shook it firmly. "You're on."

They stood, staring at their joined hands, for a long minute, then Tim straightened and took a step toward Tara. "I've got to get Jack home before he shakes the car apart with his snoring." He leaned forward to kiss her, and Tara found herself reluctant to let him go. "Am I welcome back at your place afterward?"

Tara pretended to give it some thought. "As long as you park that little rice burner in my garage. Rebecca doesn't need to know I'm fraternizing with the enemy, and neither does anyone else. I'll leave my rig on the street."

Tim rolled his eyes. "Thanks. Man, I'll be glad when we get back to Seattle. This small town crap's for the birds."

Tara shook her head and headed back to her Jeep. "Don't count your chickens, Tim. I may well be right."

Tim laughed. "We'll see."

* * *

"What do you mean, the results are gone?" Tim stood in the waiting room staring at his father in consternation.

Samuel gazed mournfully at his son. "I mean they're gone. I don't know how they ended up in the trash can, but today was garbage day. Betty put everything out last night before she left, and Petersons' always come by early in the morning."

"So they're at the dump." This place was a disaster, Tim thought. It was a wonder the state medical board hadn't shut the clinic down long before now.

"I'm sorry, son. I figured it didn't matter, since they're not getting married, anyway."

Tim sighed. "Dad, did it occur to you that there might have been a mistake? That maybe everyone jumped to the wrong conclusion?"

Samuel looked at his son reproachfully. "I read the results very carefully. I was so astonished that little Becky Thorstein was pregnant that I read through them twice."

"But you didn't hang onto them." Which was seriously not ethical. Tim started to tell him so in no uncertain terms.

But his father had an odd look in his eyes, as if he was trying to excuse something he wished he hadn't done. "No. I told you. I saw no point."

"Speaking of which, has Becky been in to see you?"

"No, and I'm getting worried about her. She should be concerned about the baby, too."

"I think I'll go see if she'll have anything to do with me."

* * *

Tim wasn't surprised to see Tara's Jeep in front of Becky's house. He hesitated before knocking on the door, if only because he wasn't quite sure he was ready to take on both of them at once.

But then, he and Tara were supposedly on the same side of the fence now, right? He'd sure felt that way late last night, when she'd

finally come home and welcomed him in. Tim would give Tara one thing
– she wasn't holding grudges anymore.

He knocked on the door, and was grateful when Tara actually
answered it. He wasn't quite so grateful for her reaction when she saw
who'd knocked.

"What are you doing here?" she whispered sharply through the
storm door.

He figured it was obvious "I came to talk to Becky."

"Well, now's not the time to be doing it. She just got fired. Guess
why?"

"That was quick."

"News travels."

A teary, tired voice came from the back of the house. "Who is it,
Tara?"

Tara turned her head and called back, "It's nobody."

Tim raised his voice. "It's me, Tim."

Tara did not let go of the storm door handle. "The last person she
wants to see is you." While Tim had to admit he admired Tara's fierce
loyalty to her friend, he wished she'd let up a little right now.

Becky came into Tim's view and he stepped back in shock. She
looked awful. Her face was red, her eyes puffy, her long blonde hair
tangled down her back. The skirt and blouse she wore were wrinkled,
and a tissue was stuck to the bottom of her navy blue flats.

"Hi, Becky. I'm so sorry about your job."

"Thanks." Becky shrugged, then reached to open the door. Tara
made as if to keep her from doing it, but at Becky's gesture, pulled it
open for him herself. "I'm sorry, too. I'd forgotten how easily people
can condemn. Even without knowing the truth."

Tara glared at Tim, but her voice was gentle. "Rebecca, why don't
you go lie down and rest? I'll see what Tim wants."

Becky gave her friend a reproachful look. "It's okay, Tara. I couldn't
sleep if my life depended on it." She turned back to Tim. "Have you
seen Jack?"

He watched her carefully. He'd figured on tears, but not this almost
defeated attitude. He supposed he should have, given her background.
She was behaving as if she expected everyone to believe the worst of her.
"Not since yesterday. He and I went out to the Red Dog for a while."

Her smile was wan. "Could you give him a message for me?"

"Sure." He hesitated. "I don't know if he's ready to listen yet, though."

"Tell him I love him. Tell him there has never been anyone for me but him." Two new fat tears slid down her cheeks. "Tell him I'd never do anything to hurt him."

"I'll try, Becky." Suddenly he realized he could do no less.

"Thank you." She lifted her face toward him, and Tim felt his heart crack in sympathy for Becky and her plight. Tara's right, he thought. There's no way this woman could cheat on anyone.

Impulsively he reached for her and folded her in his arms. He could feel the heat of her face and the trembling of her body, and he held on tight until her shivering stopped.

As he loosened his arms and stepped back, he caught Tara's eye. She was beaming at him as if he'd just won the Nobel prize. He smiled sheepishly, then got down to business, taking Becky by the hand and leading her into the living room.

Once she was settled in the rocking chair, he took a seat on the sofa, and gestured Tara down next to him.

He leaned forward to look the tearful woman in the eye. "Okay, if I'm going to get to the bottom of this, I need to know a few things. You up to answering a few questions?"

Becky looked at him quizzically. "Bottom of what?"

"The bottom of the mistake that was your blood test," he said as matter-of-factly as he could, hoping he wasn't raising dreams he couldn't fulfill as he saw the look of almost painful hope flash across Becky's face. "Tell me when you came in to have it done."

She answered him almost eagerly. "Last week. Dr. Samuel said it had been a while since we'd checked my iron levels, too, so I had both done at the same time."

"What day?"

"I don't – Tara, could you get me my calendar? It's in the kitchen."

Tara went to find it. A couple of minutes later she called out, "Wednesday. The eleventh." She came back out, carrying a calendar with pictures of teddy bears on it.

"Don't you have records of this at your office?" she inquired.

"I want to double-check it," Tim told her. "After this, I'm not sure I trust the recordkeeping that goes on there." He'd run up against a few issues, a few puzzling but minor omissions, with the manual records his father had always used, which was reason number four hundred and thirty-one for insisting that they digitize everything, but nothing like this. Maybe, he thought warily, because nothing he'd seen so far had caused such a disaster. But who knew what else was hiding under all that mess?

"You believe me, don't you?" Her smile was watery but more genuine.

"Let's just say I think there's something fishy going on."

Tara grinned as she sat down again. She slung her arm on the back of the sofa behind him and ran her fingers through his hair.

"Hey," he said, and jerked forward. Becky's smile went wistful, and Tim shook his head at the two of them. Still matchmaking, was she? He had to give Becky credit for persistence. He supposed he ought to thank her for it. And he would. By fixing this mess.

Tara grabbed him by the shoulders and pulled him back to her.

"I take it you two have worked out your differences?"

But it certainly couldn't hurt her feelings to tell her she'd succeeded. "You could say that. I asked Tara to marry me."

Tara scowled and pulled her hand back. "I hardly think that bet constitutes –" She glanced at Becky, and closed her mouth abruptly. Curiously, Tim glanced over at Becky, too. She had an oddly smug look on her face, in spite of everything. He reached behind him and lifted Tara's fingers back to his head.

"Don't start." But the warning in her voice was halfhearted at best.

"I won't." Becky's voice was soft, but stronger than it had been.

"We don't have time for that kind of foolishness right now," Tim said firmly, feeling a bit smug himself. Tara hadn't removed her hand again. "Do you remember if my dad said when the sample was supposed to be picked up?"

Becky wrinkled her forehead. "The next day, I think."

"Thursday. Okay. I'll check and see if it was, and if there were any other samples that went that day." Tim glanced over at Tara. She was beaming at him again, and her fingers were roaming across the back of his neck. Tim suppressed a pleasurable shiver. "What I can't figure out is how the test got run in the first place. You had no reason?"

"No," the two women replied simultaneously. Tara's indignation almost drowned out Becky's soft answer.

"I didn't think so." He looked at his watch. "I'd better get going before half the town realizes I've been here."

Becky's face crumpled, and Tim quickly added, "Jack's my friend, too, and I'm doing this as much for him as for you. I want to see you both happy again. But right now, I don't think he'd understand that my intentions are good, and I don't want to waste time fighting him over it."

Tim watched as Becky pulled herself back together, admiring her, realizing that he'd gone, in twenty-four hours, from believing she'd cheated on Jack and gotten herself pregnant, to knowing where it counted that this woman could no sooner do something like that than fly.

He rose, then pulled Becky to her feet and hugged her again. "We'll figure this out. I promise we will."

"Thank you." She hugged him back. "I mean that with all my heart."

"Anytime."

Tara followed him out onto the porch.

"You are the nicest man I've ever met, Timothy Swanson."

"Not the 'n' word!" Tim threw up his hands in mock horror.

She reached up and caressed his cheek. "The nicest. The kindest. The most heroic..."

"Shut up. You're embarrassing me." He leaned over and kissed her. It lasted a too-short, very sweet time. When he could finally bring himself to let go, he headed down the steps, noting the somewhat shell-shocked expression on Tara's face with satisfaction.

"Are you working this afternoon?"

She shook herself. "Yes."

"I might stop by."

"You do that."

Tim grinned, and headed back to his rig.

Chapter 17

After Tim drove off, Tara went back inside. She didn't have to be at work for another couple of hours, and she couldn't think of anywhere she should be more than here, supporting her friend.

But Rebecca wasn't in the living room, or the kitchen, and the door to her bedroom was closed. Should she knock? She supposed Rebecca could just be changing her clothes. She'd always been modest, even back when she'd slept over at Tara's when they were kids. So Tara knocked.

Silence. Tara knocked again.

Another silence. Tara was contemplating simply walking in, permission or no permission, when Rebecca opened the door.

But she wasn't being her usual welcoming self. Rebecca wasn't anywhere big enough to fill the doorway, but she was doing her best to block Tara from coming in.

She had changed clothes, from her workday skirt and blouse to jeans and a t-shirt. She'd washed her face but hadn't put any makeup back on, not that she used much to begin with, and her hair was pulled back from her face in a braid swinging down her back, the way she'd worn it in high school.

Her face was stern and solemn. For an instant Tara was reminded of Rebecca's father and his black and white approach to life and everything in it. "You don't have to stay, Tara. I know you have to go to work."

Ignoring that transparent attempt to hide what she knew Rebecca really wanted, Tara peered over her shoulder at the room beyond, at the open boxes stacked everywhere. Rebecca had already started packing for her impending move in with Jack, but it looked now like she'd accelerated the process instead of putting things back. "What's going on here?"

Rebecca's voice sounded as if it were coming from the bottom of a well. "I don't have a job, Tara. I can't pay my rent if I don't have a job."

"Oh." Tara digested this. "Surely you're paid up till the end of the month." Which was less than two weeks away, granted. "And you'll get unemployment."

Rebecca shook her head. "Not if I was fired."

"They can't fire you because they think you're pregnant. It's illegal." Tara reached out, but Rebecca backed up before they made contact. "Come on. You're making a rash decision."

"No, I'm not. You know who my landlord is."

Yes, Tara did. She'd never thought it was a good idea for Rebecca to put all her eggs in one basket, so to speak, but the house was adorable, and the rent was cheap, and, well, it wasn't as if there were that many options in a town this small, anyway. "Do you really think Mr. Markham will kick you out?"

Rebecca just looked at her. "He's a deacon of the church, Tara."

"He's already told you to leave, hasn't he?" But she didn't need Rebecca's confirming nod to know the infuriating answer. "He's got no legal right to evict you over this."

"Maybe not legally, but ethically he does. He stood up for me to my parents when I wanted to have my own place, even though I wasn't married. He had faith in me, that I would be upstanding and well-behaved, even without my parents' supervision. From where he stands, I betrayed that faith in the worst possible way. I can't live here anymore." She paused. "Besides, I gave him my notice after Jack proposed. He's already got another tenant lined up."

"But where are you going to go?"

Rebecca didn't answer, but went back to her packing.

Tara watched her, her fury filling her up like water in a glass. It was all she could do to keep it from overflowing onto her friend, but more anger was the last thing Rebecca needed right now, even if it was on her behalf rather than at her. She wanted to shake Mr. Markham.

She could have killed Dr. Samuel for ruining Rebecca's life like this. The man was a doctor, for God's sake. He was supposed to do good. At the very least he should have thought before he spoke. Double-checked everything. He knew Rebecca better than that.

Ultimately, though, Jack was who Tara wanted to draw and quarter. How he could not believe in Rebecca, how he, of all people, could have not questioned a result so out of character for the woman he supposedly loved... Men, she thought. If it weren't for Tim she'd give up on the entire half of the species.

After all, Jack had been the one person Rebecca had refused to give up on, when everyone around her had written him off without a second thought. Not that it mattered now, but Tara had been utterly astonished when she'd moved back to Campbell a year and a half ago and found her best friend seriously involved with the boy from the wrong side of the river. Granted, Jack was an upstanding citizen these days, with a respectable job, and a respectable lifestyle. Since his mother, drunk as a skunk as usual, according to what Tara had heard, wrapped her rig around a tree while he was at college, most people had decided to forget where Jack Rasmussen came from. Those who hadn't, saw fit to keep their mouths shut.

Except for Rebecca's parents. For them it wasn't just his past as the child of an unwed mother, or the hell raising he'd done as a teenager. The fact that he was a practicing heathen in their eyes – digging bones and claiming they were millions of years old when the Bible said quite clearly that the Earth had only existed for a few thousand years, and worse, teaching evolution to the town's children – was enough to condemn him without the rest of the so-called evidence.

Tara had been proud of Rebecca's backbone then. But it was just setting her up for a second world of hurt now. "You are not going to your parents' house now."

Rebecca smiled, but the expression didn't reach her eyes. "I've got to salvage something out of all this. Can you think of anything else?"

Tara flailed about for something, anything, to get Rebecca to change her mind. "You don't want to let Tim see what he can find out first?"

"Do you really think that's going to solve everything?" Rebecca shook her head sadly. "Tara, it's not whether I'm pregnant or not that matters."

Tara took a deep breath. The last thing she wanted to do was go deal with the Thorsteins, but she'd do it for Rebecca's sake. "No, I suppose it isn't. I've got an hour or so before the library opens for the afternoon. I'll go with you."

Rebecca merely shook her head again. "No, thanks. You go on."

Now she was hurt. "As if I would go off and leave you now." Tara pushed forward into the room. "All right. If you refuse to fight this, then you move in with me. Then you can go see them." And Tara could be there to pick up the pieces.

But she knew even before Rebecca opened her mouth what her friend was about to say. "I'm going home to stay. If they'll let me."

* * *

"Rebecca, you can't."

"I never should have left in the first place." Which was obviously true now, but she hadn't meant to say it out loud, not in front of her friend. Rebecca heard Tara expostulating in her defense, the words so much sound and fury. She could feel the tears welling up again, completely against her will.

She had to develop some backbone. But then backbone was what had gotten her into this trouble in the first place. She wished so much that she could regret having loved Jack, but she couldn't. She simply couldn't.

What she could do was move on. Or back. Back to the tiny, safe, Becky-shaped mold her parents were so determined she fit into. Maybe she shouldn't ever have tried to escape it after all. Maybe the commandment to honor thy father and mother trumped love after all. But she'd thought God wanted her to live. To shine. After all, He'd given her Jack. And the courage to defy her parents and love him. She'd thought loving Jack was God's plan for her, and she'd been so happy when he'd proposed at last. But now He'd taken Jack away. She didn't want to move back to who she'd been before, but what else could she do? "It's the only way to get them to forgive me."

Tara's mouth snapped shut. She looked appalled, and Rebecca couldn't blame her. "Of course. But not yet." Tara didn't understand. It was the one thing she'd never been able to understand because Tara's parents loved her unconditionally. She didn't understand about conditional love.

"You believe me. Tim believes me." Rebecca went back to her dresser and opened a drawer. "My parents certainly love me more than my friends do. So why shouldn't they believe me?"

Tara stepped closer. "They love you, but –"

"But they're closed-minded? But they've already made up their minds?" Her hands full, Rebecca turned to watch Tara pace across the floor. "Look at it this way. They'll probably be thrilled that Jack's turned away from me over this." Her voice shook slightly and she worked to get it under control. "I can just hear them now. 'Of course he wouldn't believe you, Becky. He never was good enough for you.' Something good has to come of all this. Maybe this is it."

"Rebecca –" Tara stopped pacing. "You know what you're doing to yourself."

Rebecca met Tara's gaze, knowing what Tara would see in it. She watched the wind go right out of Tara's sails as Tara sighed and said, "I've lost this fight, haven't I?"

"It's not a fight, Tara."

"That's not what I meant and you know it. Well, I'll be here when you need me. God knows you've picked up my pieces before. It's the least I can do for you."

The funny thing was, Rebecca couldn't ever remember picking up Tara's pieces. Except for that one time, after she'd broken up with Tim.

But Tara had picked hers up more times than she could count. When Rebecca'd wanted to be in school plays, when she'd wanted to go off to college, when she'd started dating Jack...

Every time her parents had practically disowned her, in spite of her being their only child. Being in school plays was vanity, and ungodly. Going away to college wasn't even to be thought of. It would expose her to ideas and people her parents couldn't control. They'd never said that, exactly, but Rebecca wasn't stupid, in spite of her narrow horizons.

The one thing she'd refused to give in on was Jack. Who had turned out to be the most monumental mistake of all. So maybe her parents had been right. It was time to go home and eat crow.

"I know. Go on, Tara. I'll see you later."

* * *

Two hours later, Rebecca, her shoulders slumped, trudged slowly back down the street toward her little house. No, not hers, not for much longer. She wasn't going to cry. There wasn't any point. This particular cloud didn't have a silver lining. Oh, her parents had been willing to let her move back home, all right. But not because they'd believed her. Or in her. They wanted her to come home because they couldn't believe she'd have gotten pregnant of her own free will, and they wanted to protect her and the nonexistent baby they were sure must have been conceived by rape. They'd always believed she wasn't safe, living on her own, and the story they'd concocted was that Jack had taken her against her will, then denied he was the father. She was only the innocent vessel. Well, she wasn't.

Robert Frost was wrong, although she'd known that all along. Home wasn't where they had to take you in, even when you had to go there. Not if she was going to be treated like a wayward child. Or a victim. Not if they weren't going to believe her. They'd learn the truth soon enough, along with Jack and everyone else in town.

Wrapped in her own thoughts, she didn't see the man sitting in the shadows on the porch until he called out her name.

Rebecca's head shot up. "Jack?"

"None other."

The shaft of hope spearing through her hurt more than her parents' condemnation. Maybe he'd finally thought things through and realized she didn't lie. Not to him. She hurried up the walk, watching him as he rose from the porch swing. "Don't you have to be at school?"

"I'm on lunch. I thought we'd better talk."

Or maybe not. Rebecca faltered at the undercurrent of anger in his voice, then made herself step forward. "Okay."

Jack remained seated in the middle of the porch swing. Rebecca, not knowing what else to do, leaned uncomfortably against one of the pillars holding up the porch roof.

"Who was he?"

No, definitely not. Her heart sank to the grass. How was she supposed to answer a question like that? Why was he even asking her? Her own anger, long buried, began to spark. "Who was who?"

Jack snorted. "You don't want me to get specific."

Rebecca stared down at her tidy gray sneakers, refusing to acknowledge that he still had the capacity to hurt her beyond measure. She was never going to allow anyone to know they'd hurt her, not ever again. Not her parents, not Jack, not anyone. After a moment, she climbed the steps.

"You're not even going to deny it, are you?" Now *he* sounded hurt. As if he had the right to be hurt in the first place.

"You didn't believe the truth the first time I told you." She went to the door. She needed to do so many things. Not one of them included letting Jack stomp on her heart again.

"Great. Okay. So this is where I say I'm supposed to give you the benefit of the doubt." Jack sighed heavily. "Okay. I give you the benefit of the doubt."

Rebecca raised her head up to meet his eyes and stared steadily into them. Wonder of wonders, he dropped his gaze. As if he knew he was wrong? She could not get her hopes up. Could not. Would not.

Whatever dim hopes she'd allowed herself were dashed by his next words. "Are you willing to take another pregnancy test?"

She stared at him, but remained silent. She literally could not think of words that could hurt Jack as much as his question hurt her. She would not falter. Would not.

But she didn't owe this man anything any more. She wasn't even sure why she was still standing here taking this from him. Ingrained, that's what it was. She'd been trained from earliest childhood to take whatever her parents told her at face value. Whether it was good or bad or true or false or hurtful or, or – not caring. Caring based on misapprehension was what she'd learned to distrust. And now she'd transferred those attitudes toward Jack.

She almost felt sorry for him, fighting upstream all this time, expecting no one to believe in him. Least of all her. But the operative word was almost. She could not feel sorry for someone who couldn't see what was as plain as the nose on his face.

"Are you?" he demanded again.

Rebecca chose her words carefully. "Considering that I never took one in the first place, what you're asking of me is impossible."

Jack swung to his feet, the porch swing rocking madly in his wake. Rebecca reached out to steady it and he jerked back. No, she thought.

Not sorry. If the man couldn't get far enough past his own history to see that she was different from the people who'd mistreated him in his past, that she would never betray him like that, he had no right to expect her to do so.

"I heard Dr. Samuel, Rebecca."

She shrugged, knowing it was useless. The backbone she'd fooled herself into thinking she'd had for years now finally snapped into place. So this was God's plan for her, was it? Well, then, she would not turn down this gift. "You heard a mistake."

"Fine." He stepped down off the porch. "I knew you wouldn't do it."

The words slipped out before she had a chance to stop them. "Then why did you bother to come here and ask me?"

"I thought you loved me. I thought I could trust you." Turning his back on her, he strode away before she could tell him the same thing.

The porch swing was still rocking. She turned around and sank onto it, and watched Jack as he marched to the corner and disappeared from her view.

Her eyes filled with tears, but her heart filled with determination. If God didn't want her to love and be loved, if He wanted her to stand up alone in this life, there must be a reason. She simply had to find out what it was.

Chapter 18

Jack glanced up as the door to his classroom opened, not really caring who came in, then flinched when he saw who was standing in the doorway. He called out, "All right, everybody, second warning, time to get going." It was getting late, anyway, and with the usual groans and complaints the kids finished winding their games down and gathering things up.

Tara had to have come directly here after closing the library for the evening, and looked surprised to find the room still buzzing. But she backed out of the way as his students piled out the door, arms loaded, still chattering madly. Some of them glanced at her curiously. Jack steeled himself as she stepped through and closed the door after her.

"Holding class late today, I see," she said.

"Hello, Tara." He gestured toward the door. "That was the chess club."

"I noticed. The chess sets all over the place sort of gave it away." She smiled at him, but it wasn't her usual cheerful grin. It felt put on. Fake.

He supposed she was going to try to meddle and wondered if he could head her off at the pass. Sometimes he really hated living in a small town. He shrugged. "Someone has to sponsor them."

"And the science club, and the math club... The kids like you. They're always talking about that cool Mr. Rasmussen when they come into the library."

He shrugged again, refusing to respond, although it was always good to hear that sort of thing. "They're good kids."

Her smile became a shade more genuine. "How are you doing?"

Was she asking for herself, or for Becky? "Fine."

"I'm sorry about what happened." She sounded like she meant it. Jack didn't fool himself that she felt that way on his behalf, though. She was here for Becky, and she wasn't going to get anywhere.

"Yeah, me, too." He started to gather his own things up. Maybe she'd get the hint and decamp, too.

"Rebecca's moving in with me."

He glanced up at her, surprised in spite of himself. "Why?"

Tara glared at him. "Why do you think?"

He didn't answer, but he knew why. He'd always told her she needed to get out of both the job and the house, but she'd refused to listen. If she – if they – well, she'd made her bed, and she could damned well lie in it.

"She's not pregnant, Jack," Tara said flatly.

He snorted. "That what she told you, too?"

"That's what I know."

"Did you see the test results?"

She hesitated. "No. But Jack –"

He cut her off. "Dr. Samuel did."

She held up a hand. "But you know they're wrong. You were there when the blood was drawn. Rebecca told me so." He had to give Tara credit for persistence. He just wished she'd find another cause to vent it on.

But he had been there for the blood draw, and no one, not Becky, not Dr. Samuel, had said anything about a pregnancy test. He shoved the niggling doubt back down in his mind. Maybe it was a byproduct of the rubella test. He'd learned the hard way that the benefit of the doubt never got anyone anywhere. It was a lesson he'd had pounded into him at his mother's knee. "That doesn't mean he didn't run the test."

Tara plunked into a chair and put her head down on the table. Her voice was muffled, but he could hear her quite clearly. "I should have known better."

She should have, but he heard himself ask, anyway, "Known what?"

She straightened back up and looked him square in the eye. "You're bound and determined to see the absolute worst of her, aren't you?" She stood back up, still glaring at him. "You're so damned sure of yourself, that you're right and everyone else is wrong, all black and white, no benefit of the doubt. No wonder Rebecca fell in love with you. You're just like her father." She paused, looking more frustrated by the second. "And Rebecca's just like her mother. I swear, I wash my hands of the both of you."

He just wanted Tara leave him alone. "Glad to hear it."

"Do you know what state she was in when she came to the library this afternoon? To ask me if she could stay with me?"

He had a darned good idea. Becky'd looked like she'd lost her last friend when he'd watched her walking up the street. But she'd surprised him with her resolve. Somehow he'd expected her say yes, to be grateful for a second chance to prove herself, but she'd refused. Not angrily. Just simply and straightforwardly, the way Becky did everything.

"I'm going over to help her finish packing tonight, as soon as I leave here."

"Good for you." The sooner she left, the sooner he'd be alone. Which is where he should have been all along.

Tara's voice stiffened. "When has Rebecca ever been less than honest with you? With anybody?"

Jack didn't look up. "There's a first time for everything. Better to find out now than after I married her."

"I guess." Tara strolled closer. She was supposed to be headed the other way. "I don't suppose there's any way you'd be willing to talk about it." She held up her hand again when he opened his mouth. "I mean really talk about it. About why no one gets a second chance with you."

Now she'd stepped right over the line. "Did she send you here?" He rose.

She backed up a step, and a brief flash of shame washed over him. He knew he could be intimidating – he couldn't help his height and bulk – but all he wanted was for her to go away. Tara knew better than to be frightened of him. He watched her straighten her spine, oddly relieved. "No," she told him, her voice firm.

"It's a good thing." When she stared at him, he added, reaching for a controlled tone, "I like you, Tara, and I know you and Becky are good friends, but you really don't want to go there. Not now."

She shook her head, obviously disgusted with him. Hell, he was disgusted with himself, and he didn't want to go into why. "I take it that means you aren't willing to try to work things out with her?"

If only there was something to work out. He'd be glad of it. "She refuses to prove she didn't cheat on me, Tara. What's left to work out?"

But no, Tara had to keep pushing. In an odd way he admired her for it, and for her loyalty to Becky. Becky was going to need all the loyal friends she could get. But she wasn't going to get a cuckolded fiancé. If he hadn't been the fiancé in question, he'd have been a loyal friend himself. He had a vision of Becky raising a child by herself, fighting her parents for her child's sake every single solitary step of the way. Then he thought of the dreams he'd had of Becky pregnant with *his* child, *his* children, of the real, normal family they could have raised together, so unlike the way he'd grown up, and winced. Losing that dream hurt, too. More than he wanted anyone to know.

Tara obviously saw his expression, and must have taken it for a chink in his defenses. Well, dammit, it was, whether he wanted to admit it or not. "Why won't you admit there could have been a mistake?" she demanded.

Jack steeled his spine. If it took rudeness to get her out of here, then he'd be rude whether he wanted to be or not. "There's a mistake, all right. She's pregnant. I'm not the father." He picked up his satchel. He'd had more than enough of this. If he didn't get out of here he wasn't going to be responsible for his actions. "I need to lock up."

Tara's face fell. Well, and he wasn't responsible for her feelings, either. He gestured her pointedly toward the door. But, Tara being Tara, she apparently couldn't help getting in the last word. God help Tim if he actually did marry her. "I guess it is a good thing you dumped her. You certainly don't deserve her."

He didn't reply. He couldn't.

* * *

"You've got to talk some sense into him," Tara declared later that night. Becky, thank God, wasn't moving in till tomorrow, or so Tara'd told Tim when he'd come by after his hours at the clinic to help with the heavy lifting. He suspected Becky just wanted one more night in her own home, and he couldn't blame her. But he did wonder how things were going to work out with her established in Tara's spare bedroom. He hoped Becky wasn't going to be a prude about his presence in Tara's bed, because he had no intention of giving this up. Ever.

He lay on his back, his arm around Tara, her body curled into his, his breath gradually slowing down, and gave her suggestion some thought. "It's kind of hard to talk to someone who refuses to listen. Look what happened when you tried."

Tara stroked his chest with her fingertips, as if willing him to say yes. Tim was almost ashamed to admit that he'd be willing to do just about anything for her to keep her touching him, but tilting at this particular windmill seemed not only pointless but dangerous. He didn't want to lose Jack's friendship, either.

Tara's voice took on a wheedling tone. "You know him better than I do. You've been his best friend forever."

"I've seen him half a dozen times in the last five years. That's not exactly what I'd call being good friends." It was something he fully intended to rectify in the future, though. He had friends in Seattle, but, much as he liked them, they weren't the same as someone he'd known all his life.

She sighed and snuggled closer. "Did you find out anything from the lab?"

Tim snorted. "Not damned likely. The idiot clerk I talked to can't find a record of the test. Claims it never went through their office. I'm going to try again tomorrow. If whoever I get then can't find anything, I guess I'll have to keep moving up the chain until I get to someone who can. The only other thing I can think of is to wait. It'll be obvious in a few weeks, but by then I suspect things will be beyond repair. I'm not sure they aren't already, anyway." He paused, knowing what he was about to suggest was futile, but he had to say it, anyway. "This whole mess could be short-circuited if Rebecca would just agree to take the test again."

"I suppose I could ask her..." Tara's voice was tentative. "But she's already told Jack she wouldn't."

He guessed he understood that one. Sort of. "Maybe it would be different, coming from you? It can't hurt."

"Except maybe her ego."

Tim leaned up on one elbow. "It appears to me that her ego is already in pretty bad shape. You'd think she'd at least want to prove her innocence."

"You'd think she wouldn't need to." But then Tara smiled up at him, obviously ready to change the subject.

Tim grinned wolfishly down at her. "How's your ego, Tara?"

She slipped a hand to the nape of his neck and pulled his head down to hers. When her lips met his, they were warm and waiting. Long minutes later, she broke the kiss. "My ego's just fine." She reached down and caressed him. "It feels like yours is, too. Would you like to test that theory?"

"Tara, shut up." But his words held no anger, just a world of affection as he tugged her underneath him and proceeded to do what he'd told her to do himself.

* * *

The next morning at the clinic, Tim pulled Becky Thorstein's file one more time, not expecting anything to magically appear that hadn't been there before. He just wanted – heck, he wanted to have missed something, some scribble in his father's hand ordering that damned pregnancy test, a sticky note that might have come loose, something.

He took the manila folder to the storage room for some privacy, even though his father had told him he wasn't coming in today. Tim should have been glad, was glad, honestly, that his father was beginning to trust him with the clinic enough to take some time off, but the memory of the conversation he'd had with his dad in the kitchen that morning was completely overwhelmed by embarrassment, which he had no business feeling as a grown man.

His father had found him sneaking in the back door this morning, actually, and had been way more smug about catching Tim red-handed than anyone's father had a right to be.

Tim didn't understand his father's double standard when it came to Tara and Becky and their respective sex lives, but he supposed all was fair in love and war. Tim still wished he'd taken today's clothes over to Tara's last night so he wouldn't have had to go back to his folks' house this morning, but that was so much water under the bridge. Neither he nor Tara was quite ready to acknowledge ahead of time that his spending the night at her place was a foregone conclusion and not just spontaneous combustion. Not that it wasn't combustion. Just not spontaneous anymore.

He smiled briefly, thinking about spontaneity and Tara as he flipped the overhead light on, but he was dead serious by the time he opened Becky's file and examined the record of a healthy young woman. She'd had a bad case of chicken pox at age eight, which was what had finally forced her parents to bring her in to see Dr. Samuel for the first time in her life. He'd insisted she go to Kalispell General, and the staff there had been pro-active, thank God. Becky'd gotten all her inoculations and her first visits to the dentist and the optometrist as well, at the insistence of the Montana Department of Child Protective Services.

Tim knew that the complications from her bout of chicken pox had changed her life, because it had brought her to the attention of a social worker who'd also insisted she be tested to see how she was doing educationally, which proved the Thorsteins' home schooling efforts were not meeting even minimal standards. The social worker had insisted she be put into public school, against her parents' wishes. And, Tim knew, kept an eye on the situation until Becky was eighteen to make sure she stayed there.

After age eight, nothing unusual, at least not with regards to her health. Strep throat a couple of times, and she was minus her tonsils. She'd had recurring bouts with iron deficiency anemia starting in adolescence.

No record of prescription birth control, but that didn't mean anything. Maybe she and Jack had been planning on starting a family right away. Tim grimaced. She wasn't pregnant. He'd bet his life on it.

As she'd told him, his father had decided to draw blood for an anemia test while he doing the one for rubella, apparently simply because she hadn't had one in a while. But if there was any record of a pregnancy test, it had evaporated. Tim frowned. It was as if they'd all imagined those results, given that he couldn't find a trace of a record of the order for the test, no matter what he did.

He supposed his father could have neglected to record the order. But it did seem odd that he'd have forgotten it, considering that he had to have been astonished at the request.

The record agreed with Rebecca's calendar about the date she'd come in. But nothing after that. Tim guessed Samuel hadn't bothered – or remembered – to record the results of the blood test, either. Then again, the sample had been drawn less than three hours before Mark Thronson sliced his leg open at the mill. Perhaps Samuel had set the routine work aside for later and forgotten it in the hullabaloo?

It wasn't like his father. But then so many of his father's actions had been oddly unlike him since Tim had come home. So much carelessness. Or forgetfulness. The need to push his father into retirement was resting ever heavier. And all that weight was on his shoulders. Of course, the fact that somehow he seemed to have rooked himself into trying to prove Tara's side of the bet wasn't helping his cause. He couldn't quite figure out how that had happened, only that it had, and that he didn't regret helping Becky in any way he could. Didn't regret proving something that would get him off the hook of volunteering to stay.

Would it really be so bad to stay? Tim hadn't thought for days now about the new position at Harborview he'd been so excited about. He hadn't felt so involved in his work since med school, either, which he wanted to think was ridiculous and couldn't. Except for Mark Thronson and that idiot hiker up in the Cabinets, his work couldn't have been more routine. But he wanted to do so much more with his life than simply being a small-town doctor. He'd had plans. Of doing research. Of making discoveries. He couldn't do that here. Could he?

Jack did. His friend was a lot more than a small-town science teacher. His excavations and research into the Hell Creek formation fossils, out in the plains of eastern Montana, had brought new insights into the body of knowledge of that paleontologically famous region. He wrote for respected scholarly journals on a regular basis, and was invited to prestigious conferences to present his findings. Tim remembered the first time Jack had been published, back when he was still working on his master's degree. He'd practically been bouncing

off the walls. Tim had thought Jack was crazy when he came back to
Campbell after graduation, thought he was giving everything up. But
instead he'd kept building on his research as well as teaching. He'd
done it. Jack managed to keep his mind challenged here in the back of
beyond.

But it was different with medicine, wasn't it? Didn't Tim need
to be in the heart of the action to accomplish his goals? Maybe. But
maybe he didn't need to be there all the time. Or even most of the
time. Maybe he could figure something out.

He wanted to talk with Jack. Not about Becky. There wasn't
anything Tim could do to knock sense into his friend on that subject.
But suddenly he desperately wanted to talk to his friend about how he
managed his double life, and get some ideas about how he could create
a life like that for himself.

As soon as he could get out of here today. But first he had to get
hold of someone at that lab in Texas who could actually find a record
of Becky Thorstein's blood test.

Chapter 19

"Tara, can I talk with you for a minute?"

Tara glanced up from her computer screen at the library counter to find Tim square in front of her. She hadn't even heard him come in, but then she'd been preoccupied, thinking about Rebecca. If she could have, she'd have taken the day off to help her friend move, but Rebecca had nixed that idea with a vengeance. "Sure."

"Not here," he told her. "In your office."

She nodded, curious at the anger in his tone. She wasn't quite sure why she was positive it wasn't aimed at her, but she gestured him around the counter.

As soon as the door closed behind them, the room seeming suddenly very small, he said flatly, "I finally got hold of someone at the lab."

Tara sank into her chair. "And? I thought you talked with them first thing."

Tim shook his head, scowling. "I did. But this time I finally got through to someone in charge. Good grief, their bureaucracy's worse than Harborview's, and that's saying something."

"And?" Tara was about to strangle him.

"I had to go up about three steps in the chain of authority, but I finally got someone to agree with me that the discrepancy looked fishy. Especially once they bothered to check their records, and what Dad said didn't match what they claim they sent.

Tara wanted to hug him, and if she hadn't been at work she would have. "And why are you telling me this instead of Rebecca?"

He threw up his hands. "Because I can't get a definitive answer out of them, or a corrected report. Only a promise that they're looking into it and will get back to me as soon as they figure out what the screw-up was."

"Did they actually call it a screw-up?" Tara could have been amused, if it wasn't her best friend's whole future on the line.

"No, I did. Which I don't think helped the case, but I swear, the Campbell Clinic won't be using Lubbock Labs ever again. Not on my watch. What a bunch of clowns."

Tara couldn't help grinning at him in spite of everything. He looked so offended. And sounded so possessive. She wondered if he realized he'd all but taken over the clinic already.

Then he shrugged. "At least now I'm positive the screw-up started with them, not us. I was worried about that. Rebecca's specimen was shipped on the same day Mark Thronson had his accident. That took priority for everyone, including Betty."

"So there was a possibility that things could have gotten mixed up before they ever left here." Now Tara knew why he'd been pushing the lab so hard. "And since the results were lost…"

Tim stood up and started to pace, then apparently realized there wasn't room to do it properly and dropped back into the chair, rubbing his hands over his face. "It was more than a possibility, I think. Much as I like Betty Real, she doesn't work well under pressure, and the stress was thick enough to slice that day. She was canceling appointments, handling everyone who came in, and dealing with the fact that her neighbor's son might be losing his leg. Getting the specimen on its way couldn't wait, either."

"But your father should have been on top of it. I'm surprised he didn't make the connection."

Tim hesitated a long time. It was obvious he didn't want to say what was on his mind, and Tara couldn't imagine why. Nothing could be that bad. Could it? Finally, he said, "Dad's memory isn't what it used to be, but he doesn't want to admit it. It's not that he's not a good doctor, but –" he looked up at her then, his expression positively stricken. "I really hope he's not developing dementia."

Tara opened her mouth but he held up a hand. "Tara, if it was just this one incident I'd write it off as a mistake, pure and simple. But I've been going through each file before Betty enters it into the computer, and there's a pattern. It's not a good one. I've got to get him to see a specialist, but first –" He stopped, apparently unable to go on.

At that, Tara came around the desk and sat down next to him. She didn't know what to say, or to do, so she put her arm around him instead.

After a moment he said, "It's not just the records, either. Mom warned me –"

She knew it wasn't helpful, knew he knew far more than she did about this sort of thing, but she couldn't help it. "He seems okay."

"Yeah, he does, in casual conversation. But my mother's noticed, and Betty's noticed, and God knows it's staring me in the face."

"I'm sorry."

He sighed. "Yeah, me, too."

Dwelling on this was obviously not doing him any good. Tara decided it was time to distract him. She set her free hand on his knee. "At least he's got someone to take over for him."

Tim gave her a wry grin. "Going to hold me to our little bet, are you?" He laid his hand on top of hers, sandwiching her cool fingers in warmth.

"Would that be so bad?"

"I can think of worse things." He shrugged, looking rather uncomfortable about it.

She supposed from him, this was a concession. "Well, that's more than what you've been saying up till now."

"What do you mean?"

"You know what I mean." Poor guy. He just didn't want to give in to what she knew he really wanted. "This is the first time you've acted even remotely ambiguous about it."

"I guess." She couldn't help noticing his expression change as he saw the hope she couldn't hide. "Don't push it, okay? Not right now." He stood, pulling away from her, and tucked his hands in his pockets.

She wasn't about to say anything that would jeopardize his decision. The last thing he needed from her right now was more stress. "Okay."

"Thanks. And thanks for listening to me. I swear, if I hadn't had you to talk to since I came home, I'd have combusted. And not spontaneously." His smile was genuine, if brief.

"Any time." She was glad to have his trust. "So what now?"

"I guess the next step is to talk to Dad. Wish me luck."

"Of course." She couldn't help adding, "See you tonight?"

This time his smile lasted longer. "Thanks. Yeah. Unless you think Becky will mind the extra company."

"She won't mind." Tara would make sure of it.

She followed him out of her office and watched him as he strode purposefully through the big double doors. She wouldn't have wished his problems on her worst enemy, now that she knew what he was really up against. The least she could do was support him.

* * *

Tim squared his shoulders and opened the door into what he was beginning to think of as his own office, to find his father, not at his desk, but in the battered armchair in the corner. Samuel looked up as Tim closed the door behind him, the welcoming expression on his face changing into worry.

"Sit down, son. Is something wrong?"

Tim just wanted to get this over with. He remained standing. "Dad, do you remember exactly what happened the day Rebecca came in to have blood drawn?"

Samuel looked puzzled for a minute, then his expression cleared. "Yes, I do. She and Jack came in together. He held her hand and told her jokes while I was doing it. I remember thinking at the time how well those two looked together."

"They do, don't they?"

"They did."

Tim grimaced and asked the important question, the one he'd asked before. "Do you remember Becky asking about running that pregnancy test?"

His father didn't protest that they'd been over this before. Tim wondered if he remembered, as Samuel's brow furrowed once more.

"Think, Dad. It's important."

"I am thinking." Samuel sat up straighter, not an easy task in the spring-sprung chair, one Avis had forcibly ejected from the house years ago. He glanced up toward the framed diploma hanging on the wall that recorded his graduation in 1958, with honors, from the University of Minnesota School of Medicine. Leaned back again with a sigh. At long last, he turned to his son, the worried expression still on his face.

"You know, Timothy, I can't put my finger on it. I can't remember discussing it with them, I can't remember marking it on the chart, I can't remember saying anything about them jumping the gun."

He paused, frowning. "And I would have. I know I would have. For little Becky Thorstein to have gotten herself in the family way before the wedding – well, I still have a hard time believing it."

It was time. Tim said gently, "Maybe because it isn't true."

"But –"

"Dad. Listen to me. There's no record in Rebecca's file. Neither she nor Jack remember asking you for the test. And you just said yourself that you'd have remembered if they'd asked you about something like that."

Samuel looked up into his son's eyes. Tim didn't like what he saw on his father's face. Didn't like what was likely to come next. But for the town's sake, he'd listen. For his own sake. For his father's.

"Tim, sit down. Please."

Tim pulled one of the two straight chairs in front of the big, battered desk closer to the corner where his father sat, turned it around, and sat athwart it, his arms draped over the back. The silence dragged on.

"Dad –"

"I'm going to be seventy-five on Saturday."

This wasn't news. But it was an acknowledgement. "And?"

"When you get to be my age, you forget things sometimes." Samuel paused and ran a finger around the frayed welting on the chair arm, then looked back up. "Ask your mother. She's still fussing at me over some fool thing I didn't pick up at the store for her the other day."

Tim smiled. "I remember. I thought she was going to take your head off." He deliberately sobered. "But forgetting to pick up something at the store and forgetting whether or not you ordered a blood test are two entirely different things. What if it had been for something life-threatening, the results hadn't come back, and you'd forgotten it?"

Samuel raised his head. Something in his expression made Tim proud and wary all at once.

"I've never forgotten something that important."

No, just a lot of little things, according to the charts Tim had been perusing. But they added up. He took a deep breath. "Except whether or not you ordered a pregnancy test for Becky Thorstein."

Tim hated himself for the stricken look his father gave him, but he had to go on. "Becky and Jack deserve to be happy together. If you didn't order that test, the lab screwed up, and nobody caught it, their lives would have been ruined because a well-meaning old man has too much pride to admit that maybe, just maybe, he made a mistake. They deserve more than that from you. Heck, Dad, the whole town deserves better than that. You've loved these people all your life, and taken care of them for the better part of forty-five years." Tim stopped, hating to have to say the words, but knowing it was important that they come from him.

"You say you won't make a mistake that could be life-threatening. How do you know that? Is your memory suddenly going to be perfect simply because someone is depending on you? You love these people. Could you live with yourself if you caused someone's death because you couldn't let go? Dad —"

"And who is going to take care of them?"

Tim sighed, but it wasn't the point. Then again, he was becoming less and less sure what the point was anymore. "That's your trump card, isn't it? Every time you've said that, I've backed off. Well, I'm on to you. I'm not going to back off this time. Yes, Campbell needs a doctor. But you know as well as I do that bad care is worse than no care. People are better off driving to Kalispell than they are relying on someone whose memory they can't trust."

"I'll take better notes. My memory isn't that bad." A new note entered his father's voice. It almost sounded as if he was pleading. Pleading, Tim thought. With me.

Tim wanted to put his head down on his arms and throw in the towel. Why couldn't his father understand the decision had to be his? "You just don't give up, do you?"

"I never have before." Samuel squared his shoulders. "Mark Thronson would have died before the helicopter got here if one of us hadn't been there to stop his bleeding, among other things. At the very least he would have lost his leg."

Tim shoveled a hand through his hair. He couldn't deny that. He was beginning to wonder why he was even trying.

Samuel shook his head. "Tim, we love Campbell. It's a beautiful place, full of the salt of the earth. We've lived here all our lives. But it's not the big city. It's a small, isolated town in the backwoods of Montana. You know as well as I do that a practice here isn't going to make anyone rich." He stopped. Stared into Tim's eyes for a moment, then went on. "There's no future in it for someone who doesn't love the town for itself."

Tim dropped his gaze. "No, I suppose there isn't." He put his hands on the back of the chair and pushed himself to his feet.

"Son, I can't abandon them."

Tim looked back from where he'd somehow gotten himself to the door. "No, I guess you can't. Even if they'd be better off if you did.

"But dammit, Dad, I have a life. My own life. One I've wanted ever since I was old enough to know there was something out there besides Campbell."

"I know, son."

"I need to make my own decisions."

"I know."

"Dammit, you don't! And that's the whole problem." Tim opened the door and turned back to his father. "You know, if you hadn't been so damned pushy, I might have come back of my own accord." Ignoring his father's sputtering, he strode down the hall, past a curious Betty, and out of the clinic.

Being needed was one thing. Being jammed into a Dr. Tim-sized hole against his will was entirely another. If, indeed, it was against his will at all.

But if it wasn't, then why was he fighting it? He thought he'd all but made up his mind to stay until his father pushed, and pushed, and pushed... Every time he got near Samuel he felt – and acted – like a rebellious teenager all over again. And every time he did, he shot himself in the foot.

Tim let his strides take him where they would, and found himself strolling down California Avenue toward the railroad station near the river. Past the small shops, the post office, the hardware store. Past the used car dealer where he'd bought his first ride, a '76 Oldsmobile

Cutlass with 80,000 miles on it and a peeling vinyl roof. A far cry from the Prius, and thank God for it.

He pushed open the door of the five and dime where he'd spent allowances on candy and bought his school supplies each fall. He wandered through, waving hello to Mr. Chapman as he browsed past the heavily-laden shelves. Nothing changed in Chapman's Variety, except that the notebooks for sale now sported Angry Birds instead of Superman. Baseball cards still held the place of honor at the checkout counter, and the whole place smelled of new erasers and peppermint.

He bought a couple of Mrs. Chapman's homemade huckleberry-filled chocolates for old times' sake and let himself out, munching thoughtfully.

A few doors down, the Rose Cinema – the only movie theater for at least a two-hour drive in any direction – was open for business three nights a week, just as it had been when he was growing up. Tim had taken Tara to see *Alien* there, hoping, accurately as it turned out, that she'd want to have someone to hang onto when the monster popped out of John Hurt's stomach. He smiled and strolled on, more slowly now, to where the railroad tracks paralleled the river.

The old gingerbread-trimmed railroad station at the end of California Avenue was boarded up now, and he wondered when that had happened. A small glass and metal shack next to it held a few plastic benches, and an empty rack meant to display Amtrak information. A schedule taped to the window noted that the Empire Builder stopped here three times a week at 1:20 a.m. westbound on its three-day trip between Seattle and Chicago, and an equal number of times at 6:55 a.m. eastbound.

Times did change. Tim could remember when the train came through daily, late in the afternoon. He'd taken the train to come home from college for Christmas every year, because his parents had worried about him driving over the mountains in December.

Never mind that he'd grown up driving in the snow.

Tara's parents had felt the same way, and he remembered sitting together in the cloth-covered seats, his arm around her shoulders, her hair tickling his chin, watching the snow-covered landscape fly by. Remembered the time they were delayed for three hours by an avalanche on the tracks, and necking the time away.

Tim stepped carefully over the tracks and down the embankment to the river. He stood watching the dark cold water rush past on its way to the falls west of town.

Campbell wasn't so bad. He had a lot of good memories here.

Maybe he could stay for a few years, until he could find another doctor to take his place. Until he could talk Tara into going back to Seattle with him.

Tim snorted and aimed a rock at the riffles. It wasn't that kind of decision. If he stayed, it would be for a lifetime, and he knew it. Once Campbell had its claws in him, he'd be in it for the long haul.

Like his father, content with the little challenges of a small-town practice, the enjoyment of working with the same patients year after year, treating his friends and neighbors for their broken arms and bouts of flu, seeing them off to the hospitals in Kalispell and Spokane when they needed more. Treating the injuries and frostbite of idiotic hikers. Delivering babies. And being there at the other end of life, as well. Being needed, in a way he'd never truly be needed at Harborview Hospital in Seattle, where he'd be just another cog in the machine.

He'd never wanted to be a cog in the machine. He'd wanted to make a difference.

Staying here wouldn't be so bad. Not if he had Tara in the bargain. If he stayed in Campbell, he'd have Tara. Tim folded his arms over his chest and stared at the root beer-colored water. Trying and failing to visualize the life in the city he suddenly realized he could give up without a qualm.

If that's what it took to keep Tara. He could no more give her up now than he could fly. Even if he wanted to, which he didn't. Delivering her babies. Their babies. Watching them grow. Growing old with Tara, till their rocking chair days.

He couldn't miss out on that. Even if his father made him eat crow till he threw up.

Tim scrambled back up the embankment and headed back up California Avenue toward the clinic, scraping the mud off his shoes on the pavement as he went.

His father would be thrilled, and claim full responsibility for Tim's decision, no matter how much Tim denied it. He knew that, wasn't happy about it, but he'd survive it. He'd have to endure the full gauntlet of teasing from everyone in town, too. Maybe they'd be glad enough to have a new doctor not to shovel it at him too hard. He snorted again. Right. As his mother always told him, if they didn't tease, it meant they didn't care. Still, he was going to have to deal with the fallout when everybody found out he'd proposed to Tara, anyway, and it would be easier to get both sets of it over all at once.

Now all he had to do was deal with the lab, and with Jack and Becky. Jack needed to know he was wrong. So wrong.

Chapter 20

Oblivious to the still-golden larches and the rushing Yaak River, Jack strode along the riverbank Saturday morning, fishing pole in hand. His boots knew the way, probably better than he did, and he paid no attention to obstacles in his path, stepping over rocks and tree roots, impatiently brushing branches out of his way.

His life was in ruins. Again. He'd been in love with her, ass end over teakettle in love with her, long before he'd finally gotten up the guts to tell her. Pretty, shy Becky Thorstein. She'd always been there for him, even when she hadn't known she'd been doing it. She'd stood up for him against her family and her church, something he'd known was difficult for her. He'd trusted her.

And he simply couldn't understand how she'd done something like this to him. It was one thing if she wanted to ruin her own life, but why she wanted to ruin his right along with it baffled him.

He'd loved her. He still wanted to murder the man who'd gotten hold of her, but that wasn't easy given that she wouldn't tell him who the bastard was. That she was protecting him.

Jack supposed, given Becky's sense of loyalty, she wouldn't want to have the father of her child beaten to death. Unlike Jack's own mother, who hadn't even known who'd impregnated her. Who hadn't even cared to know the name of her son's father.

Loyalty? If Becky had been loyal in the first place he wouldn't be in this mess.

Hell, he still loved her. In spite of her cheating ways. And since the bastard hadn't bothered to show up and claim his rights – maybe because Becky wouldn't let him? Maybe because the jerk hadn't cared?

Jack stopped dead in his tracks, the branch scraping across his unshaven face gone unnoticed as another possibility, one he hadn't even thought to consider until now, leaping into his mind far more vividly than he could stand. She hadn't been raped, had she?

His fishing pole clattered to the ground. He sank onto a nearby boulder and put his face in his hands. It would be so like Rebecca to hide something like that, to not report it for fear that her parents would be dishonored, to keep her shame a secret as long as she could.

It wasn't as if he'd been around to protect her, either. She'd been on her own for most of the summer while he'd been selfishly gallivanting around Fort Peck looking for fossils. But he'd left her by herself before, especially while he was in college, and she'd been what amounted to independent off and on most of her life, given her parents' utter uselessness. To his knowledge she'd never had any problems. Up until this summer.

Campbell wasn't Seattle, and she didn't work at the Red Dog. Sure, tourists were getting thicker on the ground these days, but –

Why hadn't she told him? Hurt shot like needles into his already broken heart. Didn't she trust him?

He already knew the answer to that.

Nearby, the Yaak River rushed in its whitewater course down from the Cabinet Mountains, its course gilded by the larch needles and amber-colored ferns.

Jack felt as if he'd been caught up and hurtled headlong down the river like one of those needles, aimlessly darting about in an eddy before being caught up in the current and swept downstream. Out of control. Like his entire life.

There had to be some way to get hold of the situation again. He had to ask. He had to know.

She'd tell him, he thought, reaching down to pick up his abandoned fishing pole, if it was the last thing she ever did.

Purposefully, he headed back down the trail.

* * *

Jack could see Rebecca watching him warily from the living room window as he climbed out of his 4x4. He hadn't bothered to change clothes after his Saturday in the wilderness, to shave, to do any of the things he supposed he'd have done had he been feeling civilized.

He didn't feel civilized. He felt like slinging Rebecca over his shoulder and taking her to his lair, wherever that was, refusing to let her loose until she told him the truth. When she disappeared from the window as he walked up the steps, he grunted and headed for the door, and shoved it open. She was still standing there, a broom in her hand, her hair tied back in a scarf, her jeans and t-shirt smudged.

"What are you doing here?"

He cursed inwardly at the quaver in her voice, but he couldn't help himself. He grabbed her arm before she got away from him. "Were you raped, Rebecca?"

"What!?" She dropped the broom.

"You heard me." His expression gentled, and he stepped forward to run his other hand down her cheek. "I wish you'd told me." He wrapped his arms around her. She stood stiffly still, accepting his embrace but not returning it. After long moments he felt her surrender, as she leaned her head on his chest. Jack let out an enormous sigh, and tightened his arms, pulling her into his body. "It's okay, Rebecca. It doesn't matter, well, I mean it does matter, it matters a hell of a lot that some bastard would do that to you and you have to tell me who it was so I can make him pay for what he did to you, but I'd never let it come between us. I love you."

Rebecca tilted her head back and looked up at him, her arms still straight at her sides. "I wasn't raped."

It was his turn to let his mouth hang open. He dropped his arms to his sides and took a step back. "So there is someone else."

"No. There never was. There's never been anyone but you for as long as I can remember."

For as long as she could remember. His heart rose, in spite of himself, trying to force his mind to accept that she'd loved him as long as he'd loved her. "Then –" Much as he wanted to summon the anger that had sustained him for the last few days, he simply couldn't.

"Why won't you trust me?" she asked plaintively.

There it was again. Why did everyone keep asking him that? The anger and frustration he'd felt all his life at the hand he'd been dealt came roaring back and filled him, almost against his will. Trust? He didn't think so. He'd trusted his mother, and she'd let him down time after time. He'd trusted the social worker who'd tried to get him adopted more than once, only to have her let his mother pull the strings every time. He'd trusted the men she'd said might have fathered him, only to be rebuffed again and again.

He'd trusted Rebecca –

"Why should I?" The question came out less belligerently than he would have liked.

Rebecca reached out and touched his face, drew back when he couldn't help flinching. "Because I loved you. Because I would never have hurt you. You were my best friend and the man I wanted to marry."

Past tense.

So it was truly over. He'd never have Rebecca to make a family of their own, never make his life complete. His heart sank. He couldn't think of anything to say, then realized the one thing he did owe her. No matter what, and no matter what she thought it was for.

"I'm sorry, Rebecca."

She stepped up to him, stood on tiptoe. Gently pressed a kiss to his lips. Stepped back.

"No." He leaned back, opened his arms.

Rebecca's eyes shot wide open.

"I don't care. I am not giving you up." Jack looped one arm under Rebecca's knees, the other one under her shoulders. "You're mine. And if there's anyone else, that's just too bad for them." He headed through the open door, kicking it closed behind him. Surprising him, she reached out and turned the deadbolt. But he could feel the warmth of her face against his neck, and her slender arms wrapped around his shoulders, hanging on to him for dear life, and nothing else mattered. He could have told her it wasn't necessary. He wasn't going to drop her. Not now, not ever.

Gently he set her on her feet. He could feel her quivering. He didn't want to know why. She buried her face in his chest.

"Rebecca?" He caught her chin with a finger and tipped it up so that she would have to look at him. "I won't hurt you. I wouldn't hurt you for the world. I never meant to hurt you in the first place."

She smiled. The iron band around his heart loosened slightly. "I know."

Then she reached for the buttons on his shirt. Jack's breath caught in his throat. Fascinated, he watched her small hand slip down his chest until his shirt hung open. She leaned over and placed a tiny kiss in the exact center of his chest. It burned all the way to his toes. He tried to back off, holding onto control by a thread, but she snuggled closer. Her hand moved toward his belt buckle.

It took a monumental effort, but he closed his hand over hers. "Are you sure?"

She smiled up at him again, then stretched up to plant another soft warm kiss on his lips. Jack made a throttled sound and lifted his hand from hers to wrap it around her nape, claiming the kiss, taking control, nudging her lips open and sweeping through her mouth, intent only upon possessing her entirely. When he felt her fingers unbuttoning his jeans, he lifted his head up only long enough to pull her t-shirt over her head and unzip her pants.

Still kissing, still touching, their efforts hampered by their complete inability to concentrate on anything but each other, they managed to get skin next to skin, rough hands on silky curves, small soft hands on taut angles. Chest to breast, thigh to thigh. Face to face. Taking his shaking hand, she led him to her bedroom and shut the door behind him.

The uncovered glass of her window did nothing to filter the sunlight that lay across the bare mattress. Rebecca led him to it. "I already packed the bedclothes. I didn't know —"

"It's all right." It wasn't, but he needed her too badly to stop now. He'd wanted everything to be perfect for her, candles and moonlight and flowers. He wanted to slow down now, to make this last forever. He couldn't. The fire in his belly was urging him on, pushing him beyond finesse. As gently as he could manage, he pushed her down onto the bed. Followed her there. And slipped a hand down to her mound and cupped her, sucking in a sharp breath as he felt her wet heat.

"Jack?" Rebecca's voice was a thread of vulnerability. Part of him wanted never to hear anything that close to fear in her voice. Part of him wanted to howl triumph, and shamed him.

"Shh..." He laid his lips on hers again, pulled her back into another warm deep kiss. A possessive kiss. He slipped a finger into her, found her most sensitive spot with his thumb. Rubbed it gently, easily, over and over, his hand slick with her moisture.

She convulsed, her pulse pounding against his fingers. His breath stopped. He lifted his head. Felt that surge of triumph again, without the shame this time, at the wonder he saw in her face.

Then he nudged her legs apart, found himself room between them. And pulled his hand away as he touched her with himself.

Her eyes grew large as he slowly pushed his way inside, but she didn't protest. Instead she reached down and touched him as he slid in. Her soft hand threatened his control again. She was so tight. So beautiful. So slick. So – He came to a sudden halt, as she frowned in what looked like discomfort.

"Rebecca –?"

"Shh..." She reached up and covered her mouth with his once more, then arched her back. He felt himself slide all the way in.

Exactly where he belonged.

She was moving, rubbing against him. He tried to slow down for fear of hurting her, but the sensations were driving him mad. He began moving, pushing to the hilt, then pulling almost completely out, then, as if to convince himself he could, pushing in again as far as he could go. Her hands reached to clasp his buttocks, as if he needed the encouragement, and he gave into the fire, pumping and rearing like a stallion.

It was when she convulsed again, her muscles squeezing and loosening, again and again, that he finally let go, shuddering, and collapsed against her.

An eternity later, he found the strength to roll to his back, bringing Rebecca with him. She propped her chin on her hands, resting them on his breastbone, and grinned.

Jack smiled ruefully. "I'm sorry I ever doubted you."

Leaning forward, Rebecca gave him a peck on the lips. He returned it with interest. "Just see that you don't do it again."

Jack chuckled ruefully. "Yes, ma'am."

She cocked her head inquisitively at him. "Do I love you?"

He sighed. "You do. And I love you."

"Can you trust me?"

She had to ask the hard ones, didn't she? But if anyone deserved an honest answer, his Rebecca did. "With my life."

She shook her head. "With your heart?"

He sighed. "Rebecca, I know I've been stupid."

"As long as you know better than to be that way again." She slipped a hand free and tapped him on the lips.

He kissed that finger and put his hands on her elbows to bring her mouth to his for another kiss. "I'll do my best."

She nodded decisively. "And if you forget, I will remind you."

He supposed he deserved that. But if he was going to trust anyone in this life, he wanted it to be her.

Chapter 21

Tim held the examining room door open for elderly Mrs. Waite, then walked her out to the waiting room where her daughter sat anxiously, and, with a wink at his patient, told Emily, "You were right to bring her in. It could have been important. But she's fine. Her heart's as good as mine."

Tim had known long before he actually went to medical school, that when he fulfilled his dream people were going to trust him with their lives. He remembered when he'd first told his dad he wanted to be a doctor when he grew up, back when he was six years old. His father had told him it would be an tremendous responsibility, and that he'd need to live up to it. Emily's heartfelt, "Thank you, Dr. Tim. I know Mother didn't think she needed to come in, but these spells of hers worry me," was just another example. He wished they could all be so benign.

"She's in good shape." As good as a ninety-six-year-old could be, at any rate. The "spells" in question, so far as he could tell, and he'd examined her thoroughly, were simply an old woman falling asleep on the couch now and then. But Emily worried about her mother, with good reason since her father had passed away less than a year ago, and he was glad the elderly woman had someone who cared about her. "All she needs is to go home and rest."

"Oh! Of course." Tim watched as Mrs. Waite's quite possibly overly-devoted daughter took her mother's arm and all but carried her out of the clinic.

"They're a pair, aren't they?" Betty said.

"They sure are." If I had someone hovering over me like that, I'd go absolutely crazy, Tim thought, and turned to go back to the office.

But Betty was speaking again. "Walt came by while you were with Mrs. Waite."

"Walt?" Who was he? Another patient?

"The FedEx guy." She waved a cardboard envelope at him. "It's from the lab, but it's addressed to you, not the clinic."

"Thanks." He'd asked them to send the results directly to him, just in case. He didn't want them getting into his father's hands and misplaced for a second time.

Ignoring Betty's inquisitive gaze, he ducked into his office and yanked on the tab to open it.

There was a letter on top, but Tim set it aside and went straight to the results underneath. He ran his finger down the page. Rebecca's name at the top, the ferritin level test, which was a little low, they'd have to up the dosage on her iron supplement, the rubella antibody test, which was positive, so apparently the fact that she'd had the shot and therefore hadn't needed the test in the first place was another little item that hadn't made it onto her chart, no thanks to his father – and no pregnancy test. Tim let out a profound sigh of satisfaction, and only then did he take a look at the letter.

The usual salutation, then, "The HCG (Human Chorionic Gonadotropin) test returned to the Campbell Clinic were mistakenly exhanged with that of another patient. Please destroy results you received. The correct results are enclosed..."

Sloppy. Just sloppy. The Campbell Clinic would not be doing business with Lubbock Labs again. Not only had they made the mistake, but they hadn't even caught it before they'd sent the botched results. Or after, until he'd jumped down their throats. Damn. He'd never doubt Tara again.

Or his own instincts, for that matter. He'd known, even when he hadn't wanted to. And even though the results were exactly what he'd expected, he still couldn't get over it. Rebecca's whole world was ruined, Jack's trust gone, simply because some idiot at the lab made a mistake. Well, no. Not only because some idiot at the lab had made a mistake. Because his father – Tim didn't want to think about it.

His father needed to see a specialist. Tim would see that he saw the best, whether they had to go to Kalispell, or Spokane – or all the way to Seattle if necessary. They would find out what was wrong, and if anything could be done, it would be. If it was something that could be fixed, or if, God forbid, it really was dementia, slowed down, it would be done. No matter what.

Right now, though, he needed to see Rebecca. But first he had to go get Tara. He suspected Rebecca would need her friend when she found out. He grabbed his jacket off the coat tree, shoved his arms into it, and, calling to Betty in the otherwise empty for now, thank God, waiting room, he headed out the door.

Stopped halfway out. Turned around and headed back to the office. Aimed for the ancient photocopier tucked in the corner.

He waited impatiently for the machine to warm up. Made a copy of the letter and the results. Scribbled a note on a sticky pad, and left the whole business square in the middle of the desk blotter where his father would be sure to see it the next time he came in. Tim was cravenly glad he wouldn't be there to see his father confront the evidence.

He headed out the front door again, jacket flapping in his wake.

* * *

Tara wasn't in her usual place behind the counter at the library. Pete the page stood there in her place. He gestured.

"She's with the kids."

Tim headed back into the children's area. He could hear Tara's voice, singsong with the cadences of Dr. Seuss, before he saw her. She sat perched on a small wooden chair, an open book in her hands, a large circle of enthralled preschoolers hanging on her every word.

She was good at her job. He wondered how many children's lives she was changing simply by teaching them to love stories and reading. Probably every single kid in town. He remembered how Miss Iris had changed his life in a similar way, and knew it was right for her to stay here. For him to stay here. Doing what they did best.

Tara looked up at him quizzically, and he held the folded communication from the lab up briefly before tucking it back into his jacket pocket and leaning on the edge of a table to wait. He rather enjoyed the small catch in her voice as she went on with the story. He didn't think it had much to do with the predicament of Sam and his green eggs and ham.

The children were reluctant to let her go. Tim understood that sentiment all too well, and he stepped forward to meet her after the last kid finally left in tow of her mother.

"Well? It can't be bad news, considering the expression on your face."

He raised an eyebrow at her. "Patient confidentiality."

"Then what are you doing here?"

"I thought you might want to go with me. Moral support and all that."

Tara's face fell. "Oh, no."

Oh, he'd put his foot in it, all right. And how was he going to fix this? "Look, it's *not* bad news, one way or the other. Trust me." Another bad choice of words. It was trust that had gotten them all into this mess in the first place. Tim knew better than anyone exactly how *little* trust anyone in Campbell should be putting into the clinic and its soon-to-be former doctor right now. Not that anyone else did. But that was going to change, dammit. If it was the last thing he ever did, people would know they could rely on him the way they'd always relied on his father. And with the best reasons in the world. Just as they had his father.

But in the meantime Tara looked as if she were about to argue with him, and this was not the time or the place to be discussing a patient's confidential record, no matter what.

"Tara —"

Then she looked at him. Really looked at him. She knew. He wasn't sure how she knew he'd almost made things even worse, but she knew, and pulled them both back from the brink. She nodded decisively. "You're right. Come on."

Tim followed her to the desk, where she asked Pete, "Can you handle the place for half an hour or so? I have an unexpected appointment."

"Sure." Chuckling, Pete went back to the desk to calm down old Mrs. Rylance, who had archaic ideas about silence in the library.

Tara turned to Tim. "Well?"

"Do you know where she is?"

"She said she was going to spend the day at her old house, cleaning up. I told her she didn't owe her landlord a darned thing considering that he evicted her for no good reason, but you know Rebecca."

"Yeah, I do. Come on."

* * *

"That's weird." Tim pulled the Prius up in front of Rebecca's little house. Parked at the curb was a dirty red Toyota 4x4. "Isn't that Jack's rig?"

Tara nodded. "Mm-hmm. Wonder why he's here. Did your dad call him?"

"Dad hasn't seen the letter yet. He spent the morning over at Mark Thronson's house, helping his wife with the dressing on his leg." Because that was something his father could do without endangering anyone's health, Tim thought ruefully. He'd all but taken over the patient load in the last couple of days since their confrontation, and his father hadn't peeped about it. "I covered the clinic today."

"I guess we'll find out, then." Tara climbed out of the car and headed up the walk. Tim followed suit, reaching the door just as Tara rang the bell.

They waited. No footsteps, no sound at all.

"I wonder if they went out somewhere." Tim didn't think so, but anything was possible.

Tara snorted. "I can't see Rebecca going anywhere with Jack right now. Or," she added more sadly, "Jack wanting to take her anywhere."

"You have a point." Tim paused. "At least I don't hear anyone yelling. Maybe she went off by herself?"

"She told me this morning she was going to spend the day here. Since she hasn't really gone anywhere lately, I think she would have said something."

Tara reached for the bell again, but Tim put up a hand and stopped her. "Let me knock. Maybe there's something wrong with the bell."

He pounded on the door. Still no answer.

Tim looked down at her, the worry on her face mirroring what he felt. He reached out to open the door. He wasn't all that happy about entering the house without permission, but well, damn. They were both getting concerned.

To his surprise, the knob wouldn't turn. Nobody locked their doors in Campbell, at least not in the daytime. It was a practice that had taken him some effort to break when he'd moved to Seattle.

The expression on Tara's face changed. She looked almost like she was expecting him to read her the riot act. What on earth for? Then she reached up to the ledge on top of the door jamb and pulled down a key. Dusting her hand off, she slid the key in the lock.

Tim eyed her. "That's breaking and entering, you know."

She smirked. "Not if I'm not breaking."

He didn't quite see the difference. "Details."

"Tim, I'm checking on a friend. It's an entirely different matter."

The key turned. Tara opened the door and slipped inside. Tim shrugged and followed her.

"Rebecca?"

"Rebecca?"

Their calls echoed through the house. Tara glanced into the living room, empty of everything except a few pieces of furniture and some clothes strewn on the floor. "Curiouser and curiouser," she commented. "The place came furnished, but Rebecca's such a neatnik. I don't think I've ever seen her leave anything just lying around. Let alone her clothes." She started to pick something up, then dropped it and cleared her throat. "You check the kitchen. I'll go look in the bathroom."

"Fine." Tim watched Tara as she trotted down the hall. Now she was acting oddly, too. Well, finding out why could wait until they'd figured out where Becky'd gone.

"Rebecca?"

"Rebecca?"

They met back in the living room. "Her bedroom door's closed," Tara said in a stage whisper.

"Maybe you ought to leave it that way." Tim couldn't quite figure out why he was whispering back to her.

She frowned. "Maybe something's wrong."

"You're not going to be able to walk back out the front door without looking, are you?" Of course she wasn't. She wouldn't be Tara if she was. "Okay." Tim took Tara by the hand and preceded her down the hall. "Don't blame me."

"For what?" Tara flung the door open. Took one look, gasped, and slammed it shut again.

"What the hell?" Tim jumped back.

A very familiar voice boomed through the door. "Tim? That you, buddy?"

"Uh, Jack?" Tim stared at Tara, who was just as slack-jawed as he was.

"Tara?" Rebecca's voice was thick with shocked laughter.

Tara seemed to have temporarily lost her own voice, so Tim took over, even though he had to clear his throat twice before anything came out.

"Yeah, she's out here with me. We're leaving now. I'm going to slide something under the door that I think you should look at, though.

"Not that it matters anymore, apparently," he added, sotto voce, as he bent to do as he'd said.

He was still trying to get Tara to move when he heard footsteps and the rustle of paper. An almost inaudible gasp, and a "shh, honey, it's all right," in a tone he'd never suspected Jack capable of.

After a few moments, Rebecca's voice came through the door again. "Tara, are you still out there?"

Tim watched Tara swallow. "Yes."

A choked laugh, then, "Could you please fetch my clothes out of the living room? Everything else is at your house."

"Uh, Tim?" At least Jack sounded like himself again.

"I'm on it," Tim answered quickly.

"Thanks."

Tim did not look at Tara as they went to fetch the clothing strewn across the living room, but he was quite sure she wasn't looking at him, either. Not out of embarrassment, mind, at least not on his part. It was to keep from breaking out into completely inappropriate laughter.

The clothes were duly passed through the barely-opened door, and a few moments later a still rather disheveled-looking but decent Rebecca stood barefoot in the doorway, tears streaming down her face, staring at the record Tim had shoved under the door. Jack stood behind her in jeans half buttoned, his chest still bare, his arms around her waist. Tim wasn't sure who was holding who up.

"Shh, honey, it's all right," Jack said in that tone Tim was quite sure he'd never been intended to hear.

Rebecca lifted her head and turned in the circle of his arms. "I know." She paused. "Tara?"

Tara cleared her throat. "I guess you two worked things out without us."

Jack had the good grace to look sheepish when Rebecca frowned at him. "I knew she didn't fool around on me. Rebecca's a straight arrow."

Rebecca blushed. "Well, you know that for sure now, don't you?"

Tim tried to put on an official voice. "I'm sorry we disturbed you, but we thought you should know right away."

"Where does the blood go, anyway?" Jack peered at the letter. "Good grief, all the way to Texas."

Rebecca smiled up at him. "We'll be sending them a sample of our own after the wedding, I think."

"I sure hope so."

Tim shifted his feet, watching them. Tara tugged at his hand. "I guess we'd better get going."

"Definitely." If this was going to be typical of his career in Campbell, he'd never survive his first year here.

Rebecca slipped out of Jack's arms and hugged Tara, who hugged her back and said, "I'm so glad things worked out."

Rebecca grinned through her tears. "Me, too. I'll call you later."

"Much later," Jack added, and Tara broke into nervous giggles.

They had accomplished their task, and it was time to get the hell out of Dodge. Tim gestured toward the front door. "C'mon, Tara. Pete's probably wondering what happened to you."

They started back down the hall.

"Oh, and Tara?"

Tara turned back at the sound of Rebecca's voice. "Yes?"

"That key? I never meant for you to actually use it."

Tara turned beet red and headed down the hall. Tim nudged her. "So it wasn't breaking and entering?"

"So sue me." But she didn't sound regretful at all.

Tim understood that. "Remind me to, someday."

* * *

After he'd left Tara at the library, Tim headed back to the clinic, musing about the fact that Tara hadn't called him on the bet. Not yet, anyway.

Not that it mattered, anyway. Just that she would have called his bluff.

Tim stepped into the clinic, to find his father standing in the middle of the reception area, the copy of the lab letter in his hand. "What are you doing here?" Tim asked. "I thought you weren't coming in today."

"I had some paperwork to take care of."

Tim watched him. It was as if suddenly all the weight of his age was on Samuel. No longer the sprightly old man; his shoulders stooped, his eyes no longer glinting, he looked ninety instead of seventy-five.

"Come into my office. We need to talk."

Feeling as if he was ten years old once more, Tim took his jacket off and hung it up, then walked down the hallway and into the office behind his father, who seated himself at his desk. Tim found himself hovering near the doorway, wishing he was just about anywhere else other than where he was.

"Dad?"

"Come in."

Tim did as he was told, closing the door softly behind him.

"Something the matter?"

Samuel gestured with the copy of the letter. "I see the lab got hold of you."

"Yes. Finally. Once I convinced them there was a problem. I don't know how long you've been working with Lubbock Labs, Dad, but we're not going to use them anymore."

Tim couldn't help smiling. Just for a second. "Turns out it didn't really matter, though. Rebecca and Jack are back together, and I have it on good authority that he knows she was a virgin."

Samuel glanced up sharply.

He supposed he should explain that one, although it wasn't really any of his father's business. "Tara and I showed up at a rather, um, inconvenient time when we went to give Rebecca the good news a little while ago."

"Young people nowadays," Samuel muttered. "You just can't wait for anything."

He'd thought his father would be pleased. "They're in love, Dad. The wedding is back on."

"That's not the point. Marriage is a sacrament, a sacred thing —" Then why hadn't his father made a fuss when Tim had suddenly stopped spending the night at his parents' house? Don't ask, don't tell, he supposed. The old hypocrite.

Suddenly Samuel stopped and sighed heavily. "That's not why I called you in here."

Tim waited. Now what? he wondered. What was the next bullying tactic going to be?

"I called you in here to tell you that you're right."

Tim dropped into a chair, feeling like the breath had been knocked out of him. Right? "About what?"

"About what I would have done to Becky and Jack if you hadn't been here to straighten things out. You're quite right, you know. I could have ruined those two young lives."

Tim supposed he'd never understand the old man. Or himself, for what he was about to say. "No, Dad, you didn't. You threw a monkey wrench in their machinery, but they straightened it out all by themselves. The letter from the lab was a nice touch, but Jack was ready to marry her, anyway. Whatever she did to get him to trust her again worked. It wasn't your fault."

"But I put them through it. And, as you said, what if I'd forgotten something important in a life or death situation?"

"Do you really think you would have?"

Samuel lifted his worried gaze to his son. "I don't know, Timothy. I just don't know.

"I hate to leave the town without a doctor, but I don't have a choice. I can't rely on myself anymore. I won't put my burdens on you —" Tim opened his mouth, but his father waved a hand. "No, son, I won't do that to you. You have a right to your own life.

He settled back and reached for his coffee.

"I met your mother when she came to North Dakota to visit her grandparents. She was nineteen. I was twenty-eight, and just home from medical school. We met at a grange dance." Samuel's eyes became misty, and Tim sat back. The story was a familiar one, and beloved.

"Avis was so beautiful. Big blue eyes and golden hair. I fell in love on the spot, but she was leaving to go home to Montana in just a few days. I wanted her to stay in North Dakota with me. I proposed only two days after I met her." Samuel smiled ruefully. "Naturally, she turned me down."

Tim glanced up, startled. This wasn't the story he'd grown up on, but Samuel went on. "I tried to talk her into it. Oh, I tried.

"But she was determined to go home, to her little town in the middle-of-nowhere Montana. My parents wanted me to stay in North Dakota. I was to take over the practice of my mentor, just as I wanted you to take over mine." Samuel chuckled self-deprecatingly. "They were almost as bad as I've been with you. But I was determined to follow my love to Montana, and I defied them to do it." He took a sip of coffee.

"They forgave me. Eventually. But it was a long hard road. I told myself I'd love you no matter what career and life you chose. Even when it took you away from us. Somehow I knew you wouldn't stay here." He leaned forward. Tim watched him, his heart in his throat. "But here I find myself doing exactly as they did. I'm sorry.

"Timothy, I shouldn't have pushed you to stay. You have your own life to lead. It wasn't fair for me to ask you to continue mine for me. And," he added, and Tim could see how hard this was for his father to say, "you're right that I should step down. I don't think I could live with myself if I harmed anyone else the way I harmed Becky Thorstein." He let out his breath. "Or worse."

It took Tim a minute to find his voice. When he did, it was thick with emotion. "Thanks, Dad. I appreciate it."

Samuel cleared his throat. "So, son, how do we close up a clinic?"

Tim took a deep breath, then let it out. Now was not the time to tell his father he'd decided to stay. Not until he settled things with Tara once and for all. The last thing he wanted was for her to find out he was sticking to their bet from anyone else, especially his father. "We'll manage somehow."

Samuel stood up and came around the desk. Laid his hand on his son's shoulder. "You'll know what to do."

Tim chuckled wryly. "Yeah, I guess so."
He rose, and, together, they left the office.

Chapter 22

The next evening, Tim left the Prius parked behind the clinic as his feet carried him, almost of their own volition, to Tara's house.

He stood on her front walk for a long time, fingering the little black box in his pocket. He'd driven all the way to Spokane to buy the rock inside. He'd spent the three-hour drive wondering if he was just going to keep on going back to Seattle instead, but, not much to his surprise by now, he hadn't. He truly hadn't wanted to.

Tim stared at the little white house half hidden behind its enormous evergreens. They'd have to find a bigger place sooner rather than later.

He hoped Tara wasn't too attached to this one. Maybe they could buy a few acres out on the Yaak River and build a house of their own. Not all that practical, perhaps, but if he traded the Prius in for an all-wheel-drive...

"Are you going to stand out there all night?"

The door opened, and the object of his affections stood framed by it, dressed in jeans and a well-worn Seattle Seahawks championship sweatshirt.

Tim shook his head. "I don't know. I'm still thinking about it."

Tara grinned at him and held out her hand. He strolled up the sidewalk and grasped it. She pulled him inside, closing the door behind him with her free hand.

"It's cold out there. Don't you know any better than to stand outside and freeze to death?" She leaned up and gave him a kiss. He wrapped his arms around her.

After a few moments, he said, "I guess not."

She backed up a step. "Take off your jacket and stay awhile. I've got supper if you're interested."

He sniffed appreciatively. The aroma was Italian and delectably so. "Expecting company?"

"You're not company." She tugged at his jacket and he let her pull it off of him and hang it up. "Do you believe Rebecca and Jack? I never in this world would have opened that door yesterday afternoon if I'd known what was on the other side."

He trailed her into the kitchen. "You've never been in Becky's bedroom before?"

"You know what I mean." She grimaced. "If they'd walked in on us like that, I'd have been mortified."

Tim pulled out a chair at her little table in the corner and turned it around. He sat down and leaned his arms over the chair back, watching Tara bustle around, pulling out a trivet and a bowl full of salad.

Now that he thought about it – "They didn't seem to mind all that much."

She glanced over at him. "The whole situation did seem awfully comfortable, didn't it? I wonder how long it's really been since they patched things up?"

He'd wondered that, too, but it really wasn't any of his and Tara's business. At least that's how he'd feel in their shoes, he thought. "I don't think we need to worry about it. When isn't so important as the fact that they did."

She shrugged. "True. But she could have told me. Here when I've been so worried."

Tim considered his words and decided to play it safe. "It's all over now, so everything's fine."

She smiled at him as she brought a pan brimming with lasagna to the table. The delicious odor reminded Tim's stomach that he was hungry, and it growled.

"Glad dinner meets with your approval."

He shrugged unrepentantly. "Sorry. It smells good, and food wasn't a high priority today."

"We'll fix that."

While she brought the rest of dinner to the table, Tim turned his chair around and sliced into the lasagna. Tara settled herself, and they ate in contented silence.

Finally, Tim set his fork down. "You certainly can cook."

"Thank you. I think."

"Oh, it was a compliment. I just realized that I probably should have let Mom know I wasn't going to be home for dinner."

"The parental ties getting a little tight?"

It was the best straight line he was likely to get. Tim took a deep breath. "No. Not exactly. As a matter of fact, my dad let me off the hook this afternoon. Says he understands why I need to lead my own life and that it wasn't fair of him to expect me to take over his practice."

She went very still. "Because of the lab mix-up?"

"Yes. He couldn't very well keep pretending everything was okay with the evidence staring him in the face." Tim paused, wondering if Tara would understand, but needing to make it clear to her, at least, in a way he wasn't going to be able to publicly. "It was the hardest thing I've done in a long time. I mean, it's not like I want him to have to retire. I know how much he's loved being Campbell's doctor. It's who he's been, his whole life for decades. And now he can't do it anymore. If I were in his shoes I'd be miserable. And being the one to prove it to him was awful."

Tara put her warm hand on his where it rested on the table. "It was just one mistake, Tim. He's still a perfectly good doctor."

Tim leaned forward. If he couldn't make Tara understand, he wasn't going to be able to make anyone understand. Oh, his mother and Betty, yes, but they were close enough to Samuel to see that things weren't what they should be. They'd known something was wrong before Tim had ever arrived back in Campbell. It was why his mother had been so insistent that he come home for the party in the first place. She wanted him to see. To know what to do. And to have the authority to do what needed to be done.

He wished he hadn't – no, he didn't. Just because he hated it didn't mean he wasn't the right person to deal with this crisis. "No, he isn't, Tara. If he couldn't remember whether he'd ordered a pregnancy test, that's one thing, but what if he forgot to order a test for something important? Like diabetes, or cancer? Something that could kill somebody? He'd never forgive himself. I'm not sure the town would forgive him, either.

"And you haven't seen the records he was keeping. Rebecca's chart wasn't the only one missing records, not by a long shot. When I began going through those charts so Betty could start digitizing them, I found all sorts of stuff in there that didn't have rhyme or reason. There's a pattern, almost, if you could call it that, stretching back at least six months, maybe even a year."

He took a deep breath. Tara had long since put her fork down, as had he, and her hand was at her lips.

"There's a certain amount of trust that comes with being a doctor. A certain amount of responsibility to the people you treat. He breached that with Rebecca and the pregnancy test, but it wasn't the first time he'd messed something up, or even the second or the third. It was just the first time anyone else caught it. And the mistake with Rebecca's records wouldn't have been caught if it hadn't been so obvious."

Enough. He'd probably said more than he should have about his father, but if he couldn't trust Tara, he had no business being in love with her. And he did. Trust her, that is. But it was time to go on to the part that mattered, at least so far as he and Tara were concerned. The part where he showed her he was staying because he loved her, not because he had to.

"I don't know if you know how Dad ended up here in the first place."

Tara shook her head, looking impatient. "Tim –"

He held up his hand. "Bear with me, okay? The story always was that he met my mother when she was visiting relatives in North Dakota, and she refused to marry him and stay there because she wanted to come home to Montana, so he came with her. Well, this afternoon Dad told me the story again, but it wasn't the one I'd heard all my life, or at least I hadn't heard all of it before. And he, he apologized to me. Said he was sorry for doing to me what his parents had done to him, when they practically disowned him for leaving North Dakota to come here all those years ago."

Tara spoke slowly. "So you're not going to stay."

"What? No!" He hadn't said that. Tim stared at her. She stared back, and he could almost see her mind whirring behind those sharp gray eyes. But she didn't say a thing.

She was taking it all the wrong way. And assuming the worst of him. She always assumed the worst of him. Or maybe she didn't want him to stay, after all. After all, if he stayed, she'd said she'd marry him. And maybe she'd rethought things and didn't want to marry him after all. He stood up. "I didn't say that. I'm saying that, according to my father, I'm off the hook. He doesn't expect me to stay."

"But what are you going to do?" Didn't she know? Apparently she had no idea. So much for trust. And love.

"What do you want me to do, Tara?"

She stared at him, but didn't answer.

"Well, I guess that's that. Thanks for dinner." Tim headed toward the door, the ring a lead weight in his pocket. He had to get out of there. Now.

* * *

He was gone before she could stop him. What did he think she wanted him to do? She'd been trying to tell him practically ever since he'd gotten here. She'd thought they had the whole issue settled the night she'd started out to seduce him.

And now Dr. Samuel had to haul off and tell him he was off the hook. Apparently the only reason he'd been here at all was guilt.

He certainly didn't love her enough to honor his promises. Marriage my foot, Tara snorted. Obviously that was only when he thought he was going to be stuck in Campbell. After all, who else would marry him and live out in the back of beyond?

If she'd harbored thoughts of following him and telling him she wanted him to stay, they were good and gone now.

It wasn't fair. Tara picked up the half-empty pan of lasagna and carried it back to the counter. Yanked the foil out of the drawer, and shredded the first piece before it was long enough to cover the pan.

Who did he think he was? Just because his father felt guilty didn't mean that he wasn't still needed. The town needed him. The people needed him. She needed him.

And just because he felt like he could get away with it now, he was going to walk off and leave her– them.

The bigger fool her for not knowing better. He'd broken her heart once, and she'd opened herself right up and let him smash it to smithereens again. And this time he'd not only betrayed her, but the entire population of Campbell, Montana.

Tara leaned her elbows on the kitchen counter, staring through the window into the dark, cold night. It would be winter soon. Short days and long, freezing nights. Snow up to the eaves and cabin fever. Not for the first time did she wish she belonged somewhere warm.

If Tim had loved her, they could have made their own warmth together. If he'd wanted to stay, she could have made his life worth leaving the big city for. Maybe.

Maybe not. After all, just because he hadn't betrayed her with Jack's cousin didn't mean that he didn't have some sleek, sophisticated city girl wondering when he was going to come home to her. Tara hadn't even thought to ask him, and he certainly hadn't volunteered the information.

Scowling, Tara finished the dishes and poured herself a glass of the wine leftover from the first time she'd cooked for him. She'd had more to drink since Tim had come back to Campbell than she'd had all her life. Carrying the glass into the living room, she lit a fire in the fireplace, and plunked herself down, staring into the flames.

She had home, and family, and friends. But it just wasn't enough. Damn Timothy Swanson.

* * *

Tara was surprised to see Rebecca come into the library the next morning.

"I'd have thought you'd be back at work."

"They asked me." At Tara's quizzical look, Rebecca added, "I don't want to work for people who don't trust me."

Tara could understand that. "I don't blame you. But what are you going to do?"

Rebecca smiled. "Get married."

Tara led the way back to her office, keeping an eye on the counter through the glass partition. "I know that, and I'm happy for you. I meant for a living."

"Jack says I don't have to work if I don't want to. We're going to try for a baby right away." Rebecca plucked a pencil from the jar on Tara's desk and fiddled with it. "I think he decided that getting me pregnant would be pretty nice after all."

"So is that what I accidentally got a glimpse of yesterday?"

Rebecca blushed and kept her eyes downcast. "I guess after what happened, I realized that I don't want to be judged by the kind of people to whom something like that is important." She raised her head and gazed earnestly at Tara. "Narrow-minded people. Old-fashioned people." She paused. "People like my parents and the people at the church. It didn't matter to them that I was hurting. All that mattered to them was that it looked like I'd broken one of their precious rules. It didn't even occur to them that I might not have done it."

At last. Tara had been waiting for her friend to see that particular light for a very long time. "I've always thought your folks treated you like you were supposed to be some kind of old-maid schoolteacher."

Rebecca's expression changed into something Tara had never seen before. Something defiant. And proud. And wonderful. "They never liked Jack. And do you know why? Because they remember where he came from, and don't approve of who he's become any more than they liked who he was, so he can't win no matter what he does."

Rebecca snorted. "And all because he teaches evolution. He teaches science. He digs up ancient dinosaur bones, which are solid proof that all their narrow little beliefs are wrong.

She dropped the pencil back into the jar. "I tried to rationalize it. I told myself that they're just too literal about the Bible. That they just haven't bothered to try to understand the truth behind what he does.

"And because Jack loves me, he's put up with it all this time. No more. Love me, love my husband." Rebecca straightened. The light in her eyes made Tara's heart warm.

"Good for you."

"Thanks. I knew you'd understand." She grinned. "Just like I'm being understanding about you catching us *in flagrante delicto* yesterday."

"Not all the way *flagrante*, though, right?"

Rebecca chuckled. "No, you were a little late for that. Thank goodness. Much as I like Tim, I'd rather he not have seen me quite like that."

"Much as I like you, I'd just as soon miss it, too." Tara reached out to hug her friend. "I'm so glad you two worked things out."

"Me, too. Once we got over the shock and Jack got back to his usual practical self, he knew I wouldn't have done that to him. But I think he was relieved at the positive proof."

"The letter from the lab."

Rebecca shook her head, laughing. "And I thought I was the naïve one."

"Oh." While Tara was as pleased as she could be about how her friend's life had changed for the better, the new Rebecca was going to take some getting used to.

And her next comment was completely out of left field. "So, I see Tim hasn't bought you a ring yet. You won the bet, didn't you?"

Tara knew she wasn't going to get away with an innocent, "What bet?" Rebecca was smart. She'd picked up on Tara's slip of the tongue the other afternoon. And she was going to have to tell Rebecca sooner or later, anyway. "The bet's off." Rebecca's concerned expression had Tara backing up. "I, um, really should be getting back to work."

Rebecca grasped her arm as Tara tried to slip out the door. "What happened?"

Tara shrugged. "His dad let him off the hook. Says he was wrong trying to convince Tim to stay."

"I'd heard that Samuel was finally talking about closing the clinic. I figured I'd heard wrong. Tim *wants* to stay."

Rebecca was dreaming. And she didn't know how much her words were hurting Tara. She honestly didn't, and Tara knew that. "How do you figure? He was wanting to head back to Seattle that first night in the Red Dog."

"Oh, Tara. Not once he got a good look at you."

"Look, just because you got your happily ever after doesn't mean all of us will."

"Jack agrees with me."

Tara let her breath out in exasperation. "Jack would agree with you if you said the moon was made of green cheese right about now."

Rebecca grinned self-consciously. "Maybe, but that's beside the point. He does love you."

"How do you know?"

"I just know."

Tara shrugged. "Well, thanks, but I need a bit more reassurance than that about a man who was so excited to get out of having to stay and run the clinic that he walked over to my house first thing to tell me."

The understanding look in Rebecca's eyes infuriated Tara. "You're not going to cut him an inch of slack, are you?"

"Why should I?" Tara crossed her fingers behind her back. "He's never said a serious word about us."

"I don't know what they told you in the city, but you are a beautiful, wonderful human being. You can hold your own with anyone." Rebecca leaned over and gave Tara a quick hug. "Don't you let anyone else tell you otherwise. Not even yourself.

"I'll let you get back to work now. You think about it, okay?" And she slipped out the door, her sensible flats clicking on the worn asphalt tile floor.

Tara sank down into her chair. Beautiful, wonderful human being my foot, she thought. To the people of her hometown, who knew her faults and seemed to be able to love her anyway, maybe. To Tim, who seemed to switch off and on like a light bulb, certainly not.

Maybe it was stupid to be so cautious about him. Maybe not. Still, it hurt way more than she'd thought it would to find out that he was welshing on their lives.

Chapter 23

"Hey, it's Dr. Tim!"

"Hi, Dr. Tim, how are you?"

It was that first night at the Red Dog all over again, Tim thought wryly as he walked into the community center for his father's birthday and retirement celebration. A classically boisterous Campbell welcome.

With a couple of important changes. One was the name. He supposed he'd get used to the new honorific eventually. His father had worn the moniker of Dr. Samuel with pride, and now it was his turn. This was his town, dammit, and he was their doctor. No point in trying to make himself anything but what he was.

God knew it was too late to change his mind now. He'd taken the plunge, and a very deep breath, this afternoon, and called Harborview to regretfully decline their offer of a position. And, much more to his satisfaction, he'd called and talked with his mentor at the University of Washington medical school about getting involved with his research program, even if only on a small, peripheral level to begin with, while they figured out the logistics of his working from Campbell.

Dr. Strickland had shown more interest, and pride, in Tim's change of plans than he'd expected. Not everyone, he'd been told firmly, had to be at the center of the universe to create meaningful change, and sometimes being away from the insular world of a big-city hospital could provide a useful point of view. The one thing Dr. Strickland hadn't been was surprised. Tim was beginning to wonder if his return to Campbell was unexpected to anyone but himself. Or Tara.

And while he was on the subject of Tara, the other change from his first night in town was the little black velvet box still burning a hole in his pocket. Maybe he'd been stupid to bring it along after what had happened two nights ago, but he couldn't help but hope that once Tara saw he meant to stay, she'd want him back. Oh, he was going to stay whether she took him back tonight or not, and she would be his, eventually, if it was within his powers of persuasion. But dammit, it would be so much better if she just took him back tonight. And easier, he had to admit.

But as he accepted and gave handshakes and slaps on the back, as a beer – Moose Drool, good, someone had remembered – was pressed into his hand, Tim's gaze wandered around the old community center. The place was packed to the point where he wondered if Campbell's volunteer fire chief was looking the other way. Practically everyone he'd grown up with was here, people he'd gone to school with, his teachers, his friends, the kids he'd helped Tara baby-sit when they were teenagers.

A new generation, too. The patients he'd treated in the clinic over the last couple of weeks and the folks who'd waved at him on the street, and the few strangers in town who'd decided to stay.

Mark Thronson was here on his first outing since his accident, still in a wheelchair but with bells on and an enormous grin. Little Petey Silsand, long over his virus, was running his mother ragged as he tried to sample the entire buffet table at one go.

Tim couldn't help grinning as he saw Rebecca and Jack dancing together, her head nestled on his shoulder. Jack glanced over at him, winked, and then leaned Rebecca back in a dip. By the time she was vertical again, their lips were locked. Tim nodded satisfaction. There'd been a point at which he hadn't been sure he'd ever see them together again.

He loved them all. Something he'd never have been able to admit a mere two weeks ago, when he'd come whistling into town, planning on a few days to find out what had his mother in a knot about his father and whistle his way back out again.

His father had taken care of so many of these people. And now they were in Tim's care. One of the best things in the world, to be able to see the good he was doing.

Tim took a swallow of his beer and ran his gaze over the room again. Only one person was missing. He'd been watching for her ever since he'd arrived.

The music ended for a moment, and, excusing himself from yet another well-wisher, he aimed through the crowded dance floor toward Rebecca and Jack. He tapped Jack on the shoulder, and Jack leaned away from what he was doing, scowling in a way that Tim knew he didn't mean it. "No, you can't dance with my girl."

Tim snorted. "As if I didn't know better than to ask."

"So what do you want?" Jack demanded.

A teenaged couple bounced into Tim's back, and with a "Sorry, Dr. Tim!" bounced away again.

Tim acknowledged them with a wave of his hand and got back to business. "Have either of you seen Tara tonight?"

Rebecca glanced up at Jack before she replied. Tim wasn't quite sure how to interpret that glance, whether good, bad, or worse. "No, not since this afternoon."

He had to ask. "She did say she was coming to the party, right?"

"She wouldn't miss this party for the world," Rebecca replied, obviously astonished.

"She's already missed half of it."

"Says who?"

Tim spun around. It was as if the crowd melted away from them, or at least he wasn't seeing them anymore. "Where have you been?"

"Why do you care?" As if she didn't know.

Tim strode up and took Tara by the arm before she could get away again.

"Hey!"

"Hey, yourself." The music had started again, and he whipped her into a spin. By the time he had her back in his arms, she was laughing. Why did he think her reaction was only because she couldn't help it?

"Very sneaky."

"It's the only way to catch you." And wasn't that the honest truth? She didn't answer, but she didn't stop dancing with him, either.

Tim was still trying to figure out how to bring up the topic of the ring burning a hole in his pocket when the music stopped again. Larry Silsand, Petey's father and the manager and DJ of the local radio station, KMUS (pronounced K-moose), tapped the mike. "Can I have everyone's attention, please?" Gradually the conversations died down and everyone paid attention.

"Tonight we're here to celebrate the seventy-fifth birthday of our own Dr. Samuel Swanson, who has been our doctor here in Campbell longer than a lot of us have been alive. He delivered me," Larry added, and laughed. "And my wife. And my son. In fact, you could say that the entire Silsand family has been a Dr. Samuel special delivery."

Laughter broke out. Tim glanced over at his father, who was beaming proudly, but looking wistful, too. I probably should have told him ahead of time, he thought. But it was too late now.

"And, as it turns out, we're also celebrating his retirement. After forty-five years of taking care of this town, Dr. Samuel is closing down the clinic."

The sudden silence rang through the room, and Tim could have sworn every eye swiveled from Larry to Samuel, and then to him. Next to him, Tara stiffened.

Tim cleared his throat and raised his voice. "Larry, I'm afraid you were misinformed. My father is retiring, but the clinic won't be closing." Tara's hand clamped down on his arm, but it was his father he was watching. "I'll be taking over my father's practice. I hope you'll be willing to give me your trust as you gave it to him, and I'll do my best to live up to it."

The room erupted with applause and shouts, but it was his father's reaction Tim wanted to see the most. The old man looked absolutely stunned.

With Tara following him, still hanging onto him, too, which had to be a good thing, Tim started making his way to the chair of honor. It took a while, what with the handshakes and backslaps and congratulations and all, but at last he was standing in front of his parents. His father still looked stunned, but as Tim watched his expression changed. He looked as if he was about to burst with pride. And joy. And pleasure. His mother was beaming, too, in her gentle way.

"You don't have to do this, son."

Tim grinned. "Yeah, I do, Dad. I turned down the position at Harborview this afternoon. If I don't take over the clinic, I'm going to be unemployed."

He heard a small gasp, but if Tara was surprised at this, he really didn't want to think about it. She didn't let go, though.

"I didn't want you to do this for me."

"I know. I didn't." Tim reached down and took his father's hand, surreptitiously, or maybe not so surreptitiously judging from his father's wry expression, checking to his pulse to make sure the shock hadn't been bad for him. Noting, too, that – good grief, were those tears in his eyes? "As much as I love you, Dad, I didn't do this for you. I did it for me."

"But–" Oh, so Tara had recovered her voice. He was surprised it had taken her this long. But this was his moment now. His and his father's. The ring in his pocket could wait till he was done here.

"I'm just glad you gave me the chance to show you it's for me."

Samuel's face fell. "I almost didn't, didn't I?"

"Dad, I'm glad about this. Don't you dare spoil it for me."

Avis patted her husband on the shoulder. "Let Tim have his moment, honey. He's earned it."

Samuel nodded. "So you have, son. So you have."

"Thanks." At least Samuel hadn't said "I told you so." That had to be worth something.

Tim straightened and turned back to the crowd. The music had started back up while they'd been talking, and people had begun dancing again. And chatting, and doing all the good things a community does when it comes together to have fun.

So maybe now was the time –

"Tara? What the – Where'd she go?"

* * *

"Come on," said a voice behind him.

"What?"

"Come on," Jack repeated impatiently. "I don't know how much longer Rebecca can stall her."

Tim didn't argue any further, but followed Jack across the room, through the door behind the stage, and down the hall to the building's back entrance.

He could hear their voices before he saw them, silhouetted in the open doorway. "Rebecca, let me through. I've got to get out of here before he finds me."

"Too late," Tim called out. He strode up and took Tara by the arm. "Thanks, Becky. I'll take it from here."

"It's about time you got here," Rebecca said. "She's bigger than I am." She leaned into Jack, and his arm went around her.

"You got this, buddy?" Jack asked.

Tim nodded. "I think so." *I hope so*, he thought, and watched as his friends headed back down the hall. This wasn't exactly going as planned. Tara looked spitting mad. He wondered why she wasn't spewing venom at him, but her lips were pursed so tightly that the skin around them was white. He didn't loosen his grip – he wasn't exactly in the mood to be chasing her clear across town – but he did manage to juggle their relative positions so it felt more like a hug than a come-along hold.

"Come on back inside. It's freezing out here." As a matter of fact, the first snowflakes of the season were blowing by in a brisk breeze, the clouds obscuring the moon. Pretty enough, but neither one of them had their coat on and Tara was shivering, although whether because of the temperature or the circumstances, Tim wasn't sure.

But she let him close the door. When he made to tug her back down the hall, though, she balked. "I just want to go home, Tim."

"What, don't you want to help me celebrate?"

"Celebrate?" she asked him. "Is that what you're doing? Celebrating being stuck in Campbell for the rest of your life? I thought you wanted to be somebody."

And who did she think she was? No one? Tim didn't know why Tara had come back to Campbell. Up till now he hadn't really thought about it. She'd just seemed to belong here, the way Miss Iris had as librarian before her, the way everyone who lived in their little town did. He hadn't questioned her presence, her feelings on the subject, or anything. He'd just been glad to find her when he'd come home. He'd assumed she was happy here. Why else would she have made the choice to return?

"I am somebody," he told her. "Just like you are. You matter here. I want to matter here, too." He paused. "Tara, why did you come home?"

She was silent for a very long time, so long that he wondered if she was going to speak at all. And she wouldn't meet his eyes. He put a finger to her chin and lifted it. Her eyes glistened. Great. First he'd made his father cry, and now Tara. At least his dad's tears had been happy ones.

"Tara?"

"You weren't supposed to figure it out," she said at last. "I'm here because this is where I belong —"

"Me, too," Tim said, relieved.

But she was shaking her head. "No, listen to me. I'm here because this is where I'm safe, and where I'm not in over my head. I'm here because that wide world you kept going on about when we were kids sounded like an adventure, so I tried it, and I discovered that it's a scary, lonely place.

"When I was with you, it was an adventure, but once I lost you, I didn't want it anymore, and it didn't want me. When Rebecca wrote and told me the library board was looking for someone to take Miss Iris's place, I was glad. I'm not proud I ran home with my tail between my legs, but that's what I did." She pulled away from him to stare at something he couldn't see on the wall.

What Tim really wanted to do was pull her to him again, to tell her everything was all right, but it so obviously wasn't. Instead, he said, "So all those people you help at the library every day, they're not worth anything? My dad told me how much he relied on you to help his patients get good, reliable information about their illnesses. And those kids I saw you reading to the other day? Whether or not they learn to enjoy reading isn't important?" He was certain she accomplished more every day than she realized. Than *he* realized, he thought suddenly. "Just who do you think you are, anyway?"

She turned to face him. Her spine was straight and her shoulders back, and every last trace of her tears was gone. "I am Campbell's librarian. I do a darned good job, and I'm proud of what I do. But I'm not going out into your wide world again, at least not to stay."

Tim shook his head in exasperation. "In case you didn't notice, Tara, I'm not going anywhere, either."

"Maybe not for now —"

"Okay, that's it. Come on." He headed down the hallway, pulling her after him. If this was what it took to get her to believe she was worth marrying, then so be it.

She dug in her heels, not that it did much good on the old asphalt tile. "Tim —"

"Trust me."

She rolled her eyes at that, but at least she quit fighting him.

It was just his good luck and, he knew she thought, her bad, that the music stopped just as they came through the doorway back into the crowd.

* * *

Tara stared blankly around the still-crowded community center. It felt as if everyone on the planet was staring at them as Tim dragged her over to Larry Silsand's makeshift DJ table. But when he asked Larry for the mike, she made one last desperate try to get away, anyway.

Larry gestured and scooted his chair back. "It's all yours."

Tara watched in mounting dismay as Tim reached for the microphone, perched on a stand at sit-down level. He untangled the cord, and Tara cringed at the feedback scream from the old equipment. Then he straightened, his other hand still in a death grip on hers. The man so did not know what he was doing.

But it was too late now. He had the mike, and she watched in horror as he spoke into it.

"Everybody? Sorry to interrupt one more time, but I've got one more important thing to do, and I need witnesses."

Everyone was staring at them now. Everyone she'd known all her life. And Tim was about to make a laughingstock of both of them, and she couldn't do anything about it.

She didn't dare look at him, but she knew he could feel the sweaty nervousness in her hand. It couldn't be his. She'd never seen him nervous in his life. But he suddenly squeezed her fingers so hard she couldn't help but let out a squeak, and she realized he *was* nervous. Tara opened her mouth, but he was already speaking.

"I need to ask someone a question, and I need you all to witness it, because apparently she won't believe I mean it otherwise."

Tim paused. Tara's heart was in her throat. If he really meant to do this, she was never going to forgive him. But he was.

She wasn't going to look at him, she wasn't, she wasn't — but his gaze pulled her like a magnet. He spoke directly into the mike,

228

but he was looking her right in the eye. Daring her to look away. "Tara, will you marry me?"

She'd known it was coming, but she could feel her mouth drop open. She couldn't catch her breath. He appeared to be holding his. It took her a minute or two longer, as the crowd tittered, to find her voice. "You mean it?"

"Do you really think I'd be doing this, out in front of God and everybody, if I didn't?" Laughter rang through the room, but Tara barely heard it. He added, "You did say you loved me, didn't you? I mean, it's not like this is a shock or anything."

Tara stared at him as if he'd grown two heads. She backed away, but he wouldn't let go, drat him.

Samuel Swanson's voice stopped her dead in her tracks. "Tara, we know you love him." He sure didn't sound like he had memory problems. Not where his son was concerned.

"And you know he loves you." Rebecca's voice, ringing clearly out over the crowd. And now her best friend was on the devil's side. "You can't deny it now."

Tara struggled to find her voice again. "Can't I?"

And lost it again completely when Tim handed the mike back to an evilly-grinning Larry and dropped to one knee, still hanging onto her hand for what felt like dear life. His dear life, she thought suddenly. And hers. "No more than I can."

He reached into his pocket with his free hand and brought out a small black box. Thumbed it open and held it out to her.

"I could no more deny my love for you than I could abandon the clinic to go back to Seattle. You're my heart, my soul, and my common sense."

"Certainly your common sense. You wouldn't have any, otherwise." She stopped as the rest of his statement sank in. "You really mean it, don't you?" she whispered.

He rose. Whispered, "Yes," into her ear, and grinned. "And don't you dare tell me you ever thought otherwise." He straightened again, and waited, the open ring box still in his hand. "Well?"

He was insane. But he really meant it. He was hers. "Do I have a choice?" She didn't wait for him to do it, but plucked the ring out of the box and put it on her own finger. "At least it fits."

Tim burst out laughing. So did their forgotten audience. But while the sound was still bouncing off the walls, he leaned over again and told her, "No choice at all."

Not that she wanted one in the slightest. "Then I guess I'll have to." Before she could stop him or stop herself, not that she was likely to even in front of this crowd, she kissed him.

When they broke apart, Tim gestured at the crowd and told her, "It's public now, Tara, I've got witnesses." He signaled to Larry, who started the music back up, and pulled her out onto the dance floor.

Tara laughed. "You had to do it in front of everyone, didn't you?"

Tim whirled her out and back. "Yup. I did." He snuggled her close to him, in spite of the fast beat of the music. "Now you know I love you for sure."

"You're right." Tara sighed and leaned her head on his shoulder. "I do."

Afterword

Thank you for reading *Much Ado in Montana*. I hope you enjoyed it. Reviews help other readers find books. I appreciate all reviews, whether positive or negative.

Would you like to know when my next book is available? You can sign up for my new release email list at mmjustus.com, or follow me on Facebook at https://www.facebook.com/M.M.Justusauthor or on Twitter @mmjustus.

If you would like to read an excerpt from another of my books, *Cross-Country: Adventures Alone Across America and Back*, please turn the page.

Chapter 1

August 31, 1999

My steps are echoing. Not much room for it in an 800 square foot apartment, but when all the furniture's been hauled away to storage, and both the cats have gone to live with a friend, and it's the last night I'll be there, I suppose they're entitled to echo all they want.

I should have left today. A day or two in the grand scheme of things shouldn't matter much, but it does. I had it in my mind that I would have a round trip. One of three months, from the first of September till the thirtieth of November. And so I will.

Like Bilbo Baggins, I shall go there and back again. I have only a vague idea where *there* is. I have planned very hard to plan as little as possible. Not to schedule, as has always been my bent. Not to know exactly where I'm going to be on any given day more than a day or two ahead.

But I do know I will be back on November 30th. My friend Trish, who is keeping my two cats for me, is expecting me, and the storage people will want money again by then if I don't retrieve my belongings.

And so I sit on the floor, back propped against the wall, waiting for it to be late enough to climb in my sleeping bag resting on the foam pad cut to fit my little car, and try to sleep.

It's hard to sleep the night before the beginning of a dream.

I'm going to drive cross-country. See places I've never been, revisit old friends geographical and human, and maybe find out who I am and why I would want to do something like this.

I turn out the light and grope my way to the sleeping bag. Slide in, settle down, try to arrange my forty-year-old female hips and shoulders against the hard floor, and wonder if I've lost my mind as my family thinks, or if this really is the beginning of a new life.

I guess I'll find out. Let it be light soon.

* * *

Bright grey morning. No rain even though it looks threatening, odd weather for the Northwest in September. I rise, creaking a little, and sidestep the small pile of gear to peer out the window.

I can see my car down in the parking lot. A bright teal green 1998 Chevy Cavalier. It's a small car, but then I'm a small person, relatively speaking. I turn to stare at the suddenly larger pile of boxes and cooler and other things that are going to have to fit inside that small space.

I can do it. Owl can handle it, too. The car is named Owl by an inheritance and a stretch of good humor. The first car I ever owned was a 1966 Ford Falcon. You know how navy blue is almost black? The Falcon was navy green, with a tan interior. Owl also has a tan interior. I toyed with calling it Falcon II back when I first bought it, but decided that was pretentious. So, choosing another bird of prey, I called it Owl, thinking its namesake's silence and skill might be a good thing for it to live up to.

Another glance out the window, then I bend over to roll the sleeping bag, gather things together to put them by the front door.

I'm ready to go in less than an hour. A box of clothes, a box of food and utensils, a bright blue cooler with a white lid. A brand-new sleeping bag, a foam pad, a box of what I euphemistically call my fun and games – recreational reading, guidebooks, a road atlas, a blank stenographer's pad for journal-keeping, a cross-stitch project (I have good intentions, and, after all, I might get bored waiting somewhere), and a small container of pens, highlighter, and a couple of pictures of my cats. A small zippered case of audiotapes. Not much else.

I don't need much else, and as my mother always tells me when I'm in the midst of over-planning a trip, it's not like I'm going to outer Mongolia.

Now the apartment's really empty. I prowl around, opening closets and cupboards, trying to prove to myself I haven't forgotten anything. On impulse, I lift the lids on the washer and dryer. The washer's empty, thank goodness, but a small forlorn pile of shorts and T-shirts sits in the dryer. Great. I guess I can mail them to Karla, the friend who's playing mail drop for me while I'm gone. I pull them out, stuff them in a plastic bag, and take them with me as I lock the apartment for the last time.

* * *

A little about me. Forty years old, divorced twice – it took some experience to make me realize I don't have a talent for being married – on my own for six years and counting. Occupation librarian until a month ago, when I quit the job to pursue the dream – in other words, I couldn't get a leave of absence and I'm stubborn. Now, when asked, I call myself a writer and try not to sound self-conscious.

Youngest of four daughters by eight years, so essentially a second-generation child. Hauled from pillar to post enough to where people ask if I was an army brat, which may explain the sudden bouts of uncontrollable wanderlust.

Then again, it may simply be in my genes. I've always had itchy feet; they were born and bred into me through my father's line. Although where he got them is another story altogether, since he was the first in his family to get a job where they sent him off to places like Libya and Kuwait and Indonesia as a petroleum engineer. The rest of his family stayed put in the small town in the South where they've been since he was small, and my mother's family, short of one aunt who married an Air Force chaplain and one foray two states over when Mother was a toddler, have been homebodies as well.

I come from a short line of adventurers, then. Still, I'm the only one in the current generation who would even think of writing my own entrance visa to a country about to close to the western world – my father did that to get into Libya, but I'd certainly be willing to entertain the notion – and that's got to be worth something, even though my passport probably won't get worked over at all this go round.

I say this go round as if my passport has ever gotten a work over.

It's enough. The journey will probably change my priorities, anyway.

Owl starts up smoothly, as he has for the dozens of commutes, errands, and weekend escapes since I bought him a year and a half ago, but this is his first long-distance trip, and it's nice to hear the

uncluttered sound of his engine. I pull out of the lot and down the
alley, my last glimpse up at what used to be my bedroom window
almost costing me the whole journey when a little red truck comes
flying around the corner and we both slam on our brakes.

I've gotten used to playing dodge-em in my neighborhood, and I
swerve round on my merry way.

The few errands – things I could have done the day before if I'd
thought of it – money, the storage people, gasoline – spread themselves
out as if on purpose to give me a late start. It's noon by the time I'm
on Interstate 5, headed north out of Tacoma. Distracted, I fail to
notice the odometer as I cross the city limits, an oversight for which I
mentally kick myself when I realize what I haven't done half an hour
later.

An estimate is easily come by that evening, about 24,600 miles, but
an estimate isn't an auspicious beginning to anything.

I turn east on Washington route 18, a road that starts out four-lane
limited-access suburban and gradually narrows and countrifies itself.
By the time I've gone over Tiger Mountain Summit and come down to
the junction with I-90 eastbound to the Cascades and Snoqualmie Pass,
it's misting enough to need my windshield wipers. In September, no
less.

The Interstate is the only way over the mountains in this part of
Washington. In this section of the world it's kind of a moot point,
anyway. The only things which make it feel like an interstate are the
exits and the multiple lanes. Otherwise, it's simply a mountain highway,
gradually gaining elevation through sweeping curve after changing view.
The summit is almost anticlimactic, looking so similar to the western
slopes below, and on a rise so gentle that if it weren't for the signs
pointing to the cluster of ski areas draped on either side of the road
you might not even realize exactly where it was.

It's not till I'm on my way down the eastern slope that I notice
the disappearing act the clouds have pulled. I must have shut the
windshield wipers off without thinking about it. Suddenly the
landscape opens up – dark green Ponderosa pines, their reddish bark
and long needles a far cry from the gray-black-green Douglas firs
of wet country, standing in an almost aloof apartness on a tan grass
ground. The whole scheme of things is different.

By the time I reach the town of Cle Elum, I'm in a different version of the West. The one with cowboys and ranchers. And the set of a beloved television show.

People who like the offbeat loved *Northern Exposure* back in the early 90s, ostensibly set in Cicely, Alaska, but actually filmed in the small coal mining town of Roslyn, Washington, just a few miles north of Cle Elum. Driving onto the streets of Roslyn is like having déjà vu. There's KBHR, the radio station where Chris in the morning dispensed Kafka and tales of Wheeling, West Virginia. There's Ruth Ann's store. And Fleischmann's office. It's been several years since the show went off the air, but since the mine closed before that, *Northern Exposure* was, and is, one of the town's main sources of income. So the tourist sights – and the completely incongruous coastal Indian totem poles – have been preserved, and it's still quite possible to buy a t-shirt reading, "it's not what you fling, but the fling itself." To go into the Brick for lunch, and wonder vaguely where Holling and Shelley are.

However, the tiny post office is closed for the lunch hour, and I wait impatiently with my bag of clothes to buy a box and send them over the mountains again, to wait more patiently for me on the other side. They'll be waiting for a long time.

* * *

It's chilly on this side of the mountains, even in the sunshine, even on the first day of September. Chilly and windy and dusty. Every time another pickup goes down the partly paved, partly graveled street a small cloud rises up.

Finally, the post office is open. I see I'm not the only one waiting. Most people are here to check mailboxes. Roslyn is small enough not to have home mail delivery, and I hear bits of conversations, tail ends of stories amidst the clanking of keys and the slide of metal boxes.

On my way out of town, I look back at a place with two names and two personalities. The mural on the side of the Roslyn Café no longer has an apostrophe s. Back to the way things were before Hollywood came to town.

* * *

About 30 miles east of Ellensburg, I-90 crosses the Columbia River at a place called Vantage. The mighty Columbia looks more like a lake at this point, having been dammed to placidity by the Corps of Engineers earlier in the century. It's a desert river here, flowing between black basalt cliffs edged with the tan of wild grasses. On the bridge, a windsock stretches out. It probably spends more time horizontal than vertical in this place. I can feel the wind blowing against the car, too.

Up on the bluff, poised as if to leap hundreds of feet to the water below, stand a herd of wild horses. I pull off the road and fish out my binoculars. Horses, yes. Wild, no. These mustangs are silhouetted from metal, gracefully poised against a brilliant blue sky.

Somehow it's hard to keep from waiting to see the first one soar out into the air like Pegasus. But it's getting on in the afternoon, and I still haven't a clue where I'm going to spend the night.

A few miles further to the east, I leave I-90 for two lane U.S. 283, northeast through alfalfa fields and heavily-laden orchards. It is apple season, after all, but what I'm looking for are pears.

I first moved to Washington State in late August, 1993. The produce section of the grocery store my first day in Tacoma was full of golden-ripe, locally grown Bartlett pears. After six years in the Midwest where the only pears are picked too green and shipped in from a couple of thousand miles away, which makes the core go bad before the flesh itself is ripe, I couldn't resist them. The place was full of their scent. I bought an enormous sackful, and walked out with pear juice dripping down my chin.

I've never gotten sick on fruit before or since, but let me be the first to tell you, six pears on an empty stomach is not a good idea. Something I have to remind myself of every fall here. It isn't easy.

I spot a roadside stand and slide the car carefully off the pavement and onto the small graveled parking space. The odor in the shed-like building makes my stomach lurch slightly in remembrance, but my mouth is in control. I walk out with a bagful, and the promise to myself I won't eat them all at once.

Hwy. 283 runs through a geological phenomenon called the Grand Coulee. A few thousand years ago, at the end of an ice age, the Columbia River followed a very different course than it does now. Blocked by an ice dam, it backed up into a lake, called Lake Missoula, which makes Lake Roosevelt, the reservoir created by the manmade dam above the Coulee, look tiny in comparison. When the climate warmed, the water broke through. It crashed across the volcanic landscape in one of the greatest floods ever to cross the face of the earth. It carved a canyon in the basalt that should have taken thousands of years to create. And it left, in the form of Dry Falls, the souvenir of a waterfall that would have dwarfed Niagara.

It's a landscape that makes a human being feel awfully small. At least this human being. It isn't the last time I'll feel this way on this trip.

Sun Lakes State Park, nestled along Lake Lenore at the bottom of the steep-walled coulee, seems dwarfed by its surroundings, too. Never mind that the campground alone has over a hundred sites.

It's a place to stay for the night. My misgivings are purely atavistic. I know there's no flood poised at the top of the coulee. I know Grand Coulee Dam and Dry Falls Dam are both sturdy and secure. But I feel a bit like those folks in Johnstown, Pennsylvania, would have felt if they'd known what was going to happen to the Conemaugh Dam, back in the 1880s.

I figure if I survive the first night in a place like this, the rest of the trip will be a piece of cake.

* * *

I always awaken early when I'm camping. Something about the sun beaming down through cloth and window, the excitement of being outdoors, and my tendency, as a woman alone, to sleep with one eye open on principle. At any rate, the sun is just coming up over the wall of the coulee when I climb out of my sleeping bag and head for the restroom.

The first morning after the first night on the road. With any luck, there'll be eighty-nine more just like it. Not all in campgrounds. I have a guidebook of hostels, and another of inexpensive motels. And a short list of people who've invited me to visit along the way. But it's the principle of the thing. Since the first night went this well, it augurs well for the next. And the next. And the next.

The sunrise is gorgeous, lighting everything in pink and pearl, darkening to orange, changing to everyday light as the sun clears the coulee wall. It's perfectly peaceful.

Except for the seagull following me from campsite to restroom and back to campsite again, yelling and squawking at me every step of the way. I think he's insane. He certainly sounds it.

Maybe he's lost, sees my west-of-the-mountains license plate and thinks I'll take him back to the ocean. Maybe he's lonesome – I seem to be the first human awake in the mostly-deserted campground. Maybe he's hungry. I take a chance it's the third option, and throw him a piece of muffin. He eats it, but that was a major miscalculation on my part. Now he's back, noisier than ever, and a half a dozen of his relatives are on to me, too.

Uncle.

I break camp as quickly as possible, and head out onto the road again.

* * *

Nine in the morning at the base of Grand Coulee Dam, one of the biggest dams in the world. It certainly looks the part, hunkered down between its basalt walls, ropes of electrical wires attached to it like electrodes to the chest of someone taking a treadmill test.

They run tours, but I'm here too early. This late in the season on a weekday, they don't start till eleven. I have a long drive ahead of me today, and I don't want to hang around that long. But the museum is open, and I wander in.

It's very modern in a sixties sort of way. High ceilings, lots of glass, everything very streamlined. Lots of pictures of construction, lots of captions extolling the virtues of engineering. My father would have liked this. Actually, he probably did. My parents and I were here once that I remember – one summer when I was a teenager. All I recall from that trip now is concrete shimmering with heat and giant turbines.

It seems smaller now.

A display over in the corner seems out of place. I go over to inspect it. It's a wheelchair and leg braces, 1930s vintage. I read the label. They belonged to Franklin D. Roosevelt, President during the Great Depression back in the 1930s when the dam was built. He came out here for the dedication to give it his seal of approval. He used the chair and the braces while he was here.

I wonder what he would have thought of a museum display of something he'd tried to hide all his life, and decide he probably would have been resigned to it. He was famous. Not having a private life seems to be part of all that.

At least his affairs didn't become part of the national psyche until after he was dead.

The road southeast from the dam runs through barren, desert-like country. Not what most people would associate with Washington state, known for evergreen forests and endless rain, but actually typical for east of the mountains. Further south, irrigation kicks in again, and the land is golden with wheat. It looks like cat fur. Linnet, one of the cats I left with my friend Trish, is the color commonly described as orange, and he's the exact shade of these tawny rolling hills. I want to reach out and pet the landscape.

Rolling hills have another use as well. They're darned fun to drive on.

The car is fully loaded, of course, and being a small compact with a commensurately-sized engine, doesn't have a whole lot of get-up-and-go, but I still manage to maintain some momentum on the upsides of the hills, and to swoop over the tops and down.

I slip a tape into the machine and sing over the deserted hillsides. It's almost disappointing when I reach the interstate again.

Through Spokane, which used to be my nearest big city when I lived in Montana, and a stop for a quick lunch and gas. Then over the border into Idaho.

Goodbye, Washington. See you in three months.

Available from all major booksellers.

Books by M.M. Justus

Much Ado in Montana

Cross-Country: Adventures Alone Across America and Back

Unearthly Northwest

Sojourn

Time in Yellowstone

Repeating History
True Gold
"Homesick"
Finding Home

Carbon
River
Press

About the Author

M.M. Justus used to live in a town a great deal like Campbell, Montana. Several of them, in fact.

She holds degrees in British and American literature and history and library science, and a certificate in museum studies. In her other life, she's held jobs as far flung as hog farm bookkeeper, music school secretary, professional dilettante (aka reference librarian), and museum curator, all of which are fair fodder for her fiction.

Her other interests include quilting, gardening, meteorology, and the travel bug she inherited from her father. She lives on the rainy side of the Cascade mountains in Washington state within easy reach of one of her favorite national parks, Mt. Rainier.

Please visit her website and blog at http://mmjustus.com, on Facebook at https://www.facebook.com/M.M.Justusauthor and on Twitter @mmjustus.

80218591R00135

Made in the USA
Columbia, SC
15 November 2017